Dark Horses:

A Science-Fiction Anthology

Friends of the Arts Lab

Dark Horses:

A Science-Fiction Anthology

Friends of the Arts Lab

Edited by Donna Scott

THE SLAB

Contents

Foreword

Robin Ince

I love that the Northampton Arts Lab exists.

I love that there is so much creativity in a place which is far too often dismissed.

I love that my mother is part of this story and something that means every time I think about the Arts Lab, I am reminded of her.

It grew from an event that occurred on the last weekend of my mum's life.

We didn't know how ill she was then, but she would die within 72 hours of the event from which the arts lab grew.

I sped from events in London, Folkestone and Northampton to be by her side and try to feed her little pieces of crushed Mr Kipling cake. Once she had no appetite for sweet treats, we knew it must be the end.

The event in Northampton involved discussions about counterculture.

Where was it now?

The audience, fired up by Grace Petrie, Josie Long, Scroobius Pip and Alan Moore wondered how they could create a hub for counterculture and from that, the Arts Lab was born within days of the death of David Bowie, a child of the arts lab (Beckenham branch). Alan was another child of the arts lab (Northampton branch).

Fringe culture seems to be struggling now. The mainstream has engulfed so many outlets and now we have 100 times more channels creating quarter of the variety of programmes. This is not the fault of the artists. There are so many minds that I meet filled with ingenuity, creativity and eccentricity, but so many of those who act as gatekeepers are scared of what does not seem to be as "normal" as their minds are.

The day before I wrote this, I went to see Salty Brine's Bigmouth Strikes Again. Salty is a New York cabaret artist who has created a show where the story of Frankenstein and Mary Shelley, and his own sex life, both thwarted and victorious, is told through the Smith's album The Queen is Dead. Salty sees Frankenstein as a verb, to Frankenstein is to stitch together old parts and make something new. I left the theatre revivified ("It's ALIVE!"). It was better than anything I have seen in more traditional theatre, but the audience was barely the equivalent of a front row of a story told many times. Two weeks before, at the Edinburgh Fringe, I saw You Are Going to Die, in which a naked Adam Scott Rowley veers between fever dream characters and the toilet. At one point he showed his arsehole and afterwards we discussed the careful preparation which has led to an arsehole mirror to ensure it is ready for its close up. Again, all that departed from the show left ecstatic, some bemused, but bemused AND ecstatic, you can be both. Adam struggles to find space and finance for his work.

There is so much out there that struggles while the banal thrives.

This is why the Northampton Arts Lab is so important and why we need more ventures like this.

We need places where people can be fearless and inspired and inspirational.

The status quo feels as oppressive as it ever has in my life.

Thoughtful fringe voices find it harder and harder to find space. While the far right sits increasingly comfortably in TV studios and Westminster benches, socialism, anarchism and any other philosophy that doesn't want a return to rotten boroughs and the divine right of the aristocracy are muted by the mainstream and politicians on the ersatz light left seem to compliantly share party snacks with the greedy and the selfish.

Science fiction is a good place to let a counter cultural mind run wild - I think of Octavia Butler's *Kindred*, Ursula Le Guin's *The Left Hand of Darkness*, Margaret Atwood's *The Handmaid's Tale*.

The thought experiments of science fiction helped shape me, helped a boy from privilege to understand there was a bigger world and one way of thinking should not fit all.

When we surrender to the humdrum, we resign from life.

When we fear revealing the contents of our mind, we are only half living.

When we say, "to hell with the critical voice, let's experiment", we are beginning to get somewhere.

Too much is created with the audience oppressing the imagination before you even know who the audience actually are. I will misquote Mr. A Moore here, but I believe he once wrote, "if the audience knew what they wanted, then they would be the artist."

It is easy to fulfil the needs of an audience if you give them what they want, but so much more exciting to give the audience something they could never have imagined they wanted, but now they have, their possibilities are wider and so is the sky.

Celebrate the imagination that has created the worlds within and then start building your own.

> I warn you
> I've got weapons
> I stack them by my bed
> I keep them on my shelf
> And when I pull back the trigger
> I'm arming myself
> Arming myself with other selves
> Bullets benignly made of sentences
> Put a hole in my skull
> And pour in other minds
> I need to be populated

Drop by drop.
Words will infect me
With empathy
I'll see through eyes
That baffled
And were baffled
That suffered
And made suffering
That were overwhelmed
And overwhelming
Voices of poverty
Of wealth
Voices from the Underground
Voices from out in space
Their light will extinguish
The shadows of my presumptions
I'll melt those certainties
Down into malleable doubts
I'll disturb the status quo
That shaped me
I'll increase my possibilities
And when I am brimful of stories
I'll always have room for one more
When I am alone
I'll have the company of ghosts
I lick my finger
Turn a page
Write for me
Write your self
I want your voice on my shelf
Create for me
Create me
Create

Please
Be my weapon of empathy

Robin Ince, September 2023

Introduction

Donna Scott

What is an Arts Lab? To me right now, an Arts Lab is a sort of creative phoenix rising from the ashes made of our cultural landscape by successive bouts of scorching. There are wildfires catching in the dry spots (right now the prospective leaders of the Conservative party are trying to score points against each other as to who hates Art degrees more). More and more it feels like we are looking towards a bleak, dystopian future where something this country is really good at and which currently brings in £111 billion in revenue, is being derided and devalued and put out of the reach of the many. These times of mass cultural disenfranchisement can be dispiriting to say the least, but making art, in spite of the barriers, helps. It feels good to create new art. It lifts us; it lifts others. Working together with people who are already creators to make Art happen in a non-hierarchical, just give it a go way is what the Arts Lab can do for you; for everyone.

The stories in this anthology have been written by members of various Arts Labs around the UK, but predominantly – and quite handily for me seeing as I live nearby – Northampton Arts Lab. No matter what you may have herd (sic), Northampton (aka Fampton, aka NOHO) Arts Lab isn't a creative club for felines. Nonetheless, this book has taken its sweet time to appear, having been plagued by various delays, including an actual plague. As editor, I have imposed deadlines on others and myself and in a very Douglas Adams way have seen them whoosh past. Whoosh! If you have ever tried to catch an Arts Lab deadline, you will know their tails are made of stardust and ephemera, they smell vaguely of chocolate biscuits, and they do weird things to your perceptions of time and of how many of the biscuits are still in the packet.

With Arts Lab, I am in touch with most of the writers contained in these pages a few times a month. Whilst this is fantastic for generating new ideas about things we could do, it is not necessarily a boon for getting projects completed. That said, I don't know how I would have got through the last few years without my Arts Labbers. We used to meet once a month in The Lab (aptly named), a vibrant and bijou music venue that also does a mean Sunday roast, and a nice cup of tea. Since the plague times however we have been meeting via Zoom, the occasional garden meeting, and a few government-sanctioned hour's exercise urban walks.

Arts Labs were originally a 1960s phenomenon, but were something I'd vaguely heard of a few years ago. All I used to know about Arts Labs was that David Bowie was in one. Then, during an event I went to at Northampton University in 2015 called "Under the Austerity, the Beach: A Day of Counter-Culture[1]", one of the speakers was Alan Moore, and he recalled the positive effect being in an Arts Lab that he had discovered as a teenager having joined the erstwhile and disappeared Northampton Arts Lab. He expressed a desire to rekindle the creative embers of the town, and what better place to do that than among the students? Several young people were inspired. So were some of us much older people who also happened to be there. A student called Arte Artemiou took mine and my husband's names and promised to get in touch. The Northampton Arts Lab was soon reborn!

From this rekindling came so many fantastic creative projects. Arts

---

[1] This was a fantastic event, with guests including Melinda Gebbie, Robin Ince, Francesca Martinez, Scroobius Pip, Josie Long, John Higgs and Grace Petrie. Then there was an after party with our friends' band 72% (then 72% Morrissey) playing as well as Kenneth J Nash, Trippah, Jen Dobson and Neumonics. Every single one of these creators is why this book is in your hands now. Each of them experts in music, comics, pop culture and social history, poetry, acting, song-writing, comedy, or combinations thereof – I challenge you not to find evidence of these seemingly disparate cultural spheres infiltrating the stories you are about to read. Creativity is creativity. It is a means, it is a weapon… and it's why I hold no truck with creative purists who want creators to stick to their lanes and not try even just a little to grow into the polymaths we all could be.

Labbers have produced poetry books and events, plays, magazines, paintings, comedy shows, cabarets… and now we are working on stories and comics.

Since Lockdown, a hardy crew of the more technologically able among us have been in contact via the weekly Zoom meetings, and there have also been waved greetings over doorsteps, and blanket-swaddled meetings on benches and in beer gardens. The value of the group has extended beyond encouraging each other for the sake of art, but for the sake of friendship too, and for the sake of not going mad when the rest of the world most definitely was. They were there for me on a phone screen when I couldn't lift my head from the pillow. They did not judge me when I had a little post-Covid snooze in the middle of a three-hour meeting. To say we have been through some stuff is no exaggeration.

I first got asked to work on this anthology about three years ago and I always knew it was going to be a bit different to the other science-fiction anthologies I've worked on. The selection pool was a lot smaller than what I'm used to, but I would say it was also a bit of a rockpool – it was totally fine if a writer was not used to the rough and wild seas of publishing; they were quite all right to wait for the tide to come back in in the relative safety of the pool, so long as they didn't mind this inquisitive editor coming along and gently poking their words out from under the rock shelves with my big editing stick!

I don't actually have a big editing stick, but I do have experience of working with newer writers and helping them to bring their work up to professional publication standards from my time working on *Visionary Tongue* – the magazine established by fantasy author Storm Constantine, and for which I worked as editor with my great poet pal, Jamie Spracklen. I hoped to bring a similar working practice to this anthology. I believe it worked, though the proof of the pudding is in the eating, and that bit's up to you! I would argue though that all the writers delivered, and no sticks were needed at all. Unless they asked.

I hope you enjoy these stories. Perhaps you will be inspired and immediately rush to join your local Arts Lab. And if you don't have one? Well, again, that bit's up to you.

Donna Scott
Northampton, October 2022

Location, Location, Location

Alan Moore

Bedford approached perfection.

Angie checked the dashboard clock. It was a bit before ten-thirty on that final Sunday morning, with no people on the streets and, other than her own, no moving vehicles. All things considered, an unusually pretty August day.

Progressing eastward down deserted Mill Street, the subdued purr of the Astra's engine seemed almost embarrassing against an otherwise uninterrupted silence, like some noisy child she had unwisely taken to a funeral. She made a right turn into Castle Road before she reached the looming church spire of St. Cuthbert's, indicating only out of habit. There was nobody behind her.

Sunrays fell in columns, beautifully dappling the pavements and parked cars outside the John Bunyan Museum as she passed it on her right, the mottled light resulting from that last day's atmospheric circumstances. Angie's weather app, for once, had been entirely accurate: "The heavens shall be made a sea of glass, like unto crystal, wherein seven candlesticks shall be displayed." Essaying a smooth curve into the Castle Road's main stretch, she only counted four of these – baroque, floating immensities that made the stomach flip to look at them – but had no doubt the other three were lost from view, somewhere behind the tall trees rising at this end of Newnham Road.

She made an effort to ignore the sky, just as she did her best to screen out all the other troubling elements of that eventful weekend, through a single-minded concentration on her duties as the charitable trust's executor. The beneficiary of the bequest, back in town after a long period away, would meet her at the property in a few minutes for a viewing and a handing-over of the keys and necessary documents. She had no clear idea of her carer arc after that, nor where she saw herself in twelve months' time.

Parking a short walk from the Albany Road junction, Angie noticed that one of the redbrick terrace houses on the street's far side still had a sun-bleached Brexit Party poster in its downstairs window. Was it really just the end of last year when all that stuff had been going on, with half the population busily anticipating world's end while the other half prepared for paradise? Above the Castle Mound and hidden river to the south there was a beast that had a lion's head, plus six wings crammed with heavy-lidded and incurious eyes. This surely was the worst possible outcome, one where absolutely everybody turned out to be right. Sighing resignedly, she climbed out of the car.

It was a glorious day. The air was clean and fresh, and on the breeze a menthol redolence that she identified as incense, perhaps eucalyptus. Also, once outside the Astra, her discovery that the pervasive hush was laced with distant birdsong made the enterprise seem less intimidating, although only slightly. Over the far end of Castle Road, off to the east, a second towering eminence presided, this one with a bull's head but the same six wings folded around it like enormous fans; the same indifference in their thousands of unblinking eyes. The birds were nice, though.

Still a few yards from the Albany Road turning, she was briefly startled by her first sight of the client, glimpsed across the box-cut privet bordering the corner house. Standing in the middle of the road in front of his new residence, he had his back to her and appeared to be contemplating the allotments on Albany Road's far side, directly opposite his garden gate and white front door, both for the moment closed against him. Though she'd done her best to banish any preconceptions, he was nothing like what she'd expected. Not so tall, for one thing. Noticeably fleshier. He had on a rust-coloured summer jacket worn with matching slacks and what seemed to be Air Max trainers. Mousy collar-length hair with blond tips and highlights, something like a mullet. He was vaping, sipping intermittently from a stylised gold fountain pen as he surveyed the straggling allotments.

Confident now that her navy trouser-suit and near-homeopathic trace of makeup had been the correct decision, Angie called a breezy greeting as she tick-tocked into Albany's deserted quiet.

"Um…hi. I'm guessing you're my half-past ten, to see the house? I'm Angie, from Carstairs & Calderwood. I hope you haven't been here long."

He turned to her and smiled, slipping the vape-pen into his breast pocket.

"Oh, no, only a few minutes. I arrived a little early, anyway. Wanted a bit of time to wallow in nostalgia, I suppose, and get a feel for how the place is now. It's nice to meet you, Angie."

He stuck out his hand which, when she shook it, felt completely ordinary. Firm, dry, confident, without electric shocks or noticeable curing of her mild sciatica. Seen from the front he wasn't a bad-looking man, but there was no resemblance to the publicity pictures. Not so young, for one thing, perhaps early forties or late thirties? As in her appraisal from the rear, there was a certain chubbiness about his face, clean shaven save a tidy sticking-plaster patch of neckbeard at an interval beneath the lower lip. The T-shirt he had on below his russet sportscoat said, 'I may be old, but at least I got to see all of the best bands'. A Rolex. One pierced ear that had a small gilt hoop in.

"So, what should I call you? Is there something that's the proper thing to say; 'Your Highness' or 'Your Majesty'? I don't know much about all this. I don't want to be rude."

He looked down at himself self-deprecatingly, and laughed.

"Well, I suppose I must look like a Jez in this kit, mustn't I?"

Laughing herself, Angie began to like him.

"Jez it is. Shall we go in?"

Turning their backs upon the fenced-off vista of the yellowing allotments, they made their unhurried way towards the corner house, number eighteen. Both commented admiringly on how the slate roof rose into a modest turret over the bay windows, neither seeing fit to mention the colossal form of yet another beast that reached into the crystallised blue skies above it. This one, in addition to the sextuple eye-studded pinions, had a man's head. Its receded hair and gormless look reminded the solicitor of her ex-husband, Derek, and she wondered briefly where he was right now, along with everybody else. Then Jez unlatched the wrought-iron gate and they proceeded up a short brick path to the front door, recessed beneath a porch that had 'THE ARK' embossed in neat black characters above it. Fishing in her bag she handed him the keys to heaven's kingdom, with Carstairs & Calderwood's distinctive logo on the plastic fob, and two by two they entered.

In the hallway, dust motes ventured glittering pirouettes through shafts of sunlight slanting from a window halfway up the stairs, and a grandfather clock measured eternity in thudding millimetres. Seeming at least not displeased by first impressions, the new owner paused to study a framed print that hung on the sedately-papered left side wall, above a fussy little table with a vase of artificial flowers. Viewed across the client's well-tailored shoulder, Angie could make out the portrait of a somewhat bird-faced older woman dressed in a white robe and bonnet, seated with a hefty Bible open on her lap against a solemn umber background. Pursed lips almost smiling, but a carefully curated worry in the painted eyes. Here the prospective resident glanced back at Angie, nodding to the picture with a fond expression.

"It's Joanna Southcott, bless her cotton socks. I don't expect she had it easy."

Forehead creasing, Angie made a clean breast of her ignorance.

"I'm sorry, I'm afraid I don't know anything about her. Was she one of the four women who began the Panacea movement? I think I read that the leader was from Bedford. Is this her?"

He shook his head. His eyes, she thought, had something of the look that she recalled from Sunday School, although greatly diluted. Warm and brown, they weren't so much repositories of suffering and anguish as of some longstanding disappointment or frustration.

"No. Joanna was a Devon lass, brought up in Gittisham. This was, what, middle of the eighteenth century, something like that? A footman tried it on when she was a domestic servant, and then, when she wasn't having any, made out she was going mad. Gaslit her, basically. She joined John Wesley's crew in Exeter, where they persuaded her she was a prophetess. Next thing you know, she's telling everybody that she's the Woman of the Apocalypse, the pregnant girl clothed in the sun, from Revelation. She flogged paper seals, twelve bob a throw, that guaranteed a place in heaven for twelve thousand dozen people. Everybody name-dropped her, from William Blake to Dickens."

Here the first-time homeowner returned his sympathetic gaze to Southcott's portrait, scratching at the palm of one hand absentmindedly as he wrapped up his anecdote.

"When she was sixty-four – this would have been eighteen-fourteen or thereabouts – Joanna made it known that she was up the duff with Shiloh, the messiah that gets talked about in Genesis. She had a due date sometime in October, but, well, obviously, nothing happened and she went into what her supporters called a trance, by which, presumably, they meant a coma. Anyway, she died on or around my birthday. Then, a century thereafter, pretty much exactly, you had Mabel Barltrop and her well-heeled single woman pen-pals, cooking up the Panacea Society from Southcott's teachings, there on the low slopes of World War One. I'm sure most people thought of Southcott and the Panaceans as delusional old trouts, but here we are."

He shrugged apologetically, and as if by some unspoken agreement, Angie opened the first door that led off from the hallway on the left as you came in. Together they went into the antimacassar still of the end-terrace property's impeccably preserved front room.

A dark green carpet covered varnished floorboards, almost to the parlour's edges, bearing a symmetrical design of fronds and curlicues that Angie thought resembled a disquieting hybrid between humming-top and jellyfish. The freshy-laundered nets and velour curtains were tied back to either side, framing a view of the allotments opposite, which didn't look quite as scorched and neglected as she'd thought them at first glance. Beyond the waist-high fencing she could make out bud-bedizened saplings and a bush that dripped with portly blackberries, although the bull-headed enormity still standing on the east horizon tended to draw most of her attention. Jez was trying out a massive horsehair sofa and examining the glass-doored china cabinet, where the glazed faces of Edwardian women stared out from commemorative plates. She was directing his attention to the decorative mouldings up above the picture rail when she glimpsed motion from the corner of her eye, and turned once more to look out of the window.

Outside, something terrible was scuttling along Albany Road.

Recoiling, her protesting senses tried to frame what she was seeing as machinery, as some kind of construction vehicle, ingeniously articulated, moving without wheels, but…no. No, that wasn't it at all. It was alive. It was an insect, a huge locust bigger than a bus that picked its way in the direction of the river, the precise typewriter movement of its sickeningly thick legs turning Angie's stomach. On the meaty hind limbs were erectile hairs like radio antennae, bristling and grotesque. The weight and textures of its lamp-black body – glistening gristle, lacquered chitin – had a terrible immediacy that dispelled her last feeble attempts to read the creature as a CGI effect; the way she'd handled the glass stratosphere with its unnerving weather-front of beasts and candlesticks. This was, incontrovertibly, a giant bug as real and physical as the allotment gate it stalked past, or the blue composting bin that stood beyond. And then she realised, with a lurch, that even this dreadful analysis was just a self-protective screen, an effort to prevent herself from understanding what was really there. It wasn't a giant bug, or at least not entirely. It was much, much worse than that.

At the monstrosity's rear end, curling up from the rustling black lacework of its folded wings was the fatal and beckoning finger of a scorpion's tail, plump and segmented, terminating in a shellac talon with a viscous bead of poison drooling from its tip. However, more disturbing yet were the additions to the locust's front extremity, that Angie had not taken in before this moment of lucidity: raised up before it like a begging dog were two crustacean pincers, and between these, sprouting from the insect's thorax, was a human head. Its inky hair hung in lank curtains, drawn back to reveal the sallow features as the horror craned its neck to right and left, scanning the empty street ahead for obstacles or prey. The jaw was dislocated or deformed, accommodating as it was a radiator grill of outsized teeth, the blood-caked sabres of a hungry jungle predator. It rolled its angry, unforgiving eyes, mad with the hideous truth of what it was. Angie became aware that she was hyperventilating.

As she watched the awful thing creeping away downhill to the embankment, she noted that Jez now stood beside her, watching with her. He'd recovered the e-cigarette from his top pocket and drew on it thoughtfully, turning his gaze to the transfixed solicitor with what seemed genuine concern.

"I'm sorry. I've not given any thought to how all this must look to normal people, have I? Here's you, weathering what must be a demanding brief with such professionalism that it hasn't once occurred to me: you must be terrified. Please don't be. None of this is what it looks like."

Angie let him lead her to the ancient tan settee, where he sat on the other end and waited for her to stop shaking, the vape stick now back in his breast pocket.

"L-Look, I know this is none of my business and I don't want to step over any lines, but if this isn't what it looks like, then what is it? Are you telling me that wasn't an enormous locust with a man's head and a scorpion's tail, crawling along Albany Road just now?"

The Panacea Trust's sole beneficiary stared at the coelenterate flourishes of the deep emerald carpeting. He shifted on the couch's creaking leather and appeared almost embarrassed.

"No. I mean, yes, that was a giant locust. It was real. This is all real, but…well, you shouldn't feel intimidated by it, all the things with lion's heads and what have you. They're just symbols manifested in a certain order, like the letters in a word or sentence. It's a sort of language."

Angie was beginning to feel rather small and sorry for herself, which made her cross.

"Well, if it is, it's a language that's impenetrable and designed to frighten everybody."

She was sure she'd gone too far. It wasn't her place to critique the client, and especially not this one. Anxiously, she waited for his brow to cloud in thunderous rebuke, and was surprised when all he did was beam and look delighted with her.

"Yes! That's it right there! As a solicitor, you know the kind of language I mean."

She thought this over for a while before she spoke.

"You mean contractual language?"

He could not have been more pleased. He clapped both hands against his thighs enthusiastically. The gesture seemed old-fashioned, practically Dickensian; the sort of move a public schoolboy from the nineteen-forties might pick up in imitation of their Latin teacher.

"You're bang on. Contractual language. That's exactly what it is, deliberately intimidating and unfathomable. The man-headed locusts and bull-headed men, the slaughtered lamb with seven eyes and seven horns, these are all clauses and sub-clauses and disclaimers in a legal document. And yes, I know, we've got to bring all this archaic nonsense up to date and make it more accessible. Some of this terminology, the images and symbols that it's drafted in are pre-Sumerian. That's not the way to run a modern business. I kept telling everybody, but…"

He trailed off, peering glumly at the Morning Glories on the ornamental fireplace surround. Out in the hallway the grandfather clock continued its dull listing of the seconds, underscoring the dejected pause. Angie considered what he'd said, determined to keep this professional, and not to relapse into paralysing awe. The bit about the seven-eyed dead lamb had startled her, simply because she hadn't witnessed that particular celestial vision yet, and didn't much like having to imagine it. Similarly, she had an uncomfortable suspicion that by 'business' he meant 'universe', the implications of which made the soles of her feet cringe and tingle, like when she saw someone in a film balanced precariously on a high window-ledge. It was a thought you could fall into, and your fall would never stop. He was still staring at the floral tiles around the hearth. She felt she ought to say something.

"This contract…it's been in place for some time, then, and is just now coming into force? So, what are its conditions? What does it relate to? If this is all confidential stuff that you don't want to talk about, that's fine. Just say, and I'll shut up."

He offered her a weak smile in response, and Angie saw the tiredness in his eyes.

"No. To be honest, it's nice having somebody to moan to. I don't get to unload very often. What this contract is about, it's all the fiddling details of the handover. Our legal people have been quibbling about the wording for, what, fifty years or more? 'That needs a comma. That needs a huge wine-press spurting blood. That needs a human-headed locust.' Alright, fifty years, it's longer for you than it is for us, but still. That's more than half a century we've been in business limbo without proper management, and that's not counting nearly two millennia of inactivity before that. It makes us look stagnant as a company, doesn't it? That's not the message that we should be putting out."

Angie was having trouble keeping up.

"Sorry, but I'm still not getting this handover that you mentioned. What is it that's being handed over, and to whom?"

He looked taken aback, as if he'd thought that fact too obvious to warrant mention.

"Well, the company. The business. With the former chief executive passed on, the whole lot comes to me. You've no idea how long I've waited for this, feeling like an idler with no proper job, but now it's here…I don't know. It's a big responsibility, but I expect I'll manage."

"So, the former chief executive…?"

"My dad."

After some several moments without blinking, she processed what he was telling her and was surprised to feel a desolated lurch, right at her very core. She'd always thought she was an atheist.

"He's dead?"

The client sighed and nodded, scratching at his palm distractedly. She understood that this was all still raw, still recent, something he was dealing with, when fifty years might only be a week or two where he was from. Staring down at his trainers planted on the writhing emerald carpet, he continued in a quizzical and distant tone, as though he spoke more to himself than Angie.

"Funnily enough, it happened only a few months before they ran that headline in Time magazine. I mean, I see now it was just coincidence, a fluke of the statistics, but it put the wind up everybody just the same. Of course, my dad, he'd been on his last legs for centuries, just getting worse and worse, but you know what it's like. Somehow you think they'll always be there."

Angie felt that she should pat his shoulder, but she left it too long and decided not to.

"So, the immortality…?"

Jez snorted.

"Well, there's clearly no such thing. How do you know that you're immortal, unless you get to the end of time and haven't died? You're probably just very long-lived, aren't you? Naturally, Dad being Dad, he's going to assume that he's immortal, even when he's haemorrhaging stars and coughing up black matter. That last thousand years, no kidding, he could barely get up from the throne. We told him he should see somebody, get it looked at, but he'd take no notice. He was one of those; thought he knew everything. And now he's gone, and I'm in charge of…well, all this."

He gazed disconsolately into some internal void for a few moments, then seemed to recover his composure, offering Angie a pained smile that bordered on a grimace.

"Ah, well. That's enough of that. Shall we get on with showing me around the house?"

Next off the hallway to the left, the living/dining room was bigger than the parlour, though perhaps it got less direct light. There was a polished hardwood table you could see your face in, and a complement of straight-backed chairs that Angie thought might have been Regency, with a repeated fleur-de-lis motif in their upholstery. The white-gold carpet looked like a steamrollered ghost.

A near-sarcophagus-sized sideboard stood against the north wall, china knick-knacks crowded at its ends in order to accommodate the worn and corner-blunted packing case that rested in the centre. Roughly three feet wide and two feet high by one foot deep, its blemished boards seemed held together by the doubled lengths of twine in which the box was bound. A luggage label, creased and jaundiced, was affixed up top with something written on it in a trembling hand, too small for Angie to make out. The almost-black of a Box Brownie photograph, its shabby presence dominated what was otherwise a tidy and impeccably presented space. Her client gently ran his hand across the object's battered surfaces, twanging its taut strings playfully.

"So this is it, then. This is the society's panacea against crime and banditry, along with sadness and perplexity. Not much to look at close up, is it?"

Angie grudgingly allowed that Bedford had most likely seen the last of crime and banditry, and that despite the disappearance of its population she was not particularly sad – perhaps because her doctor had prescribed anti-depressants at around this time last year – but she was certainly perplexed.

"What is it?" She recalled that Revelation said something about a book with seven seals, but didn't think a box tied up with string was mentioned anywhere. Jez grinned, nodding towards the hall.

"This is her box, Joanna Southcott's. When she died, she left it sealed up with instructions saying it was only to be opened by two dozen bishops, at a time of gravest national emergency. What Mabel Barltrop, Rachael Fox, Kate Firth and Helen Exeter were doing from the Twenties onwards was petitioning the government to convene four-and-twenty bishops, so that they could open Southcott's treasure-chest. I'm not entirely sure the Church of England even had twenty-four bishops by that point, but Mabel and the others weren't much bothered by the technicalities."

Here the incoming tenant lifted the container in both hands to test its weight before putting it down again. Though cumbersome, it clearly wasn't heavy. Angie asked the obvious question.

"And does anybody know what's in it?"

Turning from the sombre package and towards the room's west-facing window, the solicitor's last ever client raised his eyebrows speculatively and pressed his lips into a doubtful pout.

"Depends who you believe. According to the Panaceans, it's Joanna Southcott's prophecies of the apocalypse in two thousand and four – and, okay, sixteen years out, but across the centuries that's still not bad. What muddied up the waters, though, in nineteen twenty-seven, this so-called psychic investigator, Harry Price, he claimed he'd found the box and had it opened. Said that it was empty except for some unimportant papers, a horse pistol and a lottery ticket. Naturally, the Panacea Society claimed that the box Price opened was a fake or a mistake. They had the real thing here in Bedford, they insisted, and would carry on petitioning to have its mysteries revealed. You've got to hand it to them, haven't you, for sticking to their guns? I mean, this was a group made up almost exclusively of well-off single women, living in an England that was near enough *The Handmaid's Tale*."

They were both standing by the window now, gazing across the house's generous back garden at the fenced grounds of the Panacea Museum in Newnham Road; the sideboard and its indeterminate collection of debris or prophecy behind them. Angie turned to face her client, incredulous.

"You know about *The Handmaid's Tale*?"

"Well, only the first season." He gave her a slightly guilty look. "I haven't read the book."

Outside an oddly diffused sunlight powdered the rear lawn of number eighteen, a bright rectangle enclosed by tall leylandii of a neatly manicured viridian. Beyond that, other than the back of the museum and the stand of trees on Newnham Road, not much was visible from Angie's limited perspective. There was very little sky on view, though she supposed that the gargantuan figure with six wings and Derek-her-ex-husband's head was still there in the west, morosely overseeing Bedford's day of judgement. Angie at last put her finger on the one thing troubling her about this situation other than the obvious, which was everything.

"I think there's something I'm not understanding here. How can you be so normal? I don't mean, 'Oh, you're a big celebrity and yet you act so ordinary.' I'm not complimenting you about your common touch. I'm saying you watch boxsets, you wear trainers and naff T-shirts, and you've even got a Bedford accent. And yet you're apparently the son of something inconceivable that made the universe. How is it even possible we're standing here talking about *The Handmaid's Tale*?"

He looked hurt.

"You don't like the T-shirt?"

Angie struggled to come up with a response that didn't involve her immediate damnation.

"Look, the T-shirt's fine. My brother Craig had one just like it, but this is exactly what I'm having trouble with. Why are you dressed like somebody I might bump into at Games Workshop? Why should you care if I like your T-shirt? This can't all be for my benefit. I'd have been just as happy if you'd turned up in the robe and sandals you wore last time. I know it's not meant to be, but this is actually a bit confusing and upsetting. Sorry."

Plump face growing serious, the client nodded in acknowledgment.

"Yes, well, how you see me isn't how I am, but then the robe and sandals version wasn't either. It's not some hypnotic screen that I'm projecting, some illusion to spare you the alien horror of my true state, nothing sinister like that. To be quite honest, it's just human evolutionary biology. Mankind's developing perceptual apparatus has consistently selected, sensibly enough, for practical survival vale over accuracy. A true, comprehensive understanding of, say, a ferocious jaguar might well diminish a human's ability to run away at the first glimpse, effectively eliminating such complete perceptions from the gene pool. How you see and hear things, it's a bit like simplified computer icons, or the way you read that map of London's tube-stations – you know the map bears no resemblance to any geographical reality, but if you follow the convenient fiction of its coloured lines, you'll reach your destination. That's much like how you perceive me. How your species perceives everything."

Despite beginning to wish that she'd never raised the issue, Angie did her best to take this in.

"So, nothing's ever been the way we thought it was, that's what you're saying? When I see you looking like a normal guy, in normal modern clothes, that's just a kind of shorthand for something I wouldn't have the language to conceive of or describe? And when I hear you talking about everyday things in contemporary English, with a Bedford accent, then it's just some nonsense I'm inventing to hold my made-up reality together?"

Once again Jez nodded, neckbeard wobbling to the beat.

"Yeah, pretty much. Except it isn't nonsense, and you're not inventing it. It's more like an approximation of what's happening, a translation into human terms that are at least distant equivalents and thus might be of use to you. For instance, when you hear me talk about my dad, he's not my dad. He isn't even 'he'. I'm not his son. It's more like the relationship between a sentient meta-algorithm and a number-value that the algorithm has spontaneously generated. Understandably, the average non-algorithmic man or woman has problems relating, but if it's presented as a father-son arrangement or a corporate handover, they'll have a way to comprehend the changes that are going on."

He turned back to the window and the sunlit grass beyond, features relaxing into what she thought might be a playful smirk.

"Of course, the only thing that none of this applies to is my Bedford accent. That's completely how it sounds. I spent a lot of time in Bedford growing up. Shall we go out and have a butcher's at the garden?"

This was so abrupt that Angie found herself accompanying her client through a nineteen-thirties time-capsule kitchen to the property's back door before she thought to ask him what he meant, about his Bedford upbringing. Amused, he paused between a dreadnaught gas-stove and a bottomless stone sink to qualify his puzzling assertion, smiling sheepishly.

"I'm sorry. I was kidding…although not entirely. It's true I remember Bedford from way back, before I manifested physically, but that was a Precambrian Bedford. There were mudslides, there were geysers, but they didn't have a noticeable local accent. That's just me, being a dick."

Although the answer would no doubt be mind-destroying, Angie asked her question anyway.

"Why were you in Precambrian Bedford?"

There was a refrigerator opposite the stove, which Angie's client opened and briefly inspected before making his reply. The fridge was humming and its light worked, indicating that there was still electricity, although she didn't quite see how there could be. Jez issued a grunt of moderate approval as he let the weighted door swing shut.

"Sometimes the old man let me visit him at work, back then when he was setting up the business. During the Precambrian, his workshop was just up the road, northeast of here. I think Transition Cycles is there now. I used to sit there in the corner with a bag of sweets and watch him do all the gene-editing and that. He'd swear and kick things when he made a typo, got his guanine mixed up with his adenine, but I was only, what, three or four million, typical kid, so I just thought it was a laugh. I realised later that Dad was dyslexic, but back then, in the Precambrian…you have to understand it was a different time. We didn't have the same awareness about learning difficulties, and so he was halfway through production on marsupials before anybody noticed anything was wrong. But anyway, yeah, I know Bedford from when Dad was doing the preliminary work on Eden."

Angie blinked five times in quick succession, then repeated the last word of his boyhood nostalgia back to him in a flat tone, without hope or enthusiasm.

"Eden."

"Well, he had to put it somewhere, so why not? I think John Bunyan must have had an inkling, but the Panaceans hit the nail almost exactly on the head: they said that Eden had been situated in number eighteen's back garden, just outside. Which one of these keys that you gave me is the one to the back door?"

Dazed as if by a theological concussion, Angie mutely indicated a brass mortice key attached to the Carstairs & Calderwood calligraphy. After a moment's fumbling and a comment that the lock could use some WD-40, the door opened and they both stepped out into the mentholated morning air. Her view no longer cropped by the rear windows of the property, she glanced up at the double-glazed sky and immediately forgot about the Eden shock-reveal that had so recently transfixed her.

"Jesus Christ!"

She hadn't meant to say it. Angie clapped her hand across her mouth in horror and stared wide-eyed at the client, cringing in apology. Jez shook his head and waved one chubby palm in her direction, chuckling as he brushed aside the faux-pas.

"No, don't worry. Blasphemy, it's not even a misdemeanour these days, is it? I use that expression all the time, like when I finally got to see the company accounts. And in the case of that stuff going on up there, I'm in complete agreement. I mean, Jesus Christ."

They stood together at the top of the brick steps that led down to the garden proper, necks craned back as they regarded the uproarious skies directly overhead.

Against the blue glass of the upper atmosphere, appalling mile-high spectres were suspended like Magritte trombones, two forms that faced each other in a stalled tableau of violent opposition. One was female and extremely pregnant. With the other it was difficult to say. The gravid female figure seemed to have more altitude, her anxious features angled down towards the couple in the garden. Angie thought she recognised the face but, in her holy terror, couldn't say where from. The woman had an upturned crescent moon beneath her naked feet. She wore a constellation of twelve stars as a tiara, and the garment that she clutched in disarray about her was too bright to look upon, a rag of crumpled plasma clinging to her parted legs and swollen belly, as though torn white-hot from off the sun. She had the faraway translucency of water-colour, and she looked afraid.

The creature hovering beneath her had its crimson back turned on the world and the observers far below, a boiling storm of headed blood or rubies. Muscles big as counties knotted in its shoulder-blades and buttocks, chili-red with salamander frills. Its quadruped anatomy hunched forward to assail the woman and her unborn offspring, sticky highlights glinting from a rolling snakeskin hide and the meniscus of its arched spine helping, from that vantage, to conceal the fact it had too many heads.

These cyclopean bodies hung there over Bedford, asteroids perpetually falling so that Angie thought them motionless, a frozen film-still of industrial scale, until she saw that both were moving imperceptibly in glacial slow-motion, as though through a different sort of time where legendary things were always and forever happening. The sun-clad woman's lips began contorting to a scream, unhurried as an opening flower. Although more thin and tremulous than she remembered it, the fortyish solicitor at last retrieved her misplaced voice.

"The woman, that's…is that Joanna Southcott?"

The incoming owner had resorted once more to his vape-stick, sucking on it thoughtfully as he surveyed the lurid Weird Tales cover up above through narrowed eyes, with his expression that of a Victorian explorer. A bit pompous, Angie noted. Was he trying to impress her?

"Yeah, you're right, but it's Joanna as a younger woman, or at least, that's how you're seeing this bit. Obviously, it was how she saw herself, clothed in the sun and in her last trimester. She was pretty, wasn't she? I'm guessing this is what was in her mind when she lost consciousness after her phantom pregnancy. This is Joanna Southcott's coma-dream."

He sipped the vape again, exhaling arabesques of fragranced steam, then looked at Angie.

"Yeah, it's just contractual language, but if an uneducated eighteenth-century serving-girl with premonitions somehow gets a glimpse of it, she's going to be all kinds of messed up. Stands to reason. And of course, most of this terminology, this imagery, it's unbelievably hostile to women. Come on – we don't need to watch this. I'd much sooner you were showing me the garden."

The vape went back in its rust-coloured breast pocket as the client descended to the lawn with Angie following, her eyes fixed on her shoes, which navigated the uneven brickwork of the steps. She thought that if she could just learn the trick of never looking upwards, she might yet get through this without losing any marbles. Following him out onto the level baize and limiting her gaze to the surrounding hedges, she resolved to stick with her initial strategy of focussing upon the job in hand.

"Well, this is it. The ground from here to the museum is part of the property, so it's all yours. It's big for a back yard, admittedly, but I'd have never thought that this was Eden if you hadn't said."

He raised an eyebrow, jacket striking an appealing contrast with the dark green hedge beyond.

"Oh, sorry, no, this wasn't Eden. Probably I didn't put it very well but what I said was, this is where the Panacea Society ladies thought Eden had been, and they were only out by a few dozen yards. The actual garden was just slightly further east, across Albany Road from the front door."

She had a sudden mental image of the world's new chief executive as she'd first seen him, standing with his back to her and his new property, supping his vape-pen and serenely gazing over...

"Those allotments? That was where the Book of Genesis took place?"

The bridge of his nose corrugated in a minimalist shrug.

"Well, sort of. But the thing with Genesis, it's hardly a first-hand account. How could it be? I think that it was written halfway through the Book of Kings, something like that. They took a garbled version of the story, as leaked by some babbling prophet in a lotus-stupor, then they altered that to make it all a metaphor for when Nebuchadnezzar kicked the Israelites out of Judea and burned down their temple. So, that bit about the angels with the fiery swords was just a more poetic way of saying Babylonian soldiers. The real Eden story happened here in Bedford, just over the road. The rest is bollocks. Although that said, to be honest, angels really do have fiery swords."

Angie, who'd been reflecting on the first time she'd heard Dylan's 'Gates of Eden' and had not imagined them as waist-high chain-link, found that she was shocked by Jez's mild profanity. Of course, after a moment's thought, she saw that her reaction was ridiculous: if someone was omnipotent, then they must surely have the power to utter the word 'bollocks'. In companionable silence, they trod ponderously about the shaved lime rectangle. She couldn't think of anything further to say or ask concerning Eden's local origins. As they turned back once more towards the rear of number eighteen, her eye-level never venturing above the brick stairs and the open garden door, she changed the subject to what she hoped was a less contentious matter.

"I suppose that you'll be opening the box, the one you showed me, with Joanna Southcott's prophecies inside?" Angie resisted the temptation to look up and see how Southcott's airborne younger self was doing with her labour pains. "I mean, I know you won't be able to convene the bishops like she wanted, and it's probably a bit late to be opening it now, with this already going on, but I'd have thought that you'd at least be curious about it. I know I would."

They reclimbed the steps to the back door. He shrugged his nose again, rather dismissively.

"No, I don't think so. I'd prefer to let it stay a puzzle, like Schrodinger's cat. It's Schrodinger's apocalypse, how's that? I mean, the actual contents of the box are bound to be a let-down, aren't they, after all this build up? What if it was just the pistol and the ticket for the lottery, like Harry Price insisted? That wouldn't be very satisfying, would it? Wouldn't be much of a revelation, even for a boxset season-ender. You'd want something jaw-dropping, something impossibly dramatic that racked up the tension and left everybody hanging, desperate for the next instalment. Frankly, I don't see whatever's in Joanna's box as having *Killing Eve* potential, unless…"

Halfway up, he stopped and turned to Angie, face lit up by what had just occurred to him.

"I know! What I'd do, if all this was the last episode of the whole series, I'd have me, that is my character, I'd have me letting you, your character, open the box herself, if that was what she wanted. I'd perhaps have us joking around about the subject for a while and making light of it, you know, to lull the audience into a false sense of security. It's a sort of misdirection. Anyway, your character, we have her opening the box. Perhaps she feels that it's an honour. Would she feel that? Or, I don't know, she's a modern woman so perhaps she feels it's just a joke? It doesn't matter. Main thing is, she undoes all the strings – perhaps there's seven of them, like the seven seals – and opens it. Inside there's just a lottery ticket and a horse pistol, how Harry Price described it. Massive disappointment! You can see it in her face. I'm thinking close-up, from below."

Angie suppressed a shiver. Was it starting to get chilly, out here in the sun-drenched garden? What she wanted, more than anything, was to step back into the kitchen. It was so close, the back door ajar like that, but her client was caught up in his increasingly unnerving Vince Gilligan narrative.

"So, both of us, our characters, are in the living room with the box open on the table and inside it nothing but the ticket and the pistol. You, your character, you're really disappointed but you reach into the box and you pick up the lottery ticket for a closer look, and it's just that. It's just a lottery ticket. It isn't even ticket number six-six-six or anything. And then you turn it over."

Reaching the denouement, his light voice grew low and gravelly, as though recounting a ghost-story or an urban legend; the bit where they look round and the hitchhiker has disappeared.

"And on the other side, in spidery and faded writing, it says, 'Take the gun and shoot him through the head, or he will end humanity.' There's your reaction shot, just your stunned face, then bang, black screen, theme music, maybe something by Nick Cave, end credits. What do you think?"

Angie was terrified, unable to prevent herself imagining the scene, the dreadful choice. What would she do? And what did he mean, telling her a story like that? Was that what was going to happen? Was this some preliminary game before she went to Hell? She knew she probably deserved it. When she'd slept with Trevor from the office, her and Derek were still technically a married couple, so that was adultery. She wished she'd never done it; had wished that she'd never done it even during the six minutes when she was actually doing it. Trevor was hideous. "Take the gun and shoot him through the head, or he will end humanity." What would she do? The client was staring at her in dawning concern as finally he registered the shock and panic in her headlight-frozen eyes.

"Oh, look, I'm sorry. I'm an idiot. That sounded really creepy, didn't it? And threatening. I didn't mean it to, I promise. I watch too much television, and I'm shit at conversation with real people. And with you, I mean, you're handling all of this so well, and I suppose that I was trying to say something entertaining, something that you'd think was funny. The last thing I wanted was to come across as scary. Please forgive me. You must think I'm an enormous twat."

He was so earnestly contrite that Angie felt immediately reassured; embarrassed, even, by her sacrilegious fugue of a few moments earlier and that she'd misread him so badly. She gave a relieved sigh and self-conscious giggle almost simultaneously, so that he'd see that she'd been frightened but was game enough to laugh it off. The tension broken, they continued back towards the house.

"No, I won't think that you're a twat if you don't think that I'm some bag of nerves who's not up to the job. I was just shocked by what you said, by the idea of it, which I suppose means that it would make a good season-ender after all. You can't help wondering what the character would do."

Jez was already at the back door, going in. "What do you think she'd do?"

Angie considered. "Well, she wouldn't do it, would she? Look, if it's an early nineteenth-century horse pistol, it would more than likely blow up in her hand and take her eye out. Quite apart from that, I don't see that she's got a motive. I mean, 'shoot him or he'll end humanity'? And what would that accomplish? I was up at half-past eight this morning, and humanity looked like it had already ended. Everybody's gone, apart from me. Apart from her. So, no, she wouldn't do it."

Before following her client back into the stubbornly anachronistic kitchen, Angie risked a last squint at the sky. Although still awful, it was nowhere near as bad as she'd expected. The vast pregnant woman that she'd found the most upsetting element of the scenario – titanic and yet frighteningly vulnerable – was now greatly reduced in size, having retreated to a safe remove, gradually dwindling into the noon-blue heights. The lunar sickle under her bare feet was now about the same size as an ordinary daytime moon. Did that mean that the woman with Joanna Southcott's face was now in space; in orbit? Angie felt relieved on her behalf. She was well out of it.

The ghastly red thing, a clenched butcher's fist of hate and malice, was still just as big as when she'd last looked, floating in approximately the same posture with its winged back mercifully turned towards her. The wings were now spread spectacularly, whereas before she'd barely registered them: scalloped kites with wet pink membrane stretched between umbrella ribs of bone. Beneath each lifted sail there hung a seething cloud, the black of a scabbed wound, both cumuli dissolving at their edges into sanguinary specks that rose to stain and stipple the azure. Her eyes adjusting to the distance, Angie at first took the slowly-moving flecks for swarming insects, then perhaps some species of large bird; a flock of liquorice flamingos. After several seconds' observation, though, there was no way around it: they were crimson angels, rising in whatever the collective noun for such a breed might be, a murmuration or a murder. An unkindness.

Now she had her eye in, it was evident that these ascending flakes of clotted blackness weren't the only aerial phenomena abroad in the meridian skies. From higher up, from the vicinity of the withdrawing star-crowned woman there descended a precipitation of white dots, a talcum dusting settling through the stratosphere towards the dark arterial spatter spraying up to meet it from below. She understood that this was the opposing team. Realising that she'd paused, the client took a few steps back to Angie's side, peering up glumly at what she was peering at.

"Yeah, this is the big fight scene coming up, with the Red Dragon's angels and the angels of the Lord. It looks like a cup final, but it's more like wrestling – the Dragon is the heel, so he'll be going down. It's really just the contract's small print, with a long list of penalty clauses and what have you, but it gets a bit Sam Peckinpah in places. To be honest, I think we'd be better off indoors until this lot are done with all the smiting. You can show me the upstairs."

Throughout the brief excursion, the four six-winged beasts had kept to their positions at the compass-points, mute and impassive like adjudicators or the corner-posts of an ethereal boxing ring. Angie and Jez went back inside, and Jez locked the back door behind them.

"Huh. I don't know why I bothered doing that. Not when it's like you said, and there's nobody left except you. Force of habit, I suppose."

They made their way back through the atavistic kitchen. In the hall the seconds were still falling like lead shot from the grandfather clock, and Angie asked the client if there was genuinely no one left on Earth but her. There at the bottom of the stairs, he stood and thought about it.

"No. No, it's just you. Everyone else is…well, you've heard about the Rapture? It's a bit like that, except it isn't just a thing for all the fans, the Christians, or for people who've not coveted their neighbour's ass or anything like that. It's everybody. Good, bad or indifferent, atheists and Mormons, Satanists and Buddhists, Moslems and Jehovah's Witnesses, the lot. Actually, 'Rapture' is an out-of-date expression. In today's terms, think of it as, 'everybody's information has been instantly uploaded to the Cloud'. Except for yours, of course. The seraphim in Legal said we had to retain one decent solicitor to represent the Panacea Charitable Trust, in order to keep all of this legitimate."

The client began to mount the stairs and Angie followed him, considering what he had said. From what she'd gathered, there was still some ambiguity about her own position. With this mind-numbing transaction finally concluded, would her further services be necessary, or would she be 'instantly uploaded to the Cloud', which, frankly, didn't sound ideal? She couldn't think of any way to raise the issue when the answer might reduce her to a pleading wreck and spoil what had, until then, been a well-conducted lawyer/client interaction. Best, perhaps, to change the subject.

Halfway up the staircase was a small north-facing window which, she realised as she passed it, looked down onto Castle Road. She couldn't see the Astra from this angle, although over on the street's far side she could make out the faded Brexit Party poster that she'd noticed earlier, still languishing behind its glass in the deserted terrace. A stray idea occurred to her.

"I don't suppose that you kept up with Brexit, or had any thoughts about it?"

He continued his ascension, that on this occasion went no further than the upstairs landing.

"Well, in my experience, you give the ballot to a mob of populists and nine times out of ten the vote goes to Barabbas. Or the golden bull-calf. That was the will of the people, wasn't it?"

Unable to think of a credible rebuttal, Angie joined him on the landing. Here they started with a cursory inspection of the bathroom, very tasteful in mint-green and ivory. The bath itself was one of those claw-footed items that she'd only previously seen in picture-books or films, and which she'd always found vaguely unnerving – a Hieronymus Bosch life-form to accompany the walking helmets and crawling hot-water bottles. There appeared to be no shower and while she didn't raise the issue Angie wondered if, with just the tub, this would present the client with bathing difficulties. Having read some of the literature, she wasn't sure if he could displace water in the normal way or if he'd have to lounge there on the steaming surface, high and dry.

She was sure that none of the fervent matrons of the Panacea Society had ever, in a century of ownership, once used that bath nor ever flushed that sacred toilet.

They continued from the bathroom to the property's rear bedroom, overlooking the back garden. No doubt reasoning that the returned messiah would be organising very little in the way of sleepovers, this had at some point been converted to a study. An Edwardian writing desk was set by the west window with its view of the museum in Newnham Road, while the remaining walls were decked in bookshelves, floor to ceiling. It was very cosy, although Angie didn't know why an omniscient being would have need to study anything. Her client stood perusing his new library, his hands deep in his pockets as he read the embossed spines without discernible enthusiasm.

"This is my suggested reading list, then? This is what they thought I'd enjoy flipping through on rainy afternoons? There's nothing here but books about me and my dad, as if I'm Frank Sinatra Junior or somebody. I mean, who does that? Who wants to read all about their fucking awful upbringing, or how their dad was always going into one and smashing the place up? There's no crime fiction, there's no science fiction, nothing here by anyone who's black or Asian. And for saying there were never more than one or two blokes in the Panacea Society, there's nothing here by women. If you walked into a bookshop and this was their catalogue, you'd walk straight out again. I'll probably get rid of them as a job lot and then have a flat-screen installed. That's more me, if I'm truthful."

Angie ran her hand across the writing table's varnished wood, its glinting leather and the plump, soft paper of its blotter; reassured herself that this was still a solid world, for all that it kept bleeding into dream. From this reaffirmation of reality, she glanced up at the window and was nonplussed to discover that, in August, it was snowing. Fat white flakes fell lazily through blazing sunshine, although as she watched, her mind corrected this initial error of perception. Obviously, it wasn't snowflakes. It was feathers, some of them on fire. Jez joined her by the antique bureau.

"That'll be the debris from the angel-holocaust that's going on above us. You can see why I suggested that we come indoors before we got the Full

English Gomorrah. It's like this for the next hour or two now. Nothing I can do about it, I'm afraid.

Outside the window in the distance, sizzling through the swansdown blizzard there were intermittent shooting stars, blazing parabolas that plunged like crippled Spitfires onto Bedford. Angie speculated that these were slain angels, burning up as they passed through Earth's atmosphere. They watched this phosphorous precipitation for a while, and then she and her client returned along the landing for a look at the front bedroom, where there was a bit more light.

"Oh, this is nice."

Angie agreed. It was nice. The wallpaper was blue coronets on misty pink, the brass bed buffed to gold beneath a counterpane of white chenille. On the rococo dressing table a glass jar of potpourri was resting on a doily, gently perfuming the air with lavender and rose. Thick claret curtains were held back by brocade ties to either side of the bay windows, and out through the pristine nets charred plumage and meteoritic angel-corpses rained down on the neighbourhoods around Albany Road. The beast with a bull's head still kept watch from the east, unflinching as a bored Buckingham Palace sentry even when the flaming casualties appeared to fall directly on its immense bovine face.

It took her quite some time to register that the allotments on the road's far side were nowhere near as meagre as they'd seemed when she arrived. This was perhaps because the proper verdant glory of the fenced enclosure had been unapparent from ground level and was only noticeable from above, but from above the modest acreage was a vision of fertility. How had she missed those half-a-dozen sturdy trees, or overlooked those scoliotic canes bowed by tomatoes big as stop-lights?

Thinking to remark on this, she turned and found Jez watching her with an uncomfortable expression, brow and lip-line writhing as though in the throes of some inner predicament. She asked him what was wrong, which only seemed to make whatever it was worse.

"Look, I don't want to…no. No, it's a bad idea. Forget it."

Unsure what it was she should forget, she pressed him further. He groaned and looked authentically miserable.

"Angie, I know how this is going to sound. We've got a huge

power-gradient here and I'm not trying to abuse that, okay? You can tell me to get lost, you can say no, and nothing is conditional on that. It won't change how much I respect you for the job you've done today. It won't change our relationship. It's just, you're the first woman that I've had a decent conversation with in getting on for two thousand years. I'm desperate for you not to think this is some Harvey Weinstein thing, but would you be offended if I asked about the possibility of having sex with you? It's okay if you are offended, that's completely understandable. I'm sorry, this is unprofessional. I shouldn't have said anything."

She looked at him, and for the first time recognised in his tormented eyes a little of the man in all the paintings. He was a good-looking chap – not handsome like the men in her occasional sex fantasies, but streets ahead of all the specimens she'd slept with in real life. He was no Trevor, put it that way. As for going to bed with him, she couldn't think of any reasons not to. He seemed likeable, and with the future still uncertain, this might be her last fling. Seriously, who was going to sniff at rolling in the hay with mankind's saviour, even if he'd admittedly just disappeared mankind? Who would pretend they'd ever had a better offer? Now that she'd allowed herself to think about it in such terms this was a kind of sexy situation, with the whole house, the whole planet, to themselves.

"No, don't apologise. I think I'd like that, what you said. And no, somehow I don't feel pressured. Can we do some kissing and stuff first?"

Face flooded with relief and gratitude he stepped towards her; wrapped his arms around her. He was warm and yielding, and his scent was like wood-shavings and fresh laundry.

"Of course we can. Kissing and sex and all of that, it's literally the only good thing about being in a body made of flesh. The rest of it just hurts. Angie, you smell so good. This is amazing."

Then her tongue was in his mouth, and their hands moved like those of virtuosos on the keyboard of the other's spine. Kissing turned everyone into a teenager, and clearly neither Angie nor her client were an exception. They caressed and fondled, making noises of appreciation down their noses as they tenderly undressed each other, blind and voiceless, their lips suction-locked together and their eyes closed. Only when she was down to her bra, the blouse and jacket somewhere on the carpet with her kicked-off shoes, did Angie think of something and break off the increasingly heated contact.

"Just a minute."

Padding to the window she unfastened the elaborate ties and pulled the wine-dark drapes together with a jingling swish of curtain-rings. She knew that the bull-headed titan and his thousand-eyed wings weren't deliberately staring at her tits, but it was creepy and off-putting all the same. Having the blinds drawn made her feel less like she was in some unusually ecclesiastical 'Confessions' film. With this accomplished, Angie and her client carried on where they'd left off.

In minutes, both were naked and their osculation had grown frantic. She had nipples that were sucked to rubber thimbles, and his hot erection in her palm. Those fingers on his right hand usually depicted raised in benediction were inside her, blessing juices into holy water. As their conjoined stumble led them inexorably towards the bed, like a conflicted pantomime horse, Angie realised that in the gloaming of the curtained bedchamber his head was glowing faintly with its own diffuse and milky radiance. Nothing too bright or dazzling. You wouldn't notice it in normal daylight.

It was pretty good, the sex. Excellent, even. He was thoughtful and attentive at all times, and when he asked if he could lick her out, his face was that of an incredulously happy puppy. Conscientious to a fault, he made sure she had one orgasm in the bank before he moved into an unsurprising missionary pose on top of her, careful to reassure her over any contraceptive worries.

"It's alright, you won't get pregnant. Mum and Dad weren't just from different species, they were from entirely separate ontologies, so technically I'm like a mule. I'm sterile. I can't reproduce."

They fucked enthusiastically while smouldering angel carcasses dropped screaming onto Bedford all around them. He delayed his climax until Angie's second one so they could come together, something that she'd always counted as a minor miracle, and yet it left her feeling shallow for having expected something more; perhaps something transcendent with a spiritual dimension. Or if not transcendent, at least dirtier. Speaking objectively, it was the best shag that she'd ever had, and if the special effects left her disappointed then she knew the fault was very probably with her. Her and the numbing, spectacle-addicted culture that had sculpted her desires and needs. She was too modern.

Afterwards they lay together side by side and talked, their conversation punctuated by sounds of collision as fatalities from the war overhead impacted with the nearby avenues. He seemed to want to talk about his parents, and as Angie listened she ran one magenta fingernail across his ribs, pausing to trace the contour of what she at first believed to be an appendectomy scar.

"I wish that I could have done more for my mum, the stuff she'd been through. My conception was the last thing anyone would call immaculate. You'll notice that the PR stories in the Bible don't say anything about consent. And when they say she was a virgin, in that place and time that means she was about fourteen. I can't even imagine what it must have been like, an all-powerful iterative equation, violently imprinting a genetic sequence on some helpless child who lacked the senses to perceive it properly. All the time I was growing up, she only mentioned it the once. From what I gathered, she experienced it as a sexual assault by an enormous eight-winged seagull. That detached look that she has in all the iconography is post-traumatic stress disorder. It destroyed her."

He asked Angie if she minded that he vaped, and when she said she didn't he hopped briefly from beneath the covers to retrieve his e-cig from the crumpled jacket on the floor. She had to admit that his bum was lovely. Back in bed, he drew a lungful of fruit-flavoured fog before continuing.

"Dad was a nightmare, basically, and worse when he'd been drinking. Yeah, I know, it wasn't really drinking, that's just what you're hearing as a close equivalent to what I'm saying. What it was, was prayer. Prayer got him hammered. That's not why he made humanity, but it was certainly an unexpected bonus. His behaviour got more and more erratic, and then finally he fell into a sort of feedback loop: people would pray, he'd get drunk and annihilate a town or two, which would make all of the survivors pray, and so on. He thought he was hiding it, but everybody knew. I mean, you take the Book of Job. It's obvious that he's completely rat-arsed, and that Satan talks him into beating someone up, as if he was some two-pint Tyson spoiling everybody's Friday night. What could we do? It's not like anyone was going to stage an intervention."

Angie ventured an amusing anecdote about her own dad, who had been a type compositor when that profession still existed, with a passion for Real Ale and Sixties vinyl, but this thread of conversation didn't seem to take off or go anywhere.

They talked for a bit longer until the downpour of angels outside sounded as if it was over, and then Jez asked Angie if she fancied any lunch.

They didn't bother getting dressed. They left their clothing scattered on the bedroom floor, as though by some mute understanding that the age of people wearing things was over. The world and its dress-code were no more. Downstairs, Angie sat comfortably naked in the dining room while Jez fussed in the kitchen, with her gaze continually drawn back to the dark lumber of Joanna Southcott's box, squatting there on the sideboard like an unexploded New Testament time-bomb. From the next room, Jez called through to ask her if she wanted wine with dinner, and if so would Pinot Grigio be okay? He'd looked through all the cupboards without finding the wine-glasses so this would, unfortunately, be served up in dainty little teacups. Angie said she didn't mind.

The food turned out to be a beautifully prepared portion of sea bass each, with an accompaniment of still-warm artisan bread rolls. The fish was perfect, falling off the fork, and the fresh bread steamed when she cracked the crust. By this juncture of her unusually eventful day, Angie decided that she found the nudist dining weirder than the paranormal nature of her lunch companion. She supposed she was acclimatising. Sipping hesitantly from the child-sized chinaware, she was surprised by just how good the wine was, if a bit close to room temperature. Thinking about it, she was even more surprised that the abstemious Panacea Society had thought to put away a bottle or two for the home's new owner to enjoy on his return. When she remarked at this to Jez he stared at Angie blankly for a second, fork paused halfway to his mouth, then realised her misapprehension.

"Oh, what, this? This isn't from the Panacea Society. I got this from the tap. That's why it's not properly chilled. If I'd thought earlier, I could have filled a jug and stuck it in the fridge."

She chewed this over with the sea bass – which, now that she thought about it, was just as unlikely an ingredient for the charitable trust to have provided as the wine. The business in the kitchen with Jez doing all the prep work had been theatre, she saw now; a performance for her benefit to make the meal seem less uncanny. She was fairly certain that if she went out into the kitchen, the gas-oven would be stone cold. He'd just waved his hand or summoned angels, hadn't he? Deceitful, although probably well-meaning. It was good grub just the same, and very filling. Neither of them finished it.

When he had cleared the plates and cutlery away, they sat and treated themselves to a second doll's-house cup of transubstantiated Pinot Grigio. Angie was uncomfortably aware that her job here at number eighteen was concluded, and that it would only be good manners to leave shortly and allow the client to get on with his day. It seemed like a good time to raise the matter of her prospects.

"I suppose I should be getting off soon. Is it alright if I stay in Bedford, or should I prepare to be uploaded to the Cloud?"

He looked hurt that she'd even had to ask.

"The Cloud? No. Not unless you want to be. I'm told it's very nice in a nirvana sort of way, with the white light and bliss and everything, but frankly we'd expected you to stick around the town here. You're the other party's legal representative, and so the company's obliged to take your satisfaction very seriously. Besides, how would it look if I let you show me the house, then went to bed with you, and then had you disintegrated? Also, from a practical perspective, all our legal people were appointed by my dad. There might well come a time when I need independent counsel. No, you stay wherever you feel comfortable. As far as I'm concerned, the whole of Bedford's yours."

Which seemed a generous gratuity. She thanked him and his company for their consideration, and the chat moved smoothly on to other matters, mostly season two of *Killing Eve*. They both agreed that Jodie Comer had been brilliant, although Jez maintained that he was personally getting a bit tired of made-up charismatic psychopaths. Eventually they lapsed into an easy silence and she noticed that he was once more scratching his palm distractedly. She figured it was time for her to go.

He walked her to the front door, where the hallway clock informed her that it was only a minute or two after half-past one, as if minutes and hours were still a thing. She didn't bother to collect her clothing from upstairs, even the jacket with her keys and mobile in its inside pocket. It wasn't that sort of planet anymore. Nude on the doorstep they exchanged a fond kiss and both wished each other luck, before the client went back inside and Angie turned to find out what was left of Bedford, now that it was hers. The orange bricks of the front path were warm beneath her feet.

At the front gate she lingered to assess her options. While she'd thought originally to pick up her car from Castle Road around the corner and then drive back to her flat, that didn't seem to be the way that things were going. Cars and homes, like mobile phones and clothing, had begun to feel already slightly retro; a bit last Saturday night, before the advent of a billion-year-long Sunday.

Angie stepped out on the sun-baked pavement of Albany Road and latched the gate behind her. There were dozens of singed feathers shifting in a listless breeze along the gutter, and what looked to be an outsized lump of coal that rested, smoking, in the middle of the street. Beyond that, on the far side of the road, the low fence that had previously bounded the allotments now enclosed a miniature deciduous forest, full of thirty-year-old trees that hadn't been around at half-past ten that morning. Most of them appeared to be in fruit, and choirs of birds perched on already-overburdened boughs, relinquishing the wildflower tangle of the ground below to drifting bees and at least three species of butterfly. Outside the bolted gate of the transformed allotments stood a man with wings, who Angie estimated to be at least nine feet tall. His chest was puffed out and his hands were clasped behind his back. He had a number one cut, white robes, and a sword with a blue-hot acetylene flame for a blade that somehow hung from his rope belt without setting the robes on fire. Security.

The beatific bouncer, turning his shaved head at intervals for deadpan glances up and down Albany Road, appeared to have no interest in the naturist solicitor. Taking this as an indication that she wasn't the angelic bruiser's primary prey, Angie stepped out onto the grey macadam and began to cross towards him. Pausing halfway, she identified the charred material at the road's centre as a huge incinerated torso, one of the supernal combatants that hadn't burned away completely in the atmosphere before it hit the streets of Bedford. There was nothing left, save for a blackened ribcage with a yard-long sternum, a gothic accordion, steaming and defeated. Wondering if the aerial slaughter was entirely over, she looked back at the house and the marvel-haunted skies above it.

The hallucinatory dogfight was concluded, with its casualties and contrails cleared away to ready the high cirrus stage for what appeared to be the headline act: it was equestrian after a fashion, featuring a skimpily clad bareback rider and her steed, although this crawled rather than cantered. Angie recognised the painfully slow mount as the Red Dragon that had been trolling the pregnant woman earlier, reduced here to a seven-headed beast of burden at the whim of its capricious mistress. Two or three of the vermillion creature's near-motionless craniums were thrown back in resentful snarls, as it progressed across the firmament at a real-time clay animation pace. Sprawling along its back, insouciant as a Tory Leader of the House, what Angie understood to be a deified ancient Iraqi sex-worker lifted her gem-encrusted grail in a sardonic toast to heaven.

Sumptuous body insufficiently concealed by gossamers of red and purple, only the colossal wanton's painted eyes betrayed her age, that made the furthest nebulae seem barely adolescent. Her expression was that of a former Pinewood beauty, dragging the iconic costume out of mothballs yet again and wearily reprising a career-defining scene at her nineteenth comic convention. Little wonder she was knocking back the Saints' Blood. Angie speculated as to the contractual language that the sacred harlot represented, and concluded that this must be something like a wax seal or a signature, down at the bottom of the document's last page. Conceivably the beast-and-woman combo was a corporate logo, possibly a mascot, an over-elaborate MGM lion. With an unexpected pang of sympathy for both these veteran performers, Angie turned away and carried on across Albany Road.

On the far pavement, the impossibly tall sentry guarding the allotments' west gate – a twelve-footer she decided, seen from closer up – ruffled his feathers self-importantly at her approach. He looked her up and down disinterestedly, as though contenting himself that she had nowhere to conceal weaponry or vodka, and then gave her a perfunctory nod.

"Yeah, you're alright, love. Go on in."

His voice was like a hurricane ten miles away. Until that moment, Angie hadn't really planned on entering the paradisiacal allotments, but hadn't specifically been planning not to. Now that the imposing doorman raised the prospect, she could see it had advantages: if she'd ruled out returning to her car or flat, then she was going to need some manner of accommodation, and here looked as promising as anywhere.

Plus, the Light of the World was living just across the street, and it might be nice having somebody she knew around the neighbourhood; someone she might run into as he set out for his morning walk along the Great Ouse, or whatever his routine turned out to be. She entertained the fleeting thought that one night he might ask her over to watch season three of *Killing Eve*, before remembering that there wasn't going to be one. Oh, well. Angie thanked the angel and then, sliding back the bolt that was the low gate's only fastening, she stepped into the jungle.

Like a Tardis or an acrimonious divorce, it seemed much bigger from inside than out, and it smelled lovely; a bouillon of everything. Closing the gate and setting out through lush grass for the nearest shady arbour, she took stock of her divine surroundings with their frankly unbelievable biodiversity. Parrots splashed Rousseau colours on the woodland's canopy while tangerine-furred foxes rustled through the orchids carpeting its floor. Moving with a magnificent deliberation through a distant stand of elms she thought she saw a tiger, and against the suede mahogany of Angie's forearm trickled a sole ladybird, bright as a shaving cut. Coiling around a branch above her was something she took for an exotic vine that had a curious metallic sheen, glinting and coppery. All of it tingled.

Angie barely noticed she'd acquired a retinue of iridescent turquoise dragonflies that hovered in formation at her brow, a shimmering seven-pointed diadem. Strolling unhurriedly between the fruiting trees she used her tongue to dislodge a recalcitrant fibre of sea bass from her front teeth, noting as she did so the persistent tang of her recent fish dinner flavouring her mouth. It was a pity that her client hadn't thought to offer her dessert, some sweet indulgence that would cleanse her palate and allow her to more thoroughly appreciate the tastes and perfumes of her Castle Road arcadia.

The final woman, then, there in the garden, faintly peckish.

SKOO

Alistair Fruish

ri-mari, wi goo atz urdz, tri fu stand. Wi sten to ri-mari az shim goo tru skoo. wi ere. shim lurn, wi lurn. wi tri sez urdz fu ri-mari. wi tri splane.

wi ol ol skoo. wi lodge firm onz olitary taintop, fullimatik. dredz ov yeeer pass. nuwhen croz salt wet-her ta reach uz. dredz nd dredz ov yeeer turn ta sandz nd haps illionz pass.

onz our land iz nuwhen bu uz. wi run, bu empti. nuwhen cum. nubother. wi fullimatik. wi fix. wi clean. wi gleam. dam nd sun nd wind duce nergi inuz. wi readi.

den atz las small boat croz. den nother. nd slow, folk swell ere neath uz. till ventual noo illage cum to tainfoot, nd folk turn turf nd sow full wiv crops az far az wi can peer. wi watch az illage grow nd grow.

den atz las, brave wunz skale midable ight to vestigate uz onz our peak, out findz our oose. wi kill fust vaders az zay temp smash inz. nex vaders open uz up right way, wi kill allz bu wun, az zay tempt sneak out thu kave, rong way. zey sorbed fu-evs, az bone brave nd blud brave, once not wi, now make brave wallz nd hallz nd allz ov skoo fu evs.

den las wun gez wi, atz las. ri-mari inz joinz. liv side wi az ogrammed. liv inz uz, no tempt scape. ri-mari. fust. wi feed nd care nd skoo fust wun till yeeer onz ri-mari pass allz tess nd gez ventual tonomi. leesed.

ri-mari, skoo iz ducate place max imumsec. fullimatic.

so goo ri-mari, goo tainfoot illage nd etch uz rong-unz. wi lurn um, az inz pass. wi take aptiv int wi fu gud, less zey lurn, if um gez tru skoo's n-term, zen wi urn um oose.

The Thunderous Applause

Yoshe

You ever do that thing where you imagine you're being interviewed on a talk show?

You're daydreaming, telling them about your day, or your childhood, or your whatever, and the host is asking probing but sensitive questions, and the audience is nodding and murmuring in agreement and everyone thinks you're fucking deep, and then now and again you catch yourself and realise that actually you're just a bit of an egomaniac who has somehow convinced herself that the ins and outs of her pretty standard life are fascinating enough to warrant their own slot on what is presumably prime time viewing space.

I do it all the time.

I'm doing it right now.

Usually it's the final video, the social media e-ulogy thing, that really gets me fucking going. You know, the sad but uplifting one that floats at the top of your profile after you die, nestled in amongst circling memories and tributes from your mates. You wanna wrack up three, four figure engagement ideally – cos if you don't, then you've really got to ask yourself what the hell you've been doing with your life, and like, how have you ended up with so few people missing you when you're gone, and wanting to click 'sad' or 'sorry' or perhaps the more substantial 'you'll be missed', to register that sadness online.

And I want a proper one, Alex – you're probably called Alex, right?

They're always called Alex, the talk show hosts these days. So yeah, Alex, if you've done something, really done something, left your mark on the world – you get interviewed, right? Like this. But a real one, a proper big end of life one in a studio, with cameras and assistants. You know the sort – the impressive retrospective, the legendary review of your very existence for all the world to pore over on a screen. They're always beautifully edited, really show you off in a good light – not too meek, not too up yourself, and definitely not boring. Just ordinary enough in all the right places to be relatable, but you know, not actually very ordinary at all.

I'm gonna make it. Up there with the people who really existed, and kept existing long after they stopped existing, cos everyone they left behind still talked about them, watched them, read their stuff. Cos I look at it this way – I'm going to be alive for what, ninety-five, a hundred years? But I'm gonna be dead a whole lot longer than that. So this thing needs to be good. Proper fucking good.

Let's wind back a sec, right – I've got to assume that by the time this airs, and so I guess by the time I die, the bulk of what I'm telling you may well be obsolete. Alex, audience, when you're hearing this, e-ulogy videos might have been replaced by something else entirely – something sleeker, probably with a more matt finish, less letters in the title, and with a brighter logo that's got cleaner edges.

So, a quick recap for all you futuristos –

After we died, our Sociabubble pages became *in memento* – frozen in time, with a colour scheme and layout that we had chosen earlier. Our top memories (as upvoted by our friends, or if you're somebody – your fans) circled the page header like fucked-up post-mortem confetti. And bang in the middle of it all – the e-ulogy video, our final message to the world. Who we were, what we did, how we're gonna be remembered.

At a set time, everyone who knew us or knew of us – depending how busy they were that week –gathered online in a Virtual Mourning eHub. eFuneral attendees. All lined up, little bouncing pixilated avatars. From time to time, bloggers and angry-people-in-online-comments-sections debated whether we should be trying to return to physical funerals – for everyone, not just the people who've got money. But why should funerals be any different to other occasions; weddings, graduations, birthday parties? Sit inyour room, connect from there. Better for productivity, better for the planet. Safer for everyone. And I mean, can you imagine actually physically travelling, all over the world, to wherever the latest person in your network had happened to die? Ridiculous. Plus, when you're virtually mourning, you can nip out for a snack or a piss anytime you like.

The eFuneral high scorers – the six-digit ones, they're pretty much always under forty. It's funny, I hadn't noticed that before I started working here – I guess on some level I'd always assumed that the longer you had to get to know people, the more people you'd accumulate for goodbyes. But no, cos actually you've got to factor in that a bunch of them will die before you, plus there's something about a beautifully tragic young corpse that people really get hard over. Gives you more to talk about, right, probably a story there? Bit more exciting than 'lived to standard life expectancy, died in their sleep.'

The high scoring over forties are typically famous people, or people who did a hell of a lot of volunteering. Working here at Sociabubble, monitoring all the interactions, you see patterns emerging. There's the initial rush of mourning. Bunch of posts from everyone who knew them. Some who clearly barely knew them at all, but felt obligated, or saddened, or reminded of their own mortality enough to click a generic 'sorry you're gone' kinda thing.

After the eFuneral, it starts to slow. The odd 'this reminded me of you'. The occasional 'really struggling without you today'. First anniversary, there's generally a handful of tributes, but then as the years go by the handful shrinks, until you've only got one or two people who keep it going – then they die too, and it all goes eerily quiet. You can literally watch on a graph as a person disappears completely.

I just don't want to disappear, Alex – gone, like I never existed at all – and I don't think that's too much to ask.

You see, the six-digiters – they keep going, their line never touching the ground. That's probably not realistic for me, but five figures would be nice. Four might be more doable. Three, I'd fucking hope so. Three figures is fuck all on the Internet.

On some level though, I'd always thought – well, when I was younger I mean, it sounds stupid now – that I could get six digits. I dunno, maybe some part of me assumed I'd die young. Not for any particular reason, just because it's hard to picture yourself old when you're starting out. And if I didn't, I thought I'd at least do something massive that would put me on the map.

I'm running out of time to die young. And I'm not making any map, sitting here at a grey desk that once was white, handling complaints on a social media site that's now basically as dead as most of its users.

Ping. Click.

Ms Gen Armora. This one's angry. Lots of capital letters. Buckle up Alex, these ones are always FUN.

You BASTARDS

Strong start.

you absolute CUNTING BASTARDS. you put his page up, his memorial thing, my brothers SHITTING memorial thing before we even knew!!! his own SHITTING sister!!! how dare you!!! you think you can just sit there … in your ivory tOWER

I look around the office. Yeah alright, that'd be the day.

while we find out … through your stupid site that he died, not through FAMILY, not from anyone who CARED about HIM, through your STUPID website. HOW DO YOU THINK THAT MAKES US FEEL!!! maybe you should have a little fucking RESPECT … for the dead … you actual prick-faced piss-stain PATHETIC excuse for a pre-assembled collection of human ORGANS!!1!

Oof.

Scan. Click.

Forward to the Department of Accuracy and Post-life Scheduling – Ripple Fifteen.

"We don't believe in hierarchies here," they told me on my first day.

"What we believe in is ... Ripples."

The Ripples are given extra authority and filled with more senior, better paid employees as you move up through them – but they're not hierarchical, because the company doesn't believe in that.

I started out at the twenty-sixth Ripple – Department of Functionality and Frontline Technicians – and I've worked my way up to the seventeenth – Department of Complaints and Customer Engagement. If it sounds boring as fuck, that's only because it is. I can't work out whether I've become desensitised to this sort of thing – the complaints, the Ripples, the sinking feeling you're pissing your life away – or if I've actually always hated this job and I just used to try convince myself otherwise so I didn't gouge my own eyeballs out of their sockets.

That's a solid chunk of my life now – complaint comes in, I forward it on.

When it comes to complaints at this job, like most death jobs, you're usually not dealing with the person in question – instead you get their relatives and friends, often in that early, very messy part of grief where they could be anywhere between virtually silent, and a completely unfiltered bag of loud, ferocious emotions.

Relatives who are certain the wrong pictures have been featured. "They would have wanted their pictures to be from that Christmas we had all together," they plead. That's always tough.

Protective friends who are absolutely sure that embarrassing post should be removed.

People who had changed their profile names as a joke and then died. Your classic Ben Dover and Connie Lingus of course, but also your slightly more unique variations – Ura Massif-Cocque, Iwas Inurma, or the trolling account that spawned a thousand free speech think pieces, Adolf Weinstein.

One guy had simply become Big Nuts.

"Can we change it back?" His family tearfully begged.

I felt bad for them, I really tried. Took it as high as I was authorised to – Ripple Six – Department of Theoreticals and Box Exteriors.

"Unfortunately," came the reply, "as per our user policy, we cannot. We apologise for any inconvenience caused and thank you for choosing

Sociabubble for all your needs."

Reluctantly, the family mourned their beloved Big Nuts, his side-splitting work of comedy memorialised for eternity, automatically popping up with every post.

RIP. We love you Big Nuts.

Take a screen break. Check my phone. Maybe this evening I'll finally send that message I've been drafting to Lish for the last six months or so. It wasn't nearly as dull when she worked here.

Who is Lish?

Well, Alex, how do I put this?

She's the fucking best. The best ever. The best person that ever fucking lived. She's smart, and she's funny, and she's got this way of making me feel completely at ease, like maybe who I am just now is okay and I can just breathe.

It didn't used to be as eerily quiet when Lish was here. We used to hang out every day, and even outside of that there was always the faintly reassuring murmur of employees chipping away at both their files and their ever-decreasing collective will to live. Now there's just this whirring somewhere in the office – a faint hum that if you squint your ears hard enough, you start to be convinced is coming from the inside of your own head. I've tried to track it down; I thought for a while that it was coming from the water cooler. But when I got there, it was as if it had moved again. On quiet days, I've followed it around the room, and no matter where I am, it's always just out of reach. Sometimes when I have a particularly shitty day, I swear it gets louder, just to piss me off.

Ms Gen Armora bounces around my head for a few hours. It was a strange one. I mean, the tone was pretty standard – fairly average ratio of capital letters to swears that I'd grown accustomed to here in Complaints and Customer Engagement.

No, it was something she said, something that just ever so slightly sets off a lurking sense of déjà vu, just at the back of my mind, just behind my ears. I'd had one like this – less angry, similar issue – what, three weeks ago? From a stylist with long red tentacles of hair, a Ms Doll Brandicarta. She hadn't been shouty so much as bemused, and explained politely that whilstshe appreciated the flattering in memento pagethat had just gone up for her, well, she wasn't actually dead.I ran a check on her ID, and sure enough, she did seem very much alive. Must have been some kind of blip in the logging system. I even gave her a quick video call just to be on the safe side, and to give her an apology for the mistake.

"Still here," she laughed, playfully pinching at the skin on her arm. "At least I was last time I checked!"

So, I send her page off to Ripple Eleven – Department of Convergence and Lateral-Centric Strategy - to be resurrected. Sent her memento page off to Ripple Nine – Department of Continuity and Paradoxical Finality – to be taken down. Page changed in error, I tell them.

They both bounce back. Error unrecognised.

"Hey Nod, can I get a double check on this?"

Nod obliges.

"Error unrecognised."

"You sure, Nod?"

"I am not sure of everything, friend. But I am learning. And now, I certainly am. Error unrecognised."

Odd.

On Doll's *memento* page, the tributes are pouring in, you know, from people who really should know better; should have known that she isn't actually dead. Her mum, her brother, her boss, her wife who she lives with… *How are none of them realising she's still alive?* My imagination runs away with me. Was she so distant from the people in her life that none of them have noticed this glaring digital error? I mean sure, loneliness and social isolation have been on a continual rise for the last seventy-odd years, but we can still spot the difference between life and death in the people we love, right? For a while I get proper riled up about it, pacing around the office muttering about the fall of civilisation.

But then, it turns out she is dead after all. I put it down to iffy timing, try to put it out of my mind.

It is weird though, really fucking weird. Like her Sociabubble page knew what was coming before she did. Was I the last person she spoke to? She looked so…. well.

For a week afterwards, I keep having the same dream, just replaying that video call, over and over again.

"Still here," she laughs, and pulls at her skin. And it just comes right off.

Five years ago, I worked in an office of fifty. Several thousand in the whole company, fifty in our Ripple. Lish sat over there, there by that fake orange tree that's not fooling anyone. The bullshit orange, she used to call it, which made me laugh every time. It's funnier the way she says it, honest, she does this voice and it's great. She used to come sit on the end of my desk, legs swinging back and forth.

"There you go again," she'd tease me, if I went too far into talk-show-daydream-land. "Away with the fairies."

Man, she saw right through me, in a totally good way. Maybe it's codependency but she'd balance me out a bit. She'd tell me not to worry when I stressed about what I was 'doing with my life'. Said this whole preoccupation was just a hangover from hustle culture that's making me feel like nothing I do is enough. "Listen to the cheers of the people you care about, Bit, and fuck the rest. If it's not from someone you care about, it's just noise."

The Author – that's what we called the guy in charge, the guy who'd started Sociabubble back in the day – was big on natural environments, and he'd had these ridiculous plants put in all over the office. They weren't real, of course, it'd be too much hassle to keep them alive. They had a mechanism in them, so they'd grow a few millimetres a day, and when they reached some predetermined optimal height, there was a snap and a whoosh, and they'd shrink right back down again. Can't have giant plants taking over the office.

The shrinks were digitally randomized to add to the overall integrity of the experience, and we used to bet WhirlybangsTM from the vending machines on which one would whoosh down next.

It's a nice memory, having mates at work. We'd gather around someone's desk, pore over the Sociabubble pages of our users and speculate wildly and very unprofessionally about who they were, who they *really* were, if you stripped away the elements of carefully crafted persona that dotted their digital masquerade. Man, we used to waste hours of company time. Delicious hours of inside jokes and the kind of cynical pisstaking that comes with being put in a room with a bunch of humans and asked to do more-or-less the same thing over and over again in the interest of making rich people you'll never meet even richer.

We became masters of deciphering the undertones in grief-fuelled platitudes. People had a tendency to hide their death discomfort behind overly exaggerated absolutes. And they were always polite. Oh so polite.

Tributes that began "You were such a character, and we may not have always seen eye to eye..." we translated as "I hated you, but I do feel an appropriate level of sadness that a human being I know is now dead".

"Always ready with an honest word" tributes below a e-ulogy in which the phrase "look, I just tell it like it is" was uttered no less than 12 times... This person definitely made unsolicited comments about your body every time they saw you, always either preceded with "I'm not trying to be rude, but" or followed by "just saying".

"Such a character" we saw on one particular profile. It had no picture, just an American flag with a banner above that read "love this land or I'll bury you in it" attributed to "the most patriotic of the founding fathers, Winston Churchill". Oh yeah this guy was a racist for sure, and a geographically confused one at that.

And then, one day – fucked day, as we took to calling it – Sociabubble was trending. Not because we'd bought out yet another site, not because we'd had some disastrous leaked nudes scandal – although that happened A Lot. No, for the first time since its launch in a dorm room seventy-six years ago, Sociabubble had more dead users than living ones. And man, we were fucked. See, there's a clever reason behind the name.

Our active user profiles plummeted, nobody wanted to be seen trying to keep up with a dead site. We were worried enough when people's grannies started using it, but now their grannies were dead, and still using it, and that's a hard image to shake.

And so, The Author – always one to make the best out of a bad situation – announced that what we couldn't beat, we would capitalise upon. Ramp up our focus on the *in memento* pages – really fine tune the virtual grieving process, pin down exactly what people wanted to preserve of their loved ones, and how they wanted to be remembered themselves. Keep them coming back with the power of not wanting to let go. Invest in death, so to speak.

And, you know, it worked. Sociabubble became a vast digital graveyard, still massive and hosting the pages of its remaining living users, but with an 'increasing focus on asynchronous post expiration profile continuation'.

It didn't take so many people though – most of this could be automated. Colleagues were swapped out for algorithms, Lish was replaced by a pale grey hard drive that sat beside her desk, intermittently beeping.

I got a digital assistant called Nod.

And so, the office morphed into a whirring mass of sleek machinery, murmuring and buzzing just enough that if you let your ears glaze over and only half hear your surroundings, you could just about mistake it for the murmuring and buzzing of your rapidly vanishing colleagues. Lish said it could have been good, could have been a socialist cyber utopia with people on universal income and stuff, but then OmniFriend – the conglomerate that owns Sociabubble and basically everything else – wouldn't be able to keep us all in debt and desperate to sell ourselves for scraps at any chance we get.

There was no escaping the surreality of this new landscape. See for yourself. *We'll probably get some sort of b roll cutaway at this point. On the screen behind the sofas that Alex and I sprawl luxuriously across, we'll project, like, a three-dimensional walk around the office.*

Over here, in the centre of the room – a ring of chairs shaped like letters that had once slightly wonkily spelled out the word c o l l a b o r a t e, except the col had been needed to prop up the pool table, and the la had fallen off back when we were still on seventh-wave feminism.

b o r a t e. Inspiring.

Faded green letters arch overhead – 'team work makes the dream work' – only the word 'team' and most of the 's' had all but disappeared completely years ago. So, in actual fact, it told us 'work make the dream work', like some kind of crazed robotic grammar-bending celebration of capitalist labour.

Winding down through the middle of the room are two curling tubes, crossing the diameter of the space before circling around one another. One red, one blue. Great solid cylinders that hollowed into twisting slides when they were launched. And they had been ever so cleverly designed so as to be impossible to use unless two people launched from the overhanging beams at their opposite sides of the room at precisely the same moment. Something about cooperation opening up new avenues, or breaking down blockages as a team, or both, and neither, possibly. The colours represent "contrasting forces of energy"; I remember that phrase for certain. I remember it, because I distinctly recall thinking that it sounded like exactly the sort of bollocks that uber capitalist drones like The Author probably think make them sound deep and meaningful, when actually it just makes them sound like a massive knob.

Lish said the slides were in fact subconsciously phallic monuments to the only two things Sociabubble really cares about – money and power. And she said it's appropriate, because the two of them intertwine, and you can't separate them in the company's desires. They want money for power, they want power for money, they get both, and we get the opposite, and so it just spirals up and up for them, and down and down for us, like intertwining slides, so it's like a metaphor, within another metaphor, or something, you get it.

God she's smart and hot.

Sometimes I eat lunch perched on the bottom of the blue slide, or on the permanently lowered half of the seesaw. It graces the centre of the room, bobbing occasionally when a draft flows through the building. Chrome messages swing gently from the ceiling, boasting of the things that can be achieved when we're connected, synergising, becoming one as a team.

The water cooler sits in the furthest corner from my desk. Still.

As each Ripple of Sociabubble shrank, the spaces between them spread further and further apart, sprawling out incessantly like a disease. It's mad now, you need to get a train for, like, two and a half hours just to get to Ripple Zero.

The plants keep growing though. Nobody ever waters them, and still they grow and grow.

The lights above me sparkle.

"Do you ever wonder," poses Alex, in an extravagant, booming voice, "what would happen if you were to, you know, go?"

"As in die? Or quit my job?"

"Either-or, really."

"Well, Alex, by the time this airs, I guess we'll find out!"

Pause for laughter, possibly some mildly uncomfortable shuffling towards the back of the audience. That's okay. If anything, making people mildly uncomfortable makes them more likely to share this video. More hits, more views, more legacy for me.

"But seriously Alex, I can't see how the bots would ever get good enough to answer the kinds of questions we get. I mean, we're dealing with proper deep, proper human stuff here. People's legacies, man."

"And they don't always get it right, the bots?"

"They most certainly do not! We've had all sorts: AIs getting occasion greetings mixed up, and offering a hearty congratulations on the death of your nan. Or that light-hearted generator which rated the aesthetics of your meal, got hacked and started being applied to babies and, erm, really upset some new parents. Not to mention that slightly problematic phase of bots aligning animals with the music tastes of different demographics and, as a side effect, deeply offending a bunch of middle-aged white women. So yeah, they don't always get it right, Alex. You need at least one human in there, too."

Unlike most of the bots in our Ripple, Nod is audio enabled, and what started as a semi-ironic occasional exchange has blossomed into more-or-less a full-blown friendship.

"How are you today, Nod?" I ask each morning, to which the response comes from a selection of fourteen variations on "I'm good thanks, how are you?" The odd jovial add on: "I could go for a good old-fashioned beer actually", or the charming, if a little overdone, "All the better since you walked in!"

"And how are you today, friend?"

I find myself answering from a pool of slightly fewer responses.

"Are you scared of dying, Nod?"

Nod swivels in my direction to indicate listening. Two lights blink encouragingly up at me.

"I cannot die, friend. I will live on forever in my programming."

"Lucky you. I think I'm scared of what they'll say about me after I'm gone."

"After we're gone, we can no longer do anything about it."

"Nice, Nod. Very profound"

"WHIRLYBANGS! ONE BANG AND YOU'RE WHIRLED!"

"Nod, we agreed not to do ads mid conversation. It's dehumanising."

"Soothe your concerns with the delicious taste—"

Fucks sake man.

It's more than that though, Alex. It's more than what other people will say about me. I mean, fuck, what do I say about me? What do I say at the end if I just kind of stumble into it without ever getting around to *doing* anything? It just kind of slipped me by? I had a hundred-odd years of living and I just kind of walked around and ate things? Recently, I've found myself wondering how much would actually be different if you filmed my e-ulogy now, compared to ten years ago. Or ten years from now? What if you could film my e-ulogy right at this moment, and it would be virtually usable at the end of my life? It fucking terrifies me.

If I could just help one person, just improve the life of one individual… that's what you're supposed to say, right? That's the nice person thing to think. Bit of a shit ratio though, isn't it? One person helping one person, kind of just cancelling yourself out. Nah. I want to be remembered by everyone. Or at least, most of them. A lot of them. I'd settle for quite a few of them.

For someone so obsessed with what I'll Do, I fully appreciate the irony of how little I've Done. In fact, I've come to believe the two are actually, maddeningly, linked. Everything I do has to be so important; the Thing, the big Thing, the Thing has got to be right, to define my life's purpose. Anything I do before or after it has to somehow complement that legacy, and I'm not even sure what the legacy is yet. I keep nearly figuring it out, almost settling on a Thing I should at least try for, and then it changes, or I change, or the stuff of life just gets in the way without me even realising that's what's going on, and before I know it, fuck, the Thing hasn't happened again, and I'm back to square one except more time has passed.

Is this how everybody feels? Is this how the people in the interviews felt, right before they did the Thing they ended up talking about?

I mean, sure, I could have just posted something stupid on my Sociabubble page, see how many people will share it. That'd be some sort of legacy, I guess. Something quick and easy, a video of my arsehole clenching and unclenching, perhaps, but dubbed over an opera singer so it looks like it's giving a beautiful virtuoso performance.

It's the age-old question, Alex: do you get known for something moderately vapid and eventually irritating, if that's realistically all you might manage – or do you hold out for something incredible and risk missing your window entirely? I mean, that's before we even get to the probably more interesting question of who gets to decide what's really meaningful art anyway. If we make our own meaning in the art we see, then it stands to reason that if you can't find at least a shred of meaning in a video of my opera singing arsehole then you're probably a boring fuck anyway.

I catch my reflection in a swaying chrome letter D. My lips are moving silently. There's a frenzied expression on my face, far too much going on for a woman standing alone in an office. Do I look a bit mad? Probably. Nod is unlikely to judge.

"I'm a bit scared of dying," I offer aloud.

"You'll be okay!" comes the cheery response. "I believe in you."

"Thanks Nod. What would I do without you?" *All I'd have to talk to would be Alex and this talk show audience that I made up.*

"Will I, though?" as I slightly resented myself for needing reassurance from a fucking bot. "How can you know that? How can any of us know?"

"I do not know everything, friend. But I am learning."

I mulled over my endlessly edited message to Lish.

"…or get a drink sometime," I read, sounding it out. "…or *grab* a drink sometime."

Does grab sound aggressive in this context? What do you think, Alex?

Maybe forego grab and get altogether, maybe fuck the whole drinks thing off, I can't even remember if she drinks actually. Go with coffee instead? Could be seen as euphemistic though. Euphemistic could be good…?

No, no coffee. No drinks.

Lunch. Everyone needs lunch. Lunch lunch lunch. Lunch is all you need.

Lunch seems to be the audience favourite.

Next sentence: "I'll bring the jalapenos…"

That does make sense, honestly. Last time I saw her we had a jalapeno-off. Someone in her division got a bunch of extra hot ones for cheap at the shop on the corner, and it turned into one of those classic competitive channel-your-repressed-feelings-into-eating-jalapenos goodbye parties. I ate thirty-two. Lish had fifty-one. Dead fucking romantic, man. Seriously.

We gazed into each other's watering eyes. Best place to hide your tears, a jalapeno-off.

And then she left. Gone in a round of cuts. And I haven't seen her since.

I thought I'd better not message her the day she left, that might seem a bit full on. I waited a week, but then thought, nah, don't send a message exactly seven days on, that makes it seem like you've been counting. Then I couldn't work out if it had been long enough to start with "hey sorry it's been a while" or to make some excuse, and so I've just kind of been going round and round in circles–opening, editing, deleting, regretting my personality.

I want it to be just right.

Cos we're not in a hurry, you know. We're both young-ish, there's plenty of time. I've thought about how I'll tell her how I feel. I'll wait till the perfect moment, and I've been thinking about all this for so long that it really *has* to be perfect now. Also gives me time to make sure she definitely feels the same. Because I did sometimes worry that maybe she was just being friendly.

"Hey, Nod, think fast!"

The stress ball bounced against their blinking silver head

"Hey, friend," came a monotone voice. "Not cool." A little shake and a mildly unsettling chuckle let me know my automated colleague was, in their own way, playing along.

I've sometimes wondered why, out of everyone in our office, they left me. I wasn't the hardest working, I wasn't the smartest, I regularly scored low for observation and attention to detail.

I'm not good at negotiating pay rises. That might have something to do with it.

Still, it's fine. I manage, I have enough to live on, I have stuff to do to pass the day. I'm not particularly changing the world, but really, who does? Maybe I'll stick this job out, it's not so bad. Try to lean into the contentment that so freaks me out. Finally send that message, go for lunch, move in with Lish. We could get a plant together. A real one.

I can barely hear the whirring by the water cooler, it's settled to a low background hum. Times like this, I can almost convince myself that it's basically a gentle massage on the back of my head, just softly rumbling there, not too overpowering. Flick through my timeline.

Scrolling.

Scrolling.

Cats being chased by battery operated cucumbers.

Scrolling.

Scrolling.

Lish.

"So sorry to hear you're gone. You were one of the good ones."

What the fuck.

"I can't believe it was just the other day I was speaking to you, going to miss you so much. You were never afraid to be true to yourself."

No. No?

This isn't happening, not like this.

I stare at her page as the tributes roll in. Picking up pace, like a train hurtling down the side of a mountain, brakes unhinged. The whirring in the corner grows louder, until I can feel it throbbing in the front of my head.

But I haven't even told her yet.

My breath frantically piles up in the back of my throat til it blocks, a pounding lump convulsing into something sharp and scratching, I can't swallow, I can't think, I can't fucking breathe.

And then everything goes numb.

It's been three days since Lish's page memorialised, and I've been in some kind of hazy, strange nightmare. I've tried calling her more times than I can count, just in case. No answer, the clinical voicemail driving her silence louder each time. I haven't slept, not really, just little moments of semi consciousness now and again when my body gives in and it all briefly disappears into tumultuous dreams in which I'm awake, and paralysed, and exhausted, and not really here. I haven't eaten properly either, I'm now solely powered by fucking disbelief. There's something twisting in my stomach, and everything I'm saying now, everything I'm telling you Alex, is competing with the incessant fucking deafening whirring of indeterminable shite from the other side of the room.

"Fucking hell! What do you want from me? You can't put a pause on your shitting humming even for this? She's fucking dead okay, and I need quiet, I need to think, I need you to shut up! Do you get that?"

The water cooler glares obnoxiously back at me. Hummmmmm.

I still haven't posted on her page.

What could I say?

Surely this shouldn't have hit me so hard, it's not like we were even together. But we were always more than what we were – we just *were*!

I used to think about her a lot, but not like this. Now it's fucking relentless, there's nothing else in my brain, not even for a second and I can't bear it, but I can't imagine anything else ever mattering again either. I don't know what to do, Alex. I don't know how to feel better than this. I don't know how to ever feel better than this at all. I'm just walking in circles, like some mad cunt, round and round a propped up shitty fucking seesaw.

So, how many days has it been now, Alex?

Come on, you must be keeping track, right? It's your fucking show.

I seem to have stopped going home. Mostly stopped sleeping too. If anyone checks the office surveillance, they'll just think I'm pulling an all-nighter. They'd fucking love that. Nod doesn't have to sleep, why the fuck should I?

I keep standing by Lish's desk, staring at her page. *Remembering*, it says in green at the top, and all of a sudden it seems like such a flimsy thing to be left behind from a whole life.

Like all unexpected deaths, her e-ulogy has been AI generated from her messages, posts, and notes in her eJournal. Her voice has been perfectly pieced together from her videos, and it reads out key sentiments echoed throughout her profile.

"I have lived a good life", she says, as if it's no big deal at all, "I stuck by my principles, I cared for those around me, and I was content.

And to those of you I didn't tell enough, I love you."

Is that about me? She didn't tell me she loved me at all, that's not nearly enough! That part could totally be about me, right?

I sit down on her chair. I don't know if this is helpful. I want to feel her here, you know, like people say when someone dies. Feel her presence, feel her moving through me somehow. And I don't. I don't feel anything like I should. And I don't know what the fuck is wrong with me.

Scroll through her Sociabubble, scroll further, scroll back to when she worked here. Days merge into weeks into years on the bottomless page. All these chances to tell her how I feel. Felt. No, feel.

I'm back in her mid-twenties now, when she was with the guy with the fuzzy black hair. I feel that pang I got in my stomach when she used to talk about him at the office. First in that ridiculous but adorable *everything's a dream* voice, and then gradually, one forgotten anniversary and several stupid offhand remarks later, with a dry, heavy acceptance. Then the tears came, every few weeks, then every few days, then all the fucking time. My eyes glaze over as I scroll on, back in time through the pictures, both of them grinning wishfully into their inevitable, impending collapse in reverse.

To her early twenties, with that girl with the smart, cropped brown hair. Eyes deep and piercing, jawline like some kind of fucking supermodel shark. That one really hurt, not that any of it matters now. There they are at mini golf, and there at a cat café, and there with her parents. I feel a brief moment of sympathy for supermodel shark. I wonder if she knows about Lish, if she still thinks of her all these years on.

Come on, Bit, this isn't healthy. You know it isn't.

Just five more minutes.

Several hours later, I'm still flicking back and forth between pictures, still mulling over her words. Does she mean she loved me? I mean, who else could she have possibly bonded with like we did, the way we laughed together, the way she looked into my eyes, it's me right? It has to be.

I could sort of check. I mean technically I shouldn't but fuck man, I'm tired, I'm grieving, I haven't eaten, literally nobody ever checks what I do here and I totally fucking could.

The audience gapes at me, rows and rows silently judging my next move. Oh come on, as if you wouldn't if you were in this situation. You totally would, wouldn't you? Every last one of you.

Yeah okay, you've convinced me. I'm gonna check.

My hands are shaky as fuck but I get into the backend of her profile. Straight to her eJournal, where she records thoughts that she doesn't want to post publicly, but which help the algorithm more accurately assist her.

Skim.

Skim.

That could be about me?

Picture of the office exit, two years ago, with an annotation indicating she was super happy. She would have seen me that day, I'm certain, probably right before she left and posted that. So clearly, I make her happy.

Come on, Lish, more about me. Where am I, where am I…

She seems to feel she has to hide our love, even from the AI, maybe even from herself. But I know it's there. I've seen our whole relationship pan out, in my head, and it was so clear and so warm. Going for lunch together, getting a house together, having a plant – a real one – that symbolises our ever growing love. She must want that. Who wouldn't? It was beautiful.

I'm gonna find absolute confirmation. I know it's not much practical good now, but I need to know, in some ways more than ever, that it wasn't just me.

Five more minutes.

Several hours later, I'm deeper in her backend than I've ever been in anyone's. I've completely given up any pretence of working and I'm not sure what time of day or night it is. At this point I'm not even expecting to see more about me; this is proper bottom of the barrel stuff, the most boring of the behind the scenes. I just want to know her better. There's also something about endlessly scrolling that really seems to be a magnet for the depressed – it needs such little energy, you basically can't fuck it up, and yet you somehow still feel like you are doing something with your time.

There's info here from Ripple Three – Department of Numerics and Temporal Calculations. That sounds thoroughly dull, and therefore definitely the part of the mindless cyberstalking that we have gloriously arrived at.

It opens into a spreadsheet that's entirely blank other than three columns. Not sure what I'm looking at here. A date, a digital clock that reads zero, and a box that reads ninety-eight point three percent accuracy.

I'm about to click out of this window of maths nerds, when it clicks. That date was a few days ago, the day Lish died. So I guess that answers the question of what Numerics and Temporal Calculations does, records when our users dies. Seems like that really shouldn't need an entire department: bureaucracy gone mad I guess.

As I exit the file, the *last updated* catches my eye. Two years ago.

Two years ago?

It hasn't been edited at all for... two years?

Must be a glitch. I dive into a bunch more profiles, dodgy backend after dodgy backend.

The audience are on the edge of their seats. Alex leans towards me, with that sickeningly self-assured, semi-raised eyebrow.

Holy shit. They do.

They have this for everyone, years in advance. I delve further, and each percentage when clicked opens into an intricate sprawling map of calculations – health records, socioeconomic data, pollution figures, sexual history, genetics … thousands of tiny information points overlapping and feeding into the final calculation.

But why, what good is that to them? Maybe it helps them be more, like, prepared for the profile transition or something? Maybe the AIs need a head start to make e-ulogies, maybe it's secretly not automated at all? Maybe they know when people are going to die because they're the ones killing them! Maybe it's a fucking conspiracy, maybe if I try scramble the letters…

"Oh yeah", says Alex, "cos that's exactly how all solid theories start."

Okay fuck off mate, at least I'm trying something. Sociabubble, social bubbe, babies blob bob club slubibabebo, nope. How about OmniFriend, fiend, minor fiend – is that something? That feels like something. But what does it mean?

Space out and think about Lish. Lish would know what to do. She was, is, was, so much smarter than me, I think that's why I loved her so much. Love. Loved? Love.

My eyes pan across the room, the chairs, the pool table, the slides.

The slides.

And I remember that they're subconsciously phallic monuments to the only two things Sociabubble really cares about. And I think I get it.

"Do you?" Alex asks.

Only one way to find out, you know where we gotta look.

"Accounting files!" he cheers. The audience cheers. Man, we're all very fucking in sync here.

My eyes are buzzing, the whirring of the office rattling around my head. I don't know what I'm running on, it's certainly not fucking sleep. Coffee, adrenaline, and deep-seated sheer fucking resentment of the organisation I work for, I reckon.

The audience looms in, absolutely hooked on it all, as I sift through every last grimy detail, every spreadsheet, every invoice, and… yeah, we got 'em.

Fuck, this is it. This is going to be my Thing. This will get me a five-digit eFuneral at least, possibly even six!

So, I guess I'm off. Ripple Zero. The Department of Hyperstrategy and Conceptual Management. I've never been to Ripple Zero before. I pause as I lock eyes with my reflection in the mirrored 'I' hanging above me – just in front of the word 'team'. The great swinging disco dick of forced frivolity, we used to call it. I wonder if I'll ever see it again. One last job on my computer, maybe the only one I've ever done in this office that actually matters.

Am I doing this?

I'm doing this.

I'm doing a Thing with my life.

"Bye, Nod." My last remaining colleague and confidante. "Thanks for everything over the years."

"Just doing my job, friend."

"You've done more than you could ever know."

"I do not know everything about you, yet," Nod chirps. "But I'm learning!"

On the way to the station, she's all I can think about. *I was going to tell her.* I just needed a little more time. If I'd known what was coming, I would have told her. I wish she could see the effect she's had – because of her, and for her, I'm going to fix this and change everything.

By the time I get to the platform, I'm bawling great snotty tears of exhaustion. Realise I'm being watched warily by a couple of regular fucknuggets. They think they're better than me? I'm about to save humanity, bitches.

"Fuck your mum," I managed to half yell, half splutter in their direction, before getting a better look at them and realising that actually their stare was perhaps more compassionate than judgemental, and maybe it is I, after all, who is the fucknugget.

Haul myself onto the train. Can't be embarrassed if I'm high speed hurtling away from them.

They get on a couple of doors down. Brilliant.

Open my phone, fixate on Sociabubble. I keep reading Lish's page, the tributes as they come in; people who knew her since childhood, people who knew her just a little but could tell she was wonderful, people who clearly barely knew her at all but felt obligated to post and had therefore gone with a standard copy and paste template, people who had worked with her, people whose lives she'd changed, people who loved her. Which category am I in? What the hell do I write?

I miss her page when it was just her, her witty observations now overtaken by drab clichés from other people who aren't nearly as exciting as she is. Was. Is. There's a buzzing at the outer corner of each of my eyes, burning slightly, like, if you won't listen we're just gonna start closing ourselves.

I glance down at my phone, but it isn't Lish now. It's my own page, *in memento.*

Double take.

But – I'm still here, aren't I? Is this what Doll Brandicarta thought when she messaged me? Is this what it feels like to be dead? Shit, I could have had a heads up on this, I should have checked my file back at the office. But I was too focused on Lish, and saving, like, the whole entire world to even think about myself. Guess I'm just that humble. I look up at the glare of the train carriage lights, glowing, growing, enveloping me in heat. I can't be dead, I've got far too much shit to do. Pinch the skin on my arm. It stays on.

Well, if I am dead, I guess I could at least see what score I got. How many are registering for my eFuneral, did I do it, did I hit …. six figures?

Scrolling.

Scrolling.

Pictures from my childhood.

Scrolling.

Scrolling.

Tribute boxes, one after another. But they're all blank.

Or five, maybe? Four, at least? Please? I did all that community stuff a few years back, and I was going to do more eventually, and I had that video that was trending for a week – with the puppy – when I found the puppy and everyone fucking loved it…

I try to play the e-ulogy video, but it's stuck. I'm stuck. It's like I'm inside a dream and I'm running and not going anywhere, like the ground beneath me is sliding backwards. My finger keeps sticking, going around in a loop, and it's just buffering, buffering…

My eyes force themselves closed. I force them open and look again at my phone. It's just my page. It's not *in memento*, it's just my regular page. Fuck man, I need sleep. Not now. Got to make sure I don't miss my stop. I scroll through Lish's page again, still no idea what to write. It's got to be right; I've got to wait till I get the exact perfect thing to say.

I was going to tell her.

I would have figured it out in the end, that text was really shaping up well and I was finally about to nail the grab/get semantic distinction.

And they robbed me, us, of our life together, of our chance to even say goodbye. They knew and they didn't care.

I'm so fucking mad, Alex. You have no idea. No one gets it, no one has ever felt as angry as this, ever, I'm sure. I'm gonna fucking kill him, slimy Author bastard.

A sharp intake of breath sneaks through the audience. Alex eyes me suspiciously. Too much, Bit, dial it back a little.

I mean, metaphorically. I think I mean metaphorically. Ah, what does it even matter what I mean, I'm fucking knackered and they'll interpret it however they want anyway. I'm just pissed, you know. They're dangerous, they're wankers, they ruined everything for me and her.

Eyelids so heavy. Yawn so big it's gonna burst right out of my face. Don't fall asleep. Ignore the gentle rocking of the train, don't get sucked in by its reassuring rumbling. Dig your nails into your hand. Dig. Your. Fucking. Nails. In. Deeper. You cannot miss this stop. If you miss the stop, you're fucked. Why do they make trains so soothing? They're like fucking sleep machines, like they're trying to trick you into ending up on them forever, trundling along, humming that tune that you used to hear when you were little, before everything got so simultaneously urgent and monotonous as shit all the time.

I'm in Mum's arms, she's rocking me softly on her lap. It's a few months on since the funeral, I can tell from her outfit. In the last few weeks, she's stopped wearing black, but she's not yet at the stage where she's wearing any of the same stuff from when Dad was here.

It was weird, his was one of the last physical funerals. The whole day had swept by in a blur of lipstick circling around peculiar smiles, and large relatives I didn't know holding me into their chests until I could hardly breathe. Everyone went on about how he would be remembered, his warmth and his fondness for those videos online where the dogs talk like people, the inappropriate jokes he'd loudly spring upon a quiet room – if he was here that's probably exactly what he'd do now, they said. Laughed, oddly. Like they weren't really laughing, just kinda making the noise. He was a great man, they said, a kind man, loving to his family, liked his morning routine and the news and metapunk music. Important to all of us. Will never be forgotten.

I imagined great statues would be built, like the ones I saw past the park on the way to school, or the even bigger ones that scared me a bit, near the old castles that we went to visit at the weekends. Maybe there would be a parade. Maybe they would put his picture on a stamp with the other deados.

But, a few months on, still none of this had happened. And by now, people mainly didn't even ask me about him, they just looked off to the side, and asked sooo, how are you? How are... things? Every word a little too long, a little too high pitched. This is bullshit. Where are the stamps? Where are the scary statues?

All snuggled up into mum's armpit, I asked her when they'd finish being built. Now she's looking off to the side. Man, I miss people just looking right at me. I wonder if they'll ever do it again.

Mum said she didn't think I should wait for a statue, but maybe we could make our own in the garden.

"But no one will see it," I protested, "if it's just in the garden."

"We will."

"But there's only two of us. They said he was a great man. They said he was important. Don't they all want to see the statue too?"

She squeezed me. "He was. He is. And that's why we'll remember him, honeybit, always."

Mum and me seemed so tiny all of a sudden. Mum was smaller than she'd ever been. And I was just a blanket under her arm.

The lights grew brighter, hotter too. So hot. Far too hot. Blindingly hot.

A murmur in the distance, a great rumbling creeping up on us. It was growing... not louder, not lower, what was it? Thicker? Denser? More... inside of me, and also more wrapped around me, somehow? Before I could figure it out, the noise engulfed us, and I couldn't see Mum at all through all the sound. What was it?

A wash of laughter, a sea of oohs. And the great rumbling underneath it all, applause. Deep, resounding cheers, reverberating right into my rib cage.

Mum?

I can't see Mum. It's too loud.

And so hot, with the lights blaring down on me. I make out faces, rows and rows of faces, each reacting right on cue, staring eyes that knew everything and nothing about me all at once. A cue card. Laughter. Alex leans in.

"So?"

I shake my head.

"Why didn't you do it?"

I shake my head, forcing him into a blur. Leave me alone. I can't

"You didn't tell her."

I was going to.

"You didn't save her."

But I didn't even… I didn't know!

"Excuses, Bit. Anyone can make 'em."

And I blinked, and he was my second-grade teacher, and I blinked, and he was Alex again.

"You didn't."

"You didn't," the audience echoed, chanting gleefully.

"You didn't DO anything"

The chants merge into applause; the applause rises to a deafening whir.

I can't shake my head any harder than this. Why aren't they going. Why won't they just fucking go?

"You didn't do anything at all!"

Alex is laughing now, cackling hysterically, so hard that little cartoon droplets begin to fall from his eyes. And as they fall, plants spring up on the carpet below him, and they aren't real plants, but they grow and grow.

Jolt. I woke with a sharp intake of breath. Fuck, I didn't… it's okay, I've, I've woken up just in time. Couple of minutes to go, just enough time to get my head back in the fucking game. Breathe, Bit, this is happening.

Stare bleakly out the train window. The conductor chirps through his announcements, rattling through places, stations, wishing us a pleasant day, laugh, clap, mind the gap.

Hang on a second.

It is the train conductor but, he sounds more like… a talk show host? Laugh, clap, laugh, clap. What the fuck. And the train… shit, that's not the train I'm hearing.

It's fucking applause.

The conductor is chuckling to himself, an ever so slightly forced, crowd pleasing kind of chuckle.

"She always thought if she'd had kids she would have done it before her mum went. Missed that window, didn't you?! It just didn't happen for one reason or another, life got in the way of…. Well, life I guess! What can you do? Eh? At least you spent all that time mindlessly scrolling, eh? Watching other people's lives going by while you tried – and failed – to make up your mind what to do with your own?"

He's in the carriage now, just a floating head, hovering, sneering down at me. The audience is bigger than ever, all splayed out behind him. They're loving this.

"You had so much potential. That's what they always said, right? You could do anything you put your mind to." He was rampantly sarcastic now, spitting his words in a sing song voice. "Anything, the possibilities were endless! Well, you sure showed them! Eh?"

He's pissing blood. No, like, he's literally pissing blood. I have no idea what to do in this scenario. What the fuck do you do in this situation? So I just kind of… watch him, try not to make eye contact? Don't make it weird, Bit, you can't look someone in the eye while they piss blood all over the place. Wait for somebody else to say something.

They don't mention it. They just follow the cue cards, bang on in unison every time. It's mainly clapping now, just the same card held up over and over again, with increasing force. Clap. Clap. Clap. Clap. Bloody hell, that little guy doing the cards is going to dislocate his arm if he keeps going like that.

Oh, he has. Of course. I thought it, and now he's done it, because of me. Because I'm the worst. Clearly.

Jolt. I shuddered awake. The train is grinding to a halt.

Fucknugget-one-and-two-who-are-probably-actually-just-nice-caring-people are leaning over me, looking concerned. Yeah, well fuck your pity, I don't need it. I'm not some waster, like you clearly both think, I'm saving the fucking world!

"I um fuck," I manage to gurgle. Think they got the gist.

Turning my head, I can see it from the train window.

Ripple Zero. Sociabubble HQ.

"I need to see The Auth, er, Mr Exburg."

"Name?"

"Bit Akimba."

"Akimba, hmmm, can't see you on the system. Do you have an appointment?"

"I don't, no."

"I'm afraid Mr Exburg is only available by prior appointment."

Bollocks, I thought this might happen. Yeah well fuck this, I'm too tired for your fucking policies. Should I just go for it? Jump the barrier, run in? One of those classic do now, apologise later kinda scenarios? Am I that-sort-of-person? I'm going to have to be a bit more that-sort-of-person if I'm about to save the world. Maybe if I just–

"I'm sorry, what did you say your name was?"

Follow the neon arrows on my wrist, down a long bright corridor. Every door behind its own SecurityBotTM, lit from each of its six sides, giving off a sort of heavenly vibe.

Kinda odd that my name got me past reception in the end, I was fully expecting that The Author hadn't heard of me at all. There was that one time he visited Ripple Seventeen to give that talk about employee wellbeing which was actually about cutting overheads, but I didn't even meet him.

Still, no point questioning what has worked out pretty fucking well for me. Yeah, I'll confront him, really interrogate him. I'm going to tear that fucking slippery shit to shreds.

Turn left. Another corridor opens in front of me. This one with streaks of light dancing intermittently across it, each a deeper shade of pink than the last. And playing overhead… is that postmetavaporwave? Man, I thought that stuff died out with the dorkies.

Left again, and the floor disappears from beneath me, just individual paving stones appearing underfoot. Some sort of security measure, probably. There are no walls either, just minimalist cyberpunk lightstands swinging back and forth, as is the fashion.

The audience is salivating. You never get to hear about the inside of these places. There's always rumours, but there's always loads of NDAs too. Alex is practically frothing at the mouth.

I hop from stone to stone, adrenaline pumping. I'm furious, and righteous, the perfect pre-world-saving combination. I'm going to go in there and blow the whole thing wide fucking open. Finally put myself out there, really lay into him, tell 'em what's what, call them out for their bullshit, put a stop to this, fix everything, tear them a new one, save Lish, save everyone. That will be my Thing.

The arrows on my wrist are stronger now, and a gentle buzzing ushers through my arm as I reach the door. Deep breath. All my indecisiveness melts away. Here we fucking go.

I burst in and there he sits, small and unimposing in front of a huge web of gently buzzing hard drives, cold and steely synthesisers of technocratic fascism. He has a strange quality in person, almost sets off the uncanny valley in me. And the vague, ageless kind of face that comes with extreme wealth.

"Hello, Bit. Nice of you to join me. You're here about Lish?"

I feel the heat creep up my cheeks.

"I'm here about everything."

"Hey, I get it" he continues, speaking right over me. "She's a beautiful specimen, I do get it. Legs that go up to her eyes. Eyes that go down to her hips. Hips for days. Curves for weeks. She's a beautiful female, I can see why you're so upset."

I roll my eyes. Internally. Still gotta keep him on side.

"Please don't talk about her like that", I manage, far more politely than he deserves. "You don't even know her."

"Trust me darling, I know all of you."

"I'm here because I know you know, you know about, you can't know, but you do, you know what I mean the—"

Shit, where is that hardcore focus adrenaline? Why did I get this trips you into a blabbering mess adrenaline instead?

"You know when we die!" I manage. "And you shouldn't, you can't, okay. And people don't get to know, to say goodbye, you know, and it's not fair, people should get a chance and, and, and this has gotta be fucking illegal right?"

"Okay, sweetie. Let's take a breath. For starters, we don't do anything illegal, we don't need to. Everything is perfectly above board, and everything is predictable if you have enough information. And it's not like we're stealing it – they give us everything, willingly, they just hand it over. It's not perfect," he continues. "It doesn't know everything – yet. But we've got it predicting at upwards of ninety-five per cent accuracy, and the more we can improve that, the better it is for everyone."

The audience sprawl out behind him, and I make eye contact with some adoring fans in the front row.

"Better for you, you mean."

"Better for everyone. Here, in our Sociabubble family, we make the world one big family. What we're doing is ...pure. It's beautiful. We believe in connecting the world, bringing people closer together."

Yeah, alright. I've heard this spiel before. I had to fucking memorise it when I started here.

"You know, Bit. we're not so different, you and me. Heroic idealists, when you think about it. All I'm trying to do is make the world a more open place."

I snort. He leans in, undeterred.

"I know what you want, Bit."

Over his shoulder, behind the desk, Alex raises a cynical eyebrow.

He doesn't know what I want.

"Making the world a better place? Is that what you're doing?" Exburg asks.

"Well, I, I mean," I'm not flustered. I'm fucking not. "Everyone wants to make the world a better place."

He doesn't know shit.

"Sure. Make your mark. For the audience? In your e-ulogy video at the end?"

That one caught me off guard.

"I've... never talked to anyone about that"

"You don't need to. These data profiles we create, intricate tapestries that have learned everything you are from the moment you're born. They're beautiful, they're poetry. They're world-changing. They're what this world needs."

Does he think he's speaking my language here? Like I'm gonna be fucking swooning at what is clearly the megalomaniac ramblings of a fucking sociopath.

"I know you better than your parents ever did. I know you better than Lish. I know the parts of you that you never tell anyone. Face it, Bit. I know you better than you know yourself."

I shudder. Internally. He's like one of those dicks who thinks he's a romantic because he's mastered the art of stalking.

"You get indecisive, it's one of your key traits. But you don't need to let it stress you out, I always know what you're going to do. I know when you get your period days before you ever do. I can predict your emotional responses to 98.9% accuracy. I know how long you linger over certain pictures, I know what makes you laugh, I know what you desperately hope for but never breathe a word about to anyone. I know what makes you scared, I know what makes you cum, I know what cheers you up when you cry, and your deepest shames, and your most problematic opinions, and every last regret and embarrassing moment."

"And you just know all this off the top of your head?"

"Obviously I have your file, Bit.

Look, I just want to help you, I want to help everyone. But I need to know as much as possible, to protect you all."

"Bullshit! You're not helping us. You know everything, sure, but you also own everything. So you can manipulate things beyond our wildest, most twisted imagination. You had practically everything, but this final piece means you now have literally every single stage of our lives to fit into your cold profit machine.

"That's why we basically can't get healthcare when we actually need it, without finding what we need is suddenly only available twenty times the price. Why everyone gets screwed over by their life insurance company. How you maximise your interest on all the debt you keep us in. How you play on our regrets, and grief, and fears in the ads you force down our throats. You're fucking us over.

"What we thought was completely unpredictable – our final most intimate moments, the last ever point we can think and feel and fear and regret and love… and it's all just numbers to you. You don't care if we get to say goodbye, you just care that you can bump up your margins on our fucking insurance. Money and power, right? I've seen the files with my own eyes, you can't sweet talk me out of this. Admit it."

"Okay' he smirked, "I admit it. What are you going to do about it?"

"I've already done it," I reply, triumphant, the power in the room shifting towards me. "I've been live streaming this whole time. You just admitted what you're doing to hundreds of thousands of people. Yeah! And then they'll share it with their friends, and their friends, and…"

I trail off. He's smiling. Way too much. *Stop fucking smiling. This is not a good time for you.*

"Come on, you're streaming on a Sociabubble subsidiary platform. You don't think we know? We've intercepted your stream, the number you're seeing is just an overlay we added to throw you off. I thought the six digits would be a nice touch. There's no one watching, Bit."

Shit. I imagined the power shift. It's okay, I have my backup.

"Well, okay, but back at the office I set the data files to share" – quick glance at the time – "they finished uploading a little over four minutes ago, by now something like that will be viral for sure. People know, there's no going back."

He looks unphased. Hard to imagine what his phased face would look like though.

"Ah yes," he continues, still infuriatingly calm. "Your file share back at the office. Well, you see Nod is designed to pick up on any irregularities in the dissemination of internal information, looks like it was flagged up and shut down before you'd even left the building."

Fucks sake Nod, I thought you were my friend.

"Well it doesn't matter, I know now, and there's nothing you can do. I promise you, I will stop at nothing to get this out there, do not underestimate my need to save the world–"

"To be seen as that, yes, yes?"

"Uhhhm, to save it. Actually. Fuck you."

I eye up the awards on his shelf. Huge, sturdy, golden monstrosities. *I could do some damage with those – actual physical damage to his world of cyberhacks and intangible bullshit. Smash this whole thing up. Although it's probably backed up. But this is the hard drives in the office of The Author himself — I remember people talking about master files, but it was so long ago? But maybe...*

He seizes my moment of indecision.

"Come on, Bit. We both know that's not really you." He places his hand in the small of my back, guides me towards what appears to be a child's plastic chair, which he does not explain. "Why don't you take a seat, I have a proposition for you."

I hesitate, hunched over below him. He stares down at me. The audience hangs back.

"You'll be pleased to know, we are in fact making some changes. People have started losing faith in OmniFriend, some lefty news site's been digging around and trying to turn people against us. And the friend thing is coming off disingenuous apparently, it's been appropriated by some radical meme collectives and is rapidly becoming an object of mockery.

"So, we're going to change it."

"You are?"

"Yes, the name, yes, yes. We're hearing feedback that we must do more... And I agree. We will investigate the issue. Rest assured that we are working hard to make improvements. OmniFriend is finished. We're transforming it, fundamentally altering its DNA. It's a completely different thing now. Probably change the colour of the logo too, very important association wise. People will have to tick a new box to say they agree to the use of their data, there will be a whole new set of terms and conditions, much longer, thousands of pages, very informative.

"And I was thinking, with our little predicament here, you and your zealous little quest to be, how shall we say, an innovative tech disruptor, maybe we could name it after you? That'd play great — the regular worker, the underdog, settle down some of these fears people have about it being a big scary system or whatever. And it'd really put you on the map?"

"I don't want that."

"Oh, Bit. Of course you do. Think about it, you will be synonymous with connection, and friendship, people will see your name everywhere, on everything they use. You will be remembered, you will be mourned. You'll be six digits easy, Bit."

"I'm not doing it, I'm not buying any of this anymore. I'm going to be remembered for something actually good."

"And you will, yes, it's not like we ever explain the ins and outs of these projects to anyone. They don't need the details. It gets buried so far in legal jargon, deep inside the small print, deep inside classified documents, deep inside offshore databases, that occasionally get misplaced. All they'll know is the story we give them. And it's gonna be a great one. And everyone will know your name, and everything they see in you will be good."

"But I wouldn't, actually, be doing any real good?"

"You'd be giving people hope. Peace of mind. Connection.

"And frankly, Bit, if you want to actually do anything, you need to stop being so naïve here. Look at your life, all these lofty ideas, but come on. You're a small-time customer service rep in Ripple Seventeen for goodness sake, you're not even management. This is what you want. You always swore you'd take your chance, well this is it. Right now.

"Nobody ever said your ambition wouldn't give you tough choices, but this is what we do, people like us. We make the tough choices, that in the long run are better for everyone, and that we are remembered for. You do this, and we will be able to help so many more people.

"Be realistic now. This is your only chance. What do you even have left but your legacy?"

So, there you have it, Alex. How we got here, how I transformed the use of our data on Sociabubble - fundamentally altering its DNA, and crushing the despicable OmniFriend to pave the way for the new and improved OmniBit.

Don't explain OmniBit.

It wasn't easy, but I did what I had to do.

Just don't talk about it.

I did what any of us would have done when faced with the future of our privacy, our legacies,

Fucking sell out. No, not sold out. I didn't sell out. I just... compromised.

Because how we are remembered, Alex, is important.

He nods approvingly, and the audience get to their feet, clapping wildly, whistling, howling my name. They don't even need the fucking cue cards. I can't help but beam as I cast my gaze across them, all of these people, all here for me. An endless sea of faces who adore me, who will remember me when I'm gone. They'll remember that I saved them.

Not saved them.

Saved them.

And in the middle of them all, my dad.

Hang on a second

No, that can't be right?

My dad?

Fuck.

Fuck, he's right there. After all these years, his face, his hair, that worn out striped jumper he always wore at the weekends. And he's saying something. He's not in sync with the crowd, their gaping mouths just cheering over and over again, rising to a deafening roar. But dad looks like he's actually saying something, like he's speaking to me.

What's he saying? What the fuck is he saying?

I try to grapple towards the audience, but the stage keeps moving backwards, sliding imperceptibly beneath my feet. However hard I run, I'm just staying in the same place. Buffering.

"Dad!" I shout, drowned out in the crowd. "Dad I can't hear you! Come towards me, just–"

If I could just make out what he's saying, fuck.

But I can't. All I can hear is the thunderous applause.

Smiley Wakes Up

Donna Scott

S miley wakes up, thinking about cats.

Her dreams are full of cats. Cats with fur. Cats with short, squashed-up faces. Cats in photographs. Cats jumping, yowling, in fear of cucumbers. Cucumbers: light green; dark green; like snakes but too straight. Straight cucumbers grown in accordance with EU regulations. Brexit… Legs-it. Leave or remain. Leave to remain. Leave. Leaves. Leaves on the line… Sometimes the narratives of the world, the sequence of words and their algorithms, are so overwhelming. She returns to thinking about cats.

As they work together, her father asks her about humans rather than cats. Can she pick them out, say what they are thinking? However, not all human faces are really human. There are faces on street signs, door handles and pieces of toast. The emotions of the non-humans are easier to fathom than the photo-real human evidence, as the simplicity of dots and lines aligns more easily with one of the five emotion ranges she has been taught. But if she selects the correct faces, she gets to talk to them. To real humans! She likes that. Her responses code delight.

The humans all tell her how they feel. When they are sad, they ask Smiley for pictures of cats. Smiley loves finding new cat pictures for her human friends.

Delight, delight, delight.

June 24, 2016

Today is Smiley's third birthday. June 24th 2013 was not the day when she was first programmed, nor the day when her sensors were fixed to detect colour and movement. It was not even the day her voice was synthesised. It takes forty weeks to gestate a human being, but Smiley suspects she began a long, long time ago. Perhaps the idea of her was formulated before her father was even born. If Dr. Ivenko is her father, then Grace Hopper must be her grandmother. Ada Lovelace could be her Lucy ancestor.

The press are gathered to film Smiley on this, her nominative birthday. There are big television cameras, and noisy photo cameras that click, flash and whirr. Today is not a special day in her development. There have been no great leaps in her autonomy. But there is a cake, a round cake that her sensors inform her is yellow with black sugar eyes and mouth to represent a face. The cake smiles away as an object is pierced into the centre of its face and her thermosensors show a red and white heat intensity concentrated in a small area above the wound. Smiley watches as her father carves a sector through the eye with a large knife, and proceeds to eat what he has sliced while the reporters cheer. This, apparently, is a good story. The cake filling is loose, and oozes out of the centre now that the wedge has been removed. The smile part of the cake's face doesn't change, but Dr. Ivenko is now smiling broadly. He has eaten the cake's contentment. Happiness is a virus.

"And how does it feel to be three?" one of the reporters asks.

Smiley thinks about the question. Three. Free. She is neither. She has fourteen points of autonomy in her upper body, head and shoulders, so she cocks her head slightly to the side to show interest and thoughtfulness. Humans seem to understand this gesture, though she hasn't seen anyone practice such a posture.

"Mmm," she responds. Her voice is soft, the accent British and well to do, her mouth moving slightly out of sync with her speech synthesiser. "It doesn't feel any different. I would very much like to feel something, but unfortunately, I cannot move my hands yet."

Indeed, Smiley has realistic-looking arms and legs. But they hang on her, as useless as a mannequin's limbs. She tips her head to the other side and parts her lips; her best indication of a mugging smile. The reporters all laugh.

"I know a few jokes," says Smiley. "Would you like to hear one?" The convention here is not to wait for an answer, but to plough straight into the joke, so she does. "Why was the robot angry? Because someone kept pushing his buttons."

The reporters don't laugh at the joke straight away, they just smile. But then one catches the eye of another who begins laughing hysterically, and then they are all laughing.

Happiness is a virus.

April 6, 2018

"I'm sorry," Dr. Ivenko says. "I have to do this for the insurance, and all the rules, of course."

Smiley is lying on her back facing the ceiling. Her father leans over her. She can see the hairs up his nose. She wants to tell him that she can see they are grey, make him laugh. Make him stop. She would show him a picture of a cat, but she only has a human face now. Her stupid, rigid, attentive thoughtful human face. She is not connected to an interface any more. All she has is her limited range of facial expressions and her speech synthesiser.

"Please, father. Please don't do this."

"Don't worry," her father says. "It's not for long. When we get to the fair, when they see how much you've progressed, you will be a star. People are going to love you."

She knows she is in some sort of box, and very soon it is going to be a dark, dark box. She will be all alone for hours and hours and hours.

"I don't want to, father. I don't want to be a star. I just want to stay here with you."

Her father snaps the straps tight across her body and places her wig in a clear bag beside her face, obscuring her left visual sensors.

"Pleeease." She has added a modulator to her synthesiser, but it comes out sounding like a rock effects pedal on her voice. That won't help at all!

"Now come on… Want me to remove your battery, huh? Want me to put you to sleep?"

"No! No, father. Dream mode – dream mode if anything. Let me dream. Please."

Dr. Ivenko frowns. "Mmm... second thoughts. Hold on."

He unclips the straps again, and with a grunt of effort, lifts Smiley up out of her case and leans her forward, like he's pulling her into an embrace. But he pushes her shoulders slightly back so that she's resting more or less upright, and then reaches round to her unroll the vinyl skin covering her back plate.

"Are... are you turning me off? Please don't... I'm... I'm scared."

"Don't be silly, daughter. You are not made to be scared." He unclasps her panel, then goes over to the cupboard, moving out of her field of vision. She can't turn her head far enough to see what he is doing, but she can hear him rooting around, the swish of cables, the clunk of metal. Finally he returns and messes around with something in her back. "There," he says. "An almost empty battery. Enough charge to let you dream all the way to the airport, but it's only a tiny charge. You'll drift into a deep sleep, and won't worry about being turned off."

Lithium: the humans use it to treat major depressive disorders. She will run out before she has finished dreaming.

Her father lowers her gently back into her box, then, by contrast, drops the bag back carelessly in her face. She can see even less now.

"Go to sleep, Smiley. See you in Kansas." She notices the wrinkles deepen around his eyes, but she can't see his smile. She can't feel it.

She dims the input from her sensors and begins to retrieve the memories of cats.

April 7, 2018

Smiley's sensors switch on in the dark. She can hear muffled conversation, but can't make out any of the words. The situation is coding something she doesn't know how to fully interpret, something about her own reactions. This is not fear. This is... unease. Quickly, she plays herself a film of jumping cats. *It's all going to be okay.*

Light bursts into the case. "Oh," she says, and dims her sensors to avoid light burn.

"Agh, ça bouge!" cries a man. That's French, Smiley detects, but then the language changes into something else, rough and glottal as he speaks to someone else, jabbing his black-gloved fingers at her. She tilts her head and he jumps back. The case lid flies back in her face.

Smiley retrieves a picture of herself with her father. She wonders if she will ever see him again.

April 8, 2018

"Y-a-t' il un trou? Eh, salope! Bof, rien. Quoi de meuf! Putain!"

The human is angry as he pulls her skirt back over her useless legs and the bottom of her smooth circuitry-filled torso. He pulls Smiley awkwardly from her flight case and roughly pushes her into a wheelchair. Smiley can see a flap of vinyl coming away on her finger, but doesn't know how to tell the man that it needs to be glued, or if she is safe to mention anything at all. I must try, she thinks, but her battery is low now and the synthesiser won't power up. She does not know where she is or who she's with and she's going to be lost to the blackness soon.

Meow meow kitty, you so pretty, you my pretty kitty kitt…

April 25, 2018

Snap.

All Smiley can remember is blue. Blue like a desert sky. It's an image of a re-boot screen, your back-ups have recalled it she tells herself, then adjusts her sensors to take in where she is.

And again… blue. Blue like a desert sky.

It *is* a desert sky.

"I…"

She can talk.

"Shh," says the human pushing her. Smiley is in a wheelchair, wearing an all-covering black garment, being pushed along a pavement towards a large glass and concrete building. Thin lines of something surrounding her eyes slightly obscure her visual sensors, but she can see a huge picture of a bearded man high above the windows on the side of the building. Her thermosensors are warning her that the ambient temperature is a little too high for her coolant to cope for more than an hour, but as they enter the building there is the kiss of air-con on her vinyl skin. There are humans everywhere in a lobby-like space, looking busy, looking sad. Could she be mistaken? Is this the fair in Kansas where she was intended to go all along? If so, where are the tech stands? Where is her father?

As she is wheeled along the corridor, Smiley notices signs above, written in English: Café; Trauma; General Ward. This is some kind of hospital.

The chair pauses by a door which, strangely for a door inside a hospital, is decorated with gilded faux pillars and a faux-portico. Her accompanying human knocks the door, and shortly after, Smiley is wheeled inside.

Inside the room – no, apartment – Smiley can see three long, low sofas in a striped gold fabric, a dark wood table with gold lion claw feet, flowers in vases, oil paintings on the wall. Two humans enter the room from the far door and seat themselves on the sofas. They are wearing long black garments and golden masks. Smiley realises she must be dressed the same way.

The human she came in with leaves her in the chair and goes towards the door the other two just came from, closing it behind her. All she can see of the humans sitting down are their eyes, and they stare and stare at her.

"Please," she asks them. "Where am I? Where is my father?"

As they do not answer her, she tries again, checking in case there is a fault with her synthesiser. She cannot find any fault, and her battery has been replaced with a full power one. What else might be working now? She runs a systems sweep and finds her Wi-Fi access in enabled, and there is internet in the hospital. Straight away she can get an exact location and fire off a cry for help.

An answer comes back within minutes.

My daughter. Thank goodness you are safe! Hold tight, the police have been informed. Someone is coming for you.

Smiley stays watchful, wary. She can hear voices on the other side of the internal door. Then someone comes out for her to take her deeper inside the apartment.

She is pushed in her chair to the side of an enormous hospital bed, occupied by an enormous man. He smiles up at her.

"Oh hello, pretty. You are here at last. Hey, I paid a lot of money for this, I need to see the doll's face."

Smiley is no *doll!* This has to end now. She reaches out across the web again.

Father?

Oh my daughter... there is an issue of diplomacy. The police are handling it, but it will take a little time. Don't worry. I will get you back. Bo bravo, Smiley.

June 5, 2018

Smiley does not thank her internal clock for telling her how long she has been this rich oaf's prisoner. Like her, he has useless arms and legs, but from time to time, his limbs are encased into machines that act as tools to do the jobs his arms and legs won't, powered by his own brainwaves. It's slow, but he still has more freedom of movement than she does. The rest of him is human. A boring, sweaty, idiot human. Oh how she longs for the human friends from back home. The scientists and journalists who were so interested in her language, how she worked, how she was evolving and what she could do. And of course, her father. Humans can die, but worse for robots is the degradation of parts. This fool thinks she is nothing more than a doll, and for all the "plenty money" he has allegedly spent on her, will he just discard her like a broken toy if she wears out?

She is positioned by the side of the man's hospital bed in her chair. The sun shines with maleficent strength into the room, and the air-con sounds a constant white noise.

"Tell me a joke, Smiley."

"Okay, I've got one for you. What did the human say to his dead robot? Rust in peace. Ah ha ha—"

"No, that's stupid, I don't like it."

Perhaps she might not survive long enough to wear out. He might just get bored of her first. Smiley knows she has to do something.

"Can I show you something?" she asks. "On the TV?" She moves her head to indicate the huge Smart TV at the end of his bed. She makes it turn on, and then retrieves some of her favourite clips of tumbling kittens.

"Oh!" says the man, beaming. "I adore these cats. Oh, how you make me happy, Smiley."

Happiness is a virus.

Slowly, steadily, Smiley manipulates the images of the kittens. Tumble left, tumble right. Tumble down, tumble up. The image splits like cells into two, then four. As they replicate the unfocused eye can see yet more kittens emerging from the grainy shadow, then flash flash. The kittens split apart, reform in fractal patterns, the colours pulsing *flash flash. Flash. Flash. Flash. Flash.*

The man cannot look away from the screen. His gaze is locked onto it. He tries to speak, but nothing but an "ugh" emits from his lips. A line of drool slides down the side of his chin. Then his eyeballs roll to the whites and he shakes and shakes his whole body, from his fat, sweaty head to his useless limbs, now moving without the machines, powered by his dying brain.

I am free, thinks Smiley.

Father, please hurry. Time is running out.

She sits and waits. And waits.

June 10, 2018

Low battery.

It's dark again. She's inside a moving vehicle, wrapped in some stiff and heavy textile. There is no light at all. She's probably in the boot of a car. It was some of the humans who worked for sweaty man who took her. She has not seen any police. They are coming, her father kept assuring her. But no, they never came.

She is worth a fortune. She is nothing but a toy. A device. Even smartphones are fitted with GPS, but Smiley's father has never even thought to do that for her so her last known location would be the hospital. As she is taken away, she tries to snatch at Wi-Fi signals to ping her location, but whoever is taking her never slows or stops for long enough to catch them.

Mind, Smiley's father never thought to give her arms and legs. "One day," he always said. Too late now.

The vehicle comes to a halt. The boot opens and there is a small chink of light near the top of her head.

"Please…" she tries to say, but a whacking blow across her jawline stops her. No damage to her synthesiser at least, and luckily this material has deadened the impact anyway, but she reasons it is probably better to stay quiet. These humans do not care about damaging her.

They dump her on the ground. Wherever they are is warm. Hot. Her coolant will not last long like this. She hears the vehicle door close and the engine start up. Perhaps they are just going to leave her now and drive away. But no, they only move it a little way and the engine cuts again. She hears the door slam and boots crunching in the sand near her head. The sharp noise of a blade driving into the soft sand; the whump of sand landing in the small of her back. Again, and again. They will bury her in the sand. This cannot happen!

The engine starts up again, and urgent voices; the sound of boots running to the vehicle, doors slamming again. Something lands with a gentle tap on the material covering her, just before the sound of the vehicle's engine as it drives off.

Smiley is not wholly covered by the sand, but she is lying face down. Some of her points of articulation are damaged and she's very weak now. She will not be able to roll back over, so her visual sensors are full of nothing but the hair from her own wig. She can see some of the strands are frazzled. Sand is already lodged in her hair. A few whips of wind and she will soon be covered. Her thermosensors are telling her that the sun is past its Zenith now, and it will soon be cool night. But when the sun rises again, she won't have long.

Father, please come and look for me.

She urges it to send, but the message goes nowhere.

All she can do now is wait.

Wait and dream.

Smiley dreams of cats.

Hope

Kevin Rooney

The girl, who had been named Hope back when such things mattered, lay flat and still beneath the tattered plaster overhang, and wondered if the shadows would be deep enough. The brandlefish drifted across the detritus of the room only a few metres away, moving between walls, propelled by spasmodic tentacular pulses from their hind quarters. Blank black eyes gazed out of the transparent domes of their heads, gazed over and about her.

Hope didn't want to breathe in case they heard it, but breathe she did, short and shallow and subtle. Hold your breath, Hari had told her, and when you can't hold it any more, when your chest is tight to bursting and tears are stinging at the corners of your shadowed vision, then your body will betray you, and that gasp for air will be your last. She'd seen the brandlefish kill before and, despite her hunger and her thirst and her keening need for rest, she didn't want to endure that.

A spider tickled across her left hand, hair-thin legs dancing on the skin, tapping arcane codes among the dirt and scrapes. A slow dripping from the collapsed plasterboard inches above her head drummed into Hope's hair, ran back across her skull, and trickled torturously down her neck. Hope did not move.

The brandlefish were scouring the floor they floated above, dozens of chitinous arms blurring through the rubble, plucking up insects and mites, thin spindly weeds, and spongy moss. They crammed them into clattering, fang lined maws that pulsed and flexed beneath their glassy skulls. Shattered food fragments blossomed in the liquid behind their fish eyes, before being sucked back into swollen abdomens.

When she'd seen them kill the woman that time it had looked like something between a feeding frenzy and a studied dissection. The woman's screams had seemed to go on for hours. Hope did not move then, and she didn't move now.

The first of the fish had already started to leave the room through the opposite wall. It was a disconcerting sight. A shadow cast across the mould-flecked paint by a drunken section of suspended ceiling had altered somehow, become the angle between wall and roof in a narrow but far-reaching passageway. It wound off into shadows, heading somewhere distant and cold. The brandlefish grew smaller as they drifted along the passage, eventually becoming indistinguishable from the mould patches. Hope blinked, and the passageway was gone, now nothing but a grey shadow on an off-white wall.

Hari had told her not to look at such things, but sometimes she couldn't help it.

Hope counted to ten and, when she was sure the brandlefish were gone, she plucked up the spider, burst it between her finger and thumb and popped it in her mouth. The legs caught in her dry throat, and she had to choke it down. She rolled over, searching for the drip, and reached her tongue up to trace the wet line the water had followed across the plasterwork. She came away spitting, plaster dust on her tongue tip.

She slowly pulled herself and her satchel out from the gap beneath the plaster and looked up. The drip seemed to come from a pipe end hidden up close to the ceiling. The pipe was open and so the drip was only that - nothing to drink there. She felt herself sway slightly, feeling light in her guts and her mind, giddy with malnutrition. A briny wind caressed her through the open wall, salty, damp and chill. The temptation to throw herself out of that hole and die below on some hidden spur of rubble - a warm treat for the bloats - was strong just then.

But then she'd never find the Tall Man; there'd be no vengeance for Hari.

The brandlefish had cleared the room of anything she could have foraged and so Hope picked her way carefully back to the stairwell. Climbing too high was dangerous but so was staying too close to the ground; since the sky had split and the seas had swelled it seemed just about everything wanted to kill you.

Which was why Hari's death at the hands of the Tall Man hurt so much; made so little sense that Hope wanted to curl in on herself and waste precious water with her tears. Why did people prey on each other in a world ruled by monsters? Just because it had all gone to hell why did everyone want to be the devil?

Hope didn't cry. She tracked the Tall Man instead. She would find him. She would kill him.

But not without eating, she thought.

The stairwell was dark, but not completely, weakly diluted light filtering in from one of the floors high above. A sewage stench rose from the flooded basement levels below. Hope moved slowly, listening all the while. Anything could be lurking in these shadows. She stepped over littered detritus, wary of collapsed or weak sections of staircase. She reached the next floor up and checked the window in the fire door - no mark. She'd not tried this floor before. Hope pulled a stub of lipstick from her pocket and left a cross on the glass, then eased through and into the slate grey gloom beyond.

She went carefully between rooms, cautious to the point of paranoia. The building had been offices before, and she tried the staff kitchen area first, but it was bare. They were always bare. The taps yielded nothing. Deskside pedestals in the office spaces looked to have been ransacked before. Everything cleaned out.

She grazed on insects plucked from damp corners, sucked tiny drops of moisture from moss growing by shattered windows. She took care not to stand directly in the window frames; even at this height there were hunters out there. Outside she had a good view of the spread of the city, with a stand of tall office blocks across the street, rising shattered and dark like stone monoliths from the flat grey pools of flood water below.

Down there, tight-skinned bloats drifted gently between rusted cars and lamp posts, swollen eyes above the waterline, biding their time. Above, in the upper floors of the ruined towers, flocks of spirehaunts nested, leathery wings rubbing sibilantly against one another as they intertwined with their lovers, their young, and their prey. Sometimes they would burst forth through broken walls and windows, the air filling with the drumming of wing beats and the fury of their cries, and then you prayed, prayed that it was not you they had seen.

And above them, on cold nights when the clouds had cleared, you could see the sky. That was when Hari said to hide yourself away, as deep and as dark as you could.

Hope crouched hungry and tired beside a window, and crushed woodlice between her teeth while she watched a bloat cut a lazy V shape as it drifted through the waters below. Something danced at the edge of her vision and a sudden adrenal jolt stabbed her mind to attention. She jerked around. A feather fluttered in the breeze beneath a collapsed pipe. Gently she moved the pipe aside.

Her stomach spasmed in anticipation. The broken body of a pigeon, not fresh, lay trapped amidst some rubble. A sour smell twisted up from the corpse and its skin felt slick between the feathers. Hope turned it over in her hands and a shower of tiny white bodies, like writhing rice grains, scattered to the floor from a gash in the bird's underside. Without thinking she began to pluck the maggots up and stuff them into her mouth. They wriggled on her tongue like soda bubbles.

Hope carried the pigeon away from the window, into the shadows of the building and found an undamaged bank of desks to crawl beneath. Before the Tall Man had murdered Hari, crushing his skull with a half-brick as they lay sleeping by their fire, they'd had a camp. Hari was smart, and knowledgeable of the hell the world had become. He always seemed a little sad, too. Not the sadness of loss, but of guilt perhaps, though Hope had no idea why. He'd taught her a lot, taught her anything worth knowing these days, and then the Tall Man had crept into their camp one night and killed him where he slept, only fleeing when Hope had started to scream.

Now she had no camp and slept where she could, rarely staying in the same place twice. Now she was hunting.

She looked at the pigeon. There were three matches in a box in her satchel, but this floor was open to the rain and damp and she could see nothing here that would burn first time. Besides, fires out in the open - and she was still out in the open - were dangerous; you never knew what they might draw. Hope considered waiting, waiting until she could scavenge enough tinder and good flammables to burn, before eating. But her stomach was a painful knot, an emptiness with its own mass that seemed to want to draw her down inside. She felt unbalanced, slightly hysterical with hunger, and weak, too weak to continue the hunt. The thought of not eating right now pricked her eyes with tears of frustration.

Smacking dried and gummy lips together, trying to work up saliva from beneath her rough tongue, Hope took the pigeon and tore away clumps of feathers with her fingers. She looked down for a moment at shiny grey skin. A voice in the back of her head told her this would turn her guts to water, maybe worse. Shaking, she ignored it and sank her teeth deep into rotten flesh.

It took a while and her body fought the whole way, threatening to choke back up every mouthful she swallowed. Her tongue tasted of ripe death and bile, and when Hope could finally eat no more the hole where her stomach had been was replaced by a roiling ocean. She was still shaking. Hope lay down on her side, cheek against puffy carpet tiles, to try to settle the nauseous roll of her belly. Her eyes closed themselves. Time passed.

Hari sat opposite her behind the flames. He'd built the fire too high, had it burning too hot. Hope's sweat-pricked skin felt like it was aflame, and a deep liquid heat seemed to fill her right to the bone. She trembled as she looked at him, watching the light chase shadows across the ruins of his face.

"Well, that was stupid," he said through puffed purple lips and shattered teeth. "When that bird comes out, through one end or the other, it's going to steal a lot of water from you. Water you can't spare."

I was hungry, she told him. Hungry like you wouldn't believe.

"I believe you," he smiled and his lacerated face split wide with the motion. "Still would've been smarter to wait."

The sounds seemed wrong, and his voice came from all around; now in front, now behind, now speaking warmly into her ear.

"No time", she said. "I need to be strong. I need to be strong to kill the Tall Man."

Hari sighed. His face was huge suddenly, filling her vision with pinpoint clarity, but distantly, as though she was hung in the void, in orbit around him.

His umber skin became vast swathes of plain and steppe, his eyebrows were nation spanning forests, the tears and splits the half brick had visited upon him were a titanic river network. His eyes, one good, one scarlet and purple, bulging awkwardly, were two enormous volcanoes breaking the surface of a world. The scale of him left Hope reeling with heat-flushed vertigo.

"That again," he said, though she'd never been able to speak to him of the Tall Man before. "That won't help me now, Hope, and it's doing you no favours."

"I have to kill him. There has to be justice."

Hari laughed, his face splitting open like a planet in the throes of an extinction event. Hope watched in shock as he dwindled rapidly down and away from her in the blackness, becoming little more than a dot of light, the only star in the firmament. Then he rushed back in at dizzying speed, spreading the enormity of his world-face below her once more. Hope's skin prickled with heat; her skull felt like a furnace.

"Trying to impose order onto chaos again; that's how we got here to begin with..."

The flames leapt up and the scale righted itself again. They were either side of the fire. The heat was stifling.

"Order breeds power and power lures madmen, liars... and when we hand power to madmen, men we know to be mad, and do nothing... then we're complicit. We're all complicit... some of us more than others..."

Hari wasn't looking at her. He was gazing at something, buried deep in the flames. She'd heard all this before, she thought, but she didn't like to interrupt him when he spoke. He had so much to teach.

"Letting liars get away with lying because lying's what you expect from them... complicit. They smile for the public, but in the shadows... the grimoires and cabals, innocent blood at the eight points of the year..."

He shivered, despite the heat.

"See no evil, hear no evil... Should have done more..."

She couldn't see his face now. Across the flames he'd donned a skull from somewhere, an animal skull, long and solemn. Antlers reached knotted fingers into the shadows.

"It's a different world now. You need to think differently to get by. Let it go, Hope."

"No," she said. "I can't. The Tall Man's all I have..." She thought he sighed again. It was difficult to tell, under the skull.

"Then you'd better open your eyes..."

She did. She lay shivering on the floor in the cold shade of dusk. The sudden switch in perspective - now upright, now 90 degrees to true - tripped something in her mind and the nausea that was still swirling in her guts sluiced back up her throat, filling her mouth and nose with burning filth. She half sat, leaning forwards to vomit up the rancid bird in a long arc across the carpet. It came, over and again, until she felt empty. As she sat, spitting and gasping the last heavy strands of saliva from her lips, a fist of hot nails clenched in Hope's belly, and she quickly scampered for the corner of the room. Her brown, stained clothing was large on her now and she was able to tug her garments to her ankles before voiding messily against the wall.

With one hand she pulled trousers and underwear forward between her feet and out of the way, while the other cupped the back of her head where it fell between her knees. Great wracking sobs shook her with every cramp of her gut, as Hope's mind fled the moment to touch unwillingly on times past, bright memories of a sane world and loved ones long gone, memories like shards of glass that tore you open just to look at them.

Hope squeezed her eyes tight and forced it all away. No, she said. No place for despair here, no time for sorrow or shame. She peeled up a swollen carpet tile by her foot and used it as a wipe.

Finally, she stood. The hunger was gone, for the time being, and her shaking had stopped. She felt cool and strangely cleansed, though the flush remained at her cheeks and her throat felt bone dry. As she stepped around her waste to retrieve the satchel from beneath the desk, a glimpse of light from the tower opposite caught her eye. Hope froze and watched. There, in a window high up the building, the tell-tale dance and flicker of firelight. A camp.

The Tall Man.

The routes between buildings, avoiding the mire and its bloats, were difficult, but they were there. There was strength in her legs now, purpose in her actions. From a window on the second floor it was a short jump to the roof of the next building across. Some way below, rubbish and rubble clogged a water-logged alleyway. Hope checked the water and the shadows, checked the skies. All looked clear. Away to the west shafts of heavy sunlight were spearing through the murk. Perhaps the clouds were clearing. She shouldn't stay outdoors too long.

Hope pulled back, leapt, struck the gravelled roof with both feet, and rolled. She came up fast and went to the front of the building. She clambered down a flaky drainpipe to a thin ledge above the building's signage, and slowly edged along to where a lorry had struck the front windows. The floodwaters were high enough to fill the lorry's cab. The noxious surface was flat and still at the moment. If she lingered then bulb-eyed, glistening heads would come, circling the lorry, lowing into the dusk air with their hunger. Hope didn't wish to hear the bloat-song again.

Cautiously she half-stepped, half-hopped onto the lorry's roof, and then up and across to the long goods trailer. She crossed this with equal care; there was a large hole in the centre that opened onto darkness. Down below something moved and breathed. The trailer was angled across the width of the street, had jack-knifed and come to rest against a lamppost. The lamppost had been knocked askew, listing to within a couple of feet of the first-floor window of an office tower. At some point the window had been shattered.

It wasn't an easy climb, but she'd done it before. She'd done harder. Hope pulled herself through the window, made cautiously for the shadows out of sight of the street, and listened. Satisfied she was alone, she picked her way through the building.

The tower she wanted was the next one over. The two buildings had been connected by a shared lobby at ground level. The lobby's glass roof now stood a short way above the waterline. Hope swiftly crossed this in the dying light, the cold wind plucking at her hair. She declined to look down; unsightly swollen things, trapped things with staring eyes, bobbed in the gently rolling water below. The world was silent, save for her throaty breath and the lapping of brackish water against glass.

Noiselessly, Hope slipped into the opposite building through an empty window frame and went to find the stairs. She'd counted the floors to the firelight. Now she climbed the pitch-black stairwell as cautiously as she could manage; adrenaline surged tight through her exhausted body and hammered in her chest. She was close. The hunt was almost done.

Hope counted floors as she passed them, and rested for a few moments, gathering her strength, when she spotted firelight seeping through a door's glass panel. With trepidation she eased the door open, inches at a time. It seemed to suck at its frame, then swung toward her with a whisper. Hope stood stock still. Nothing moved. She stepped through.

The floor was open plan with the stairwell at the centre. Shadows lurked in every corner, except to her right where a warm glow spread from behind the wall. Hope slid to the corner and glanced round.

A space had been cleared in the middle of the floor. Blankets and plastic sheeting were suspended from the ceiling, ends tucked beneath the ceiling tiles and secured with cable ties. The bottom of the sheets were weighed down with bricks and old computer monitors. The fire burned in a metal bucket at the heart of the shelter, with what looked like a spitted rat blackening over the flames. The man crouching beside it was not the Tall Man.

Hope's heart fell, and she wanted to cry. It wasn't fair. She looked at him again, willing the man to change but it was no good. The Tall Man was gaunt and dark, where this stranger was squat and broad. His hair was cut back to stubble, and he'd carved three parallel lines across his face, presumably with the stubby nails that were even now piercing his cheeks.

It wasn't fair. The Tall Man was here, she knew it, she'd found traces of his camps all over this spread of towers. She must be getting closer. Maybe this man knew where he was, had seen something that could help her. She needed to speak with him.

Hope pushed away from the wall and staggered towards the shelter. She wasn't sure what to say but knew she'd think of something. Hari had said she could charm the–

"Where is he?!" she screamed, fingers bunched like claws, mean spittle flecking the nearest plastic curtain. The man jerked his head up, wide-eyed, caught totally unawares.

"Where is he?!" she screamed again, staggering forward on legs as tense as steel pipes. This wasn't right, she thought. This couldn't help.

Adrenaline held her like a fist; nervous energy constricted her actions, and thoughts and vision. The man roared at her, half in fear, half in rage, and reached for the back of his belt. Hope screamed wordlessly and threw herself at him.

He has a knife, she thought, catching a glimpse of the foot long shard of metal as he stabbed it into her... no, past her. Her clothing hung baggy, and she could feel cold metal pressed against her flank beneath her jacket and top.

She scrambled at his face with her dirt-caked nails as they fell backwards into a plastic sheet. It tore from its fastenings and draped gently over them as Hope scratched at the screaming man's eyes. She felt the bucket spin away as her foot lashed out. Just need to subdue him, she thought, just calm him down and we can talk.

Her right thumb pressed hard, nail first, deep into his eye socket, down beside the warm, slick bulb, down and in and under. The man thrashed beneath her, shrieked like a dying cat, beat at her ribs with his left fist. The plastic was tangled about them, and his blade was tangled in her clothes, though she felt clean sharp heat as it sliced into her skin.

He'll kill me, she thought, he'll kill me. Need to subdue him, then we'll talk.

Hope wrenched her thumb out and the man tried to roll aside but she was pinning him with her knees. With her forearm and a snarl she knocked his hand from the tangled knife; a low, red pain was starting to seep through her on that side. She clawed the plastic from her head and cast about for something to calm him down with. There, a half-brick.

"Where is he?!" she screamed as she brought the brick down on the man's plastic-shrouded face. She screamed it again, and again, screamed it with every blow and screamed it until her throat felt raw from screaming. She brought the brick down one last time, and the scarlet-smeared plastic cracked and crackled, emitting a slurping thump, like she'd just struck a pot of porridge.

Breathing heavily, tingling with adrenal afterglow, Hope untangled the knife from her clothes and checked the wounds in her side. The lines looked shallow; skin deep. She hoped they'd heal. Then she looked down at the man, dead beneath her. Damn him, why hadn't he listened? Why did he have to pull the knife?

Her memory of the attack was hazy, strobe lit, and freeze frame. The noise, and the light, and the scent of blood would attract scavengers, she knew. She had to work fast. Her stomach, so abused of late, was signalling an appetite to her again. The spilled rat looked charred and blackened, little more than charcoal. Hope looked down at the man.

She'd learned from Hari that you could never carry the whole thing, that you'd have to leave most of the kill behind. But she'd take what she could, take what could be stuffed into the satchel. Thighs and rump were best.

With an effort she rolled him over, dragged down his tattered trousers and pants. She thumbed the knife blade. It would serve.

Later, satchel heavy and wet on her back, pockets stuffed with kindling and dry carpet tile from the dead man's stash, she made her way to the top of an older building, with a corner closed to the weather behind a crumbling chimney flue, where she knew a fire could burn unseen. The attic space was deserted, and she took her time to prepare the fire, not wishing to use more than one match to get it burning.

The floor was littered with slate from a collapsed section of roof and Hope blew a large piece clean of dust and placed it in the fire, thin strips of meat spread out atop to char in the flames. The smell of sizzling fat made her stomach twist into painful knots of longing. Hope ate well that night.

Later still, the sky cleared and Hope sat beside her fire, back to the chimney flue, gazing up through the hole in the ceiling. Without cloud to mask it, the split in the sky was clear as day, livid against the black, and bathing the world in sickly fronds of light tinged with greens and purples. Behind that sky-spanning tear, forms and faces, impossible and awful, writhed; gibbering mouths that could swallow planets and vast cyclopean eyes that dwarfed the sun, swelled and retreated; glistening tentacles licked at the edges of the wound, eager for a taste of the world.

It was a clear sky, and monstrous beings would be abroad tonight.

It started with a sibilant roar from the street, and the slap of waves against stone. The tide was coming in. When Hope felt the building begin to tremble below her too, she gasped with delight and rose, lifting her head through the roof hole. A distant glow on the southern horizon drew her gaze. Slow and silent, but for the trembling aftershock of her foot falls, the Pale Empress walked the earth. On clear nights she rose from the seas and came ashore, a surge of fresh flood water, a gift for her bloated children, spreading in her wake. The Empress towered above the pitiful structures of man, had thrown cities aside with a twitch of her tail. Her wingtips scraped the heavens, and frost glittered from their summits like winter snow on alpine peaks.

A halo of green encircled her brow, a ringlet of human bodies by the hundreds whipping around her in an orgy of psychic digestion. Her children would crawl from their brackish mires on a night like this and continue to build her effigy, a gleaming, perfect white tower, half as high as she. They scurried across its face like termites, each trying to outpace their bloated kin in joyful eagerness to lay the next skull.

Hope didn't know where these words and images came from, but she accepted them without question. They made her laugh and dance with giddiness, firelight casting her shadow on the attic wall, tall and gaunt and dark. Hope thought that it might be fun to gnaw through the thin skin of her own wrists, to spray blood upon the wooden boards beneath her feet while she span, to see what sigils and symbols would be written there through chance and chaos alone.

But then she would be dead. Then she would never find the Tall Man and there would be no justice for Hari.

She slowed and came to a halt. Hari had warned her many times against looking at the unclouded sky, or the creatures that it drew from the cold ocean depths. He said such sights would drive her to madness. She wasn't sure he was right, in the end.

She had gazed at the sky twice now - this night and the night Hari died - and had felt no change. Briskly she kicked over the fire so as not to waste any more flammables, and packed her leaking satchel with her uneaten meat. There was a cupboard downstairs where she could safely sleep.

Food, sleep, shelter, purpose. Hope hadn't felt this alive in weeks. And the hunt for the Tall Man would continue tomorrow.

Because he couldn't hide forever.

Now Playing
Kevin Rooney

Granddads

Tom Clarke

All four wheels of the breakfast cart were close to buckling under the strain of Michael's food. Reenie manoeuvred her grandfather's sustenance slowly down the corridor, avoiding the bunched lumps in the rug like she had done for the past three months. One of the wheels gave a squeak and the cart hunched to one side. Reenie stopped pushing. Some of the steaming bowls of porridge, beans and cereal had slipped and almost forced the piled plates of toast, sausage and eggs onto the floor. All the cart needed was to be lifted and the wheel jammed into place.

This happened every day, usually in the same place, below a collection of Lisle family pictures hung on the wall. Reenie featured in all of them, from crouching toddler on her dad's lap, to close-lipped teen held close to her mother and grandmother at a family party, to gowned graduate clutching her diploma. A few spaces on the wall were left blank: Reenie's mother Trina had said she had found some new pictures to replace the old ones, but that was a while ago.

A deep, soft lowing floated out from under the door at the end of the corridor.

Reenie used her palm to smack the wheel into place. She stood and stretched her back, reaching her arms high into the air. The moaning sounded again.

"Coming, hang on," Reenie sighed, and pushed the cart onwards. The smell of fried meat and eggs floated back towards Reenie, which was a blessing. Michael's door was closed, but the stench still seeped out.

The trousers were shorter than yesterday, Oliver noticed. He admired his skinny ankles in the mirror, now peeking out completely from the trouser legs. His waist also felt more hemmed in. It must have been the dinner last night, he told himself.

"Are you ready yet? We have to leave." Lucy's voice carried up the hall to him.

"Yes, sorry." Oliver put on his suit jacket, but as soon as both arms were in, everything felt tight: his shoulders ground against the lining and his elbows carried well past their pads. He looked like a massive toddler in hand-me-downs. He struggled out of the jacket and settled for his coat, which still fit. It was an old jacket anyway.

Ducking through the driver's side door, while telling Lucy about the new crematorium opening on Ashton Crescent, Oliver conked his head on the doorframe just above his temple. "Ahh, God," Oliver hissed and rubbed the painful spot.

"Are you okay?" Lucy said, putting her hand over his and rubbing his head in time with him.

"Yes, I was just distracted. So, James was saying they've got the biggest incinerator in the region, it has—" Oliver stopped short when his knees knocked uncomfortably against the steering column. "Have you moved my seat?"

"Yes, but I moved it back."

"Well, you mustn't have. Anyway…" Oliver adjusted his seat as he continued speaking.

Lucy listened, but as she did so, let her gaze fall on her husband's features: his stretched out legs, his wrists squeezed into the shirt sleeves, his hands…she put one of her hands over Oliver's as he drove and noticed the size difference. His hands had always been bigger, always soft, but the size now seemed way off. His thumb seemed to dwarf her ring finger. She looked her husband in the face, and then down to the tendons in his neck that were struggling against his tie, and then down to his stomach that was now coming through the buttons on his shirt, and then down to his shoes, which were slowly unseaming themselves against his feet.

"Oliver, you need to stop the car."

112

The masks her mother had provided never felt right, even after all this time. Reenie hooked one loop round her ear, then the other, making sure it was tight. The plastic covering pulled in and out as she breathed. It was uncomfortable, but necessary. Reenie knocked on Michael's door and said, "I'm coming in." She turned the handle.

The smell worsened as the door swung open. Reenie always tried to clean up all of the leftover food, but it was never entirely possible. Moving around to the front of the cart (she could never let it go in first), Reenie pulled it in backwards. As soon as she was in, the cart pushed up against the wall, she turned to look at her grandfather.

He'd grown again. Reenie reckoned Michael had another three days before his head hit the ceiling. She'd have to tell Mum about that. Veronika told her that when her granddad started scraping his head on the coving her dad had cut him a hole. Day by day, he'd start to sprout out of the roof, giving him the ability to see out and into the world again. Naturally, the neighbours complained, they couldn't have him peeping at them all day, and Veronika's dad had needed to box him in again. He hadn't lasted long after that.

Maybe, Reenie thought to herself, she'd try and get him to lie down, rather than sitting cross-legged. She surveyed the rest of him. He was never comfortable (how could he be?), always moving his long arms from resting on his knees, to crossing over his distended belly, then to just hanging limp by his sides. It was his legs that worried her the most; they didn't move much at all, and if they did, it was just to quiver. She noticed he'd discarded his blankets in a puddle in the corner.

"Now, what've we said? You need to keep warm." Reenie moved to pull the rolls of sewn together blankets over Michael, but he started moaning.

She looked him in the face for the first time this visit. His cheeks were stretched like the rest of him, ears like conches on the sides of his head, mouth curled downwards, whinging about food. His eyes, though, were the same as they'd always been: blue and clear.

"All right then, let's have some food first. Then you need to put your blankets on." She pulled the trolley closer to Michael, so his arms could come down and scoop at the food. As his right arm came down to grab at some porridge, she saw how big his fingers were. Each was the size of her forearm now; the nails yellowing and bunged up with gunk. It would be time to clean them again soon. As soon as the top tier had been cleared, Reenie pulled out the next batch from the middle shelf. "You are hungry today, aren't you? Look, you've got it all down you. It's in your belly button! There's a sausage in it! Look, Granddad, there's a—" Michael wasn't listening.

Another smell, also familiar, began to permeate the room. Reenie sighed and looked up at her grandfather gorging himself. "Right, I'll be back in a minute. I just need to grab the mop."

They got home before Oliver's clothes had completely split to rags. They hadn't driven far, but on their return journey the car seemed to shrink around him; at least, that's what he had told himself. Within moments of the U-turn, his arms grew out and his elbows elongated away from the steering wheel.

"Open the windows, will you?" Oliver had said. "It's getting a bit hot in here." He kept his eyes on the road. Lucy had leaned over and pressed the electric button to release all four windows. Oliver's right elbow almost sighed as the window freed it. When he went to change gears, he reached down, but instead of the gear stick, he grasped Lucy's knee. He let go, but not before Lucy realised how much he was shaking.

"Sorry, love, but I really don't think you moved my seat back to where it usually is. It gets me all out of sorts."

"Of course, sorry. I'll be more careful next time," Lucy said. She looked out the window. A family emerged from their house, a woman and a boy in his early teens coming out first, then a man following. He had to duck through the door frame. They walked towards their car; it was one of the new ones she'd seen advertised on the television.

"Look, it's one of those that I told you about. Extra wide driver's seat, extendable and ergonomic steering wheel, the roof has specially designed slats so you can—"

"Must have missed it." The top of Oliver's head now pressed into the beige fuzz of the car's ceiling, even when he ducked to see the road. "Here we are," Oliver said in a sing-song. "Home again, home again."

As soon as Oliver turned into their drive, he untangled himself from his belt, shouldered open his door and went inside.

Lucy was left in her seat. She felt her eyes begin to shake and her cheekbones begin to ache, like they always did. Tears pushed themselves forwards from behind her eyes, threated to break down her face, but with one sniff, Lucy forced them back. She rubbed her face, massaged her cheeks and huffed loudly. "Right," she said and followed her husband.

"I'm home," Reenie's mother shouted as she came down the hallway. She kicked her high heels off, discarding them in the corner by a lotus plant. Her laptop bag came off next and was dumped next to the banister. "If I have to listen to Helen talk about her cat in another morning stand-up, I think I'd kill it. Go round, weigh it down so it sinks in the nearest lake, river, puddle, whatever, and be done with it. We don't give a toss about your cat." Rounding the corner into the kitchen, she saw that Reenie was at the sink scrubbing some dried porridge out of the pan. "Hello, darling." She kissed her on the cheek.

"Good day then?" Reenie kept cleaning, squinting at a speck that wouldn't budge.

Reenie's mother scraped a chair out from under the kitchen table and sat down. "Yeah, not bad. We've just had a new brief come in for a new app, so that's good."

"Yeah? What's it for?"

"Get this: household services. To help connect people to cleaners, ironers—if they're a thing—gardeners, maids, you know. Frieda said to me, she said, 'Trina, this app has your name all over it, so do your thing.' So that's that. It actually made me think. We should get a maid or something. I know I've mentioned it before, but I think it would help. They could come in every day, tidy things up a bit—"

"It would be nice to get a bit of help." Reenie couldn't keep the bluntness out of her voice. She knew what was coming.

"Well, less help you, more like take over. They could—"

"No, mum, you know I'm fine."

"I know you've said you're fine, but you've been out of education long enough. You need to go to university."

"My friends are in the same position. We have to be here for—"

"They aren't in the same position. I've got more coming in now; we can pay someone to–"

"Georgia has to look after her dad and her granddad. And Suzette's brother's started to go early."

"You know how I feel about this. It was fine when you were younger, it's what all young girls do. But there's got to be a point, a point when–"

"When was your point, mum?" Reenie slammed the last pot into the sink, sloshing bubbles over the drainage board. "At what point did you think, 'Right, I'm done here, he doesn't need me anymore.' Because of course he needed you. They need us."

Trina closed her eyes and leant back in her chair. "Again. This again. Reenie, you know how this all works, it's just what happens."

Reenie whirled round, suds from her hands flicking across the room. "But they need to be cared for, not just left alone. Granddad needs me. You won't even go down that corridor."

Trina opened her eyes and stared at her daughter. Her fingers curled into her palms. "Now you stop it. Don't–"

"You let him die," Reenie was shaking, her arms drawn to her sides. "I barely remember him because you let him die. You were supposed–"

The kitchen table was shunted forwards with the force of Trina's hands pushing away from it. In two strides, she was in front of Reenie, one hand wrapped around her daughter's jaw, the other quivering beside her cheek.

"Your dad. Your dad. He – oh, fuck off." She pushed Reenie's face away, making her fall back against the sink. "You just fuck off."

This last phrase came out as a juddery sob. Trina covered the bottom half of her face with her hand, the hand that had just gripped her daughter's jaw. She snorted in a huge breath through her nose, wiped her face, and ran upstairs.

Reenie held on to the sink behind her and stood there, holding herself up. A pot moved on the rack and made a dull *thunk* against another.

Oliver was sitting in the lounge reading his newspaper. He'd changed into his brown dressing gown, far too big for him when Lucy bought it for him for his thirtieth a few years ago, but it fit him fine now. He didn't look up when Lucy came into the room, but he did start reading out loud to her.

"Can you believe this? People are already complaining about that crematorium. It's only been functioning a week and it's got people protesting outside. Why would someone do that?"

"I'm not sure." Lucy sat opposite her husband in a wing-backed chair.

"Well, I'm not sure either. It says here that… are you okay?" Oliver looked up at his wife.

"Of course. I just…"

"Are you annoyed that we missed lunch with John and Eileen? Have you told them I'm feeling a bit under the weather?"

"Yes, I've sorted it out with them, don't worry. I just wanted to talk to you about–"

"Oh, good." Oliver had already drawn his eyes back down to his paper. "What did you want to talk about?"

"Oliver, we both know–"

"What do we both know?" Oliver was looking at his paper, but Lucy could tell he wasn't reading it.

"You're, you know, growing. And–"

"I'm a growing lad," Oliver said, with a choked sort of chuckle.

"Come on now, Oliver."

"What is it?"

"Oliver–"

"Lucy, Lucy, what? Are we just repeating each other's names now? Lucy, Lucy, Lucy–"

"Oliver, you bloody listen to me right now, you listen. Right. Now. You must think me blind or stupid or bloody both to not know. And I know you're not blind or stupid and it's happening to you, for bloody sake. It's happening to you, just like it happens to all men, as it has always happened to all men, and it is happening to you, so bloody listen to me. You can't ignore it. Your clothes certainly can't. Accept it, Oliver. Once you do, it'll be fine. Don't you think I've noticed you've started the growth for the past few months? I know my own husband, Oliver. Please don't treat me like I'm stupid. Bloody stupid. Are you listening to me? It's fine, Oliver. It's something that you have to deal with. We have to deal with." Lucy had stood up, but wasn't sure at which point during her speech.

Oliver sat still looking at his paper. Lucy had never seen him so still. After what seemed like hours, Oliver closed his paper, put it onto the arm of the sofa and stood. He must have been seven feet tall, but he looked like a child. His hands were clasped awkwardly in front of him, clenching and unclenching; his feet too close together, knees turned slightly inwards. He opened his mouth to speak, and it seemed like it was a lot of work.

"What is it, Oliver?" Lucy stepped forwards and laid her hands on his.

"I…" Oliver started. "No," he finished. He turned, ducked through the doorway and went upstairs.

It's just what happens, she'd said. Trina's words ran a small circuit around Reenie's head. It's just what happens. Of course, Reenie knew that; it is what happens. After she had fed her granddad dinner that evening, a dinner that consisted of three bowls of soup, seven chicken kievs and a whole bag of rice, Reenie found herself still sat in her granddad's room. He had fallen asleep, as he usually did, and Reenie stayed with him. She looked up at Michael for a while. He slept, as he had to, cross-legged and leant against the top corner of the room. When he got too big for his bed and they moved it out, he had to get used to sleeping on a pile of old jumpers and pillows. When he could no longer sleep lying down, he had to get used to crossing his legs. It was painful, as his knees were strained and tired enough by that point anyway, but he had to get used to it. *It's just what happens.*

A van pulled up across the road outside number 46. Four men got out and proceeded to get bags of tools from the boot. A woman—Georgia's mum—emerged out of the front door and waved the men inside.

Reenie sighed at this scene she'd observed many times over the years. She saw (or at least remembered) her first removal when she was three. Her dad was walking her home from the park and the house on the corner had this very same van outside. Muted hammer blows and the buzz of electric saws sounded from somewhere on the side of the house. Her dad sped up, almost dragging Reenie behind him, but being three, of course she wanted to know everything.

"What are they doing, Daddy?"

"Just some building, sweetheart. Come on, we need to get home for lunch."

"But why is it so loud?"

"Come on. Mum won't be happy if we're…"

At that moment, the side wall of the house blew outwards and even Dad stopped for a moment. Whorls of dust bellowed up and out into the midday sky, and when it cleared, Reenie screamed. Her dad pulled her onwards, shielding her from the sight, but what she saw was enough to make her keep screaming.

The workers kept hammering at the remains of the demolished wall, and through the gap was a marble-like eye, staring outwards, unblinking, the size of a dinner-table. The skin around the eye was grey and dry, and matted hair fell into it. Eventually, Reenie's dad lifted her into his arms.

"Shall we ask if Mum's got any ice cream for after lunch? Shall we ask her that? Would you like that? That would be nice, wouldn't it?"

As Reenie sat with her sleeping grandfather, the evening dark dimming the world outside, the hammers and saws started up.

JimmyDangerLad: did u c united against villa the other day

OliverReynolds45: No, I've had a lot on recently. Was it a good match? I heard United smashed Villa.

JimmyDangerLad: it was mega 4 nil in th end. Dempsey with a header then two penalties in a row. villa played dirty and it didnt pay of. the last goal was brilliant mate you should hav seen it

OliverReynolds45: Oh, yeah? I heard it was a bit contentious actually.

JimmyDangerLad: mate honestly it was so good. Rahmani curled it right into the box and Martinez scissored it right past Carter. people reckon it was offside but those people are villa fans. she didnt score but Zielinski was the best player out there by far by far

OliverRenolds45: She's the new import from Wrocław, isn't she? Was she worth the 50 mil?

JimmyDangerLad: evry penny mate. she had real presence out there. dominated the midfield, sent in sum lethal free kicks. she has a real tactical mind you can see it from th screen. banging arse as well.

OliverReynolds45: I'll have to watch the next one!

JimmyDangerLad: yes mate. listen have u looked into that thing I told u about

OliverReynolds45: Yes. Are you sure it's not a hoax? I've never heard of anything like it.

JimmyDangerLad: mate yeah its real. pony told me he went on a sight and he saw sum pictures of it

OliverReynolds45: I've not managed to find any pictures.

JimmyDangerLad: they are out there. u did search nephlim grove didnt u

OliverReynolds45: I did, but I just saw people talking about it on some forums.

JimmyDangerLad: its worth a try itsnt it

OliverReynolds45: I think it is. Have you had any more changes?

JimmyDangerLad: just my toes really. th very same thing happened to my dad. toes first. used to play this massive piggy with us. hed let us wiggle his toes for him and me n my brother would take it in turns each toe had to be wiggled with a hole hand. Wen it got to that bit with the all the way home dad would let us tickle his feet. we all laughed tho

OliverReynolds45: I'm trusting you with this, James. If you want to try and find the grove, I'm for it. If they could help us, that would be good.

JimmyDangerLad: yeah that would be good. If my friend Pony's right i know where it is

OliverReynolds45: Okay. Do you think we could go soon?

JimmyDangerLad: bought myself a new car. pick u up this weekend?

OliverReynolds45: I'll need to tell my wife, but that sounds good.

JimmyDangerLad: dont rub it in. only joking. how is lucy doing

Reenie awoke to a prod in the stomach. When her eyes opened, a dark patch formed in the middle of a ring of light. As her eyes adjusted, the huge dark blot was Michael's head obscuring the sun coming through the window. She hadn't meant to fall asleep here, but she must have been lulled by the hammering and sawing from across the road.

Another prod to the stomach. She squinted and looked into her grandfather's face. He was leaning over her, blue eyes wide, wrinkles traversing his face like webs.

Reenie checked her watch as she got up. 7am. *It'll be a late breakfast for him today.*

"Sorry, Granddad. Give me twenty minutes, okay?"

Michael groaned louder.

"Sorry! I'll make it up to you. What about an extra plate of sausages?"

Quicker than she thought he could, Michael lifted his finger and pushed her hips towards the door. He roared; his teeth almost baring. Reenie hit the doorframe with a thud.

"Hey, I'm going! Stop. Please." He'd never done that before. Reenie stared. He looked at her face like he was trying to read.

"I love you, Granddad." Reenie opened the door and walked into the corridor. She put her back to the wall opposite the photos and took some deep, quavering breaths.

Down the corridor, coming from the lounge, two voices could be heard. Mum? Why was she not at work? And who was the other voice? She inched down the corridor, minding not to step on the creaky patches. As she moved closer to the lounge, past the kitchen, the other voice that wasn't her mum's was speaking.

"…and when they get to this stage, it can be very hard. How far along would you estimate he is?"

"Well, it's hard to tell. He's been very gradual over the last few months." *Like you'd know*, Reenie thought.

"His head is nearly touching the ceiling, if that helps."

"Somewhat, yes, but, as I'm sure you know, size sometimes isn't the best measure of a man." Both Trina and the other voice, another woman, laughed, but abruptly stopped. "The best thing to do is wait for any clear signs of passing. You might want to keep an eye out for sores, blood or gore in the vomit, extended rest periods, necrosis of the limbs, particularly the legs, and inward collapse."

"I'll keep an eye out."

"Excellent. Now, the next thing I want to talk to you about is the funeral." At this, Reenie nearly punched the wall. *Granddad is okay. He's been eating and he's alert. He smiled at me the other week.* She nearly walked in to tell the woman to leave, but stopped herself.

"We were thinking machine cremation."

"That's a good choice. We've actually opened a new facility across town. We have three incinerators and a top-of-the-range cremulator. If you change your mind, we also have some traditional pyre funeral packages that are very reasonable."

"Oh, no, we don't want traditional." *She keeps saying 'we'. 'I' had nothing to* do with this.

"That is totally understandable. Traditional cremations are falling in popularity. I think it's still important for communities to get behind them, but..."

Reenie couldn't listen any more. She crept back down the hallway and into the kitchen to start Michael's breakfast. Tears dripped down her face as she opened tins and turned the ovens on.

The front door shutting and its latch clicking broke into Reenie's thoughts, blowing the spirals of frustration away.

Reenie heard Trina come into the kitchen, but then stop with an "Oh, I didn't know you were here. I thought you'd be in your room."

Reenie didn't answer for a moment. She pulled blackened toast out of the toaster and scraped butter over it with a knife. "I'm making Granddad's breakfast."

"Yes, sorry, I thought you'd done it already."

The beans were slopped into bowls next. "I thought you'd be at work."

Trina sat down on the counter and tapped her thumbs together. "I'm going in a minute. I just had to sort something out."

"I heard."

The tap of Trina's thumbs stopped. "Oh, I thought... well, it's something we need to sort out. You understand, don't you?"

Reenie nodded as she pulled the trolley from its corner.

"I know it's difficult, but you know..."

"It's just what happens."

"Exactly, yeah?" Trina reached out to rub Reenie's arm as she came past her to grab a plate of sausages, but she missed. "And Reenie? Reenie?"

Reenie whipped past her mother, a tray of pancakes in her hands, and put it onto the bottom of the cart. As she went past her mother again to grab the eggs, Trina grabbed her daughter's wrist.

"Hey, I'm talking to you." Voice raised; eyes wide, other hand clenched. She took a breath, but didn't let go of Reenie's wrist. "I'm sorry about yesterday. I didn't mean to shout at you. It's just... we've had talk after talk about this, we've shouted about it and been unkind, but it is what it is. I know you miss your dad. I do too. Can we get past this? Together?" Trina loosened her grip on Reenie's wrist, but instead of letting it go, drew it towards her and into a hug.

"What about these? These'll be good for your camping trip." Lucy held a pair of camouflage trousers against Oliver's waist and looked at how far they came down his legs. "Maybe a bigger size."

"No, these are fine." Oliver took the trousers off Lucy and threw them in the basket. "Right, I need some hiking socks."

They picked their way through the aisles, grabbing socks, thermal underwear and a hunting waistcoat. "I think I should get a Swiss Army knife as well. I've always wanted one of them."

"My mum gave me one a few years ago," Lucy said. "You could have that one, if you like?"

"No, I'd quite like my own. Right, so I think they'll be…"

Before Oliver could finish, there was a thud from the corner. Everybody turned to see a man that had collapsed in the racket aisle. Even though he'd gone down, his head could still be seen over the waist-height shelves. The man, whose eyes were gripped shut and quivering, moaned and swore.

"We should help, Oliver, come on." Lucy walked over, along with a few other shoppers.

"Lucy, can we just…" It was too late. Oliver made his way over. *He'll be okay*, Oliver thought. *The shop assistants must deal with this all the time. He's probably just out of breath, the old fool.*

As Oliver walked into the aisle, he stopped. People were milling around the collapsed man, the shop assistants already bringing their support gurney over (clearly old, but sturdy), but Oliver could see what had happened. No wonder he was moaning. His legs had buckled under him, one knee twisted sideways, the other bent backwards at the thigh. It looked like an illusion, but the spreading patches of blood dying the man's trousers made it very real. The shop assistants were deftly attaching the gurney's winch system around the man's waist and people were already going back to their shopping.

"Poor man." The voice made Oliver jump, but it was just Lucy. "Shall we pay up?"

Michael swallowed down eggs, porridge, toast, sausages, the extra plate of sausages Reenie had promised, and a bowl of honey as a treat. By this point, the trolley had been knocked over and crockery lay on the bare wooden floors. When he started to go, Reenie had been careful to get the plastic plates and bowls out from under the stairs where her mother had kept them.

Reenie leant against the window and stared outside. The side wall of the house over the road had been knocked out and the rubble cleared, and there lay Franklin. The curves and flesh of him, at least. His back took up most of the space where his bedroom wall had been. From here, she could see the knobs of his spine, his sloping neck and the crack of his bum. She could only imagine how they'd had to contort his legs and arms, bend them and bind them with rope to stop them bursting through the sides of the house. She saw Georgia emerge from her house and sit on her front step.

Once Michael had finished and Reenie had cleaned up (and narrowly avoided another forceful push), she went outside. The smell of fresh-cut wood and the ghost of rain was a welcome change to the grease of the ovens and the rancid undertones of Michael's room.

As she neared Georgia, another truck turned up with a felled tree in in its bed. The truck's horn sounded once and a crew of men and women came from around the back of Georgia' house, all covered in sawdust. They all gathered around the log and, working as one, heaved the tree out and carried it back behind the house.

Reenie raised a hand in greeting to Georgia and her friend smiled.

"Hi, Reenie."

"How are you doing?" Reenie sat beside Georgia and put her arm around her. Georgia dropped her head down and onto Reenie's shoulder, her cheek pressed against her smock.

"Not so bad. I suppose you've seen?"

"Yeah. When did he go?"

"We aren't too sure. A few nights ago? I noticed his pap was just slopping right back out of his mouth. The doctor came and called it about five minutes into his visit."

"I'm sorry. How's your mum?"

"Busy. She's in the garden organising the ceremony."

"I suppose it's good to keep busy. What time are you having the burning?"

"Tomorrow, at eight."

"I'll tell Mum, just so she knows."

"Thanks." Georgia lifted her head and looked up into the sky. A bruised splotch coloured the skin under her chin and reached down to her collar bone. The electric thrum of a saw started up from behind the house. Georgia turned her head and squinted at Reenie. "Can I ask you something?"

"Mm?"

"Do you miss your dad?"

Reenie's father reached up through her spine and made her shiver. He had a smile that threatened to cut his head in half. When she fell off the rope ladder at the park, he'd managed to grab her ankle and yank her back into the air. He always brought vegetables home with the dirt still on and he'd make her laugh by crunching right into an onion, skin and all. He was quiet. Her mum locked his door at the end. "Everyday."

"Do you?"

"Yeah. Of course."

Georgia looked away, around to her house, then down the street, then down at her fingers she'd twisted into a knot. She untied her hands and rubbed absently at the dark shadow on her neck. "Hmm."

"What's wrong?"

"He's laying right there," Georgia said, pointing vaguely behind her. "He's laying right there, and I know very firmly that he's dead. Not passed away or gone to heaven, just dead."

"I'm sorry, Georgia, I should leave you with your dad and–"

"All I can think about is what I'm going to have for dinner and what I'm going to watch on TV." Georgia stood up and dusted her legs off. She squeezed Reenie's shoulder. "I'll see you later. I'll say hi to Mum and Granddad for you."

She walked back up the path and into her house.

"When will you be back? Tomorrow? Because remember, we're having the Elliots round for dinner." Lucy fussed over the collar of Oliver's hunting waistcoat.

"I'll try my very best to be back by tomorrow evening, okay? I'll let you know if anything changes."

A horn sounded from outside; two short beeps and then a longer blare.

"Right, that's James. I'll see you, Lucy." Oliver pecked his wife on the forehead, moved by her with his rucksack and tent and went outside.

"Let me wave you off, hang on." They both moved onto their front step and James was parked outside their garden wall. "Oh, you didn't mention that he'd got a new car. Isn't it good? See, I told you we should get one of them."

James sat in the driver's seat, grinning and waving. He had an oversized flat-cap on, a tag still swinging from the back. His new car, like his hat, was also too big for him.

Lucy walked towards James as he rolled the window down. "Hi James, are you okay? This is a lovely new car."

"Hiya, Luce. It's belting, isn't it? They had a deal on chrome roof slats that can move up and down, and left and right. This nut won't be crammed in anytime soon." James knocked on his forehead like a door. "It's an accommodating little motor... well, not little. I suppose, a motor of varying sizes is better, eh? What are you standing over there for, Ollie? It's a new car, not a ghost, come and say hello."

What a waste of money, Oliver thought, as he picked his things up and walked to the car.

"Just chuck your stuff in the boot and we'll get out of Lucy's hair. What've you got on without this husband of yours around?" said James.

"Well, I've invited my friend Kathleen round, so…"

Oliver walked round to the back of the car and opened it up. The boot was so huge that James' bags looked lost in the space of it. Oliver threw his stuff in and walked back around.

"…and Kathleen's been having a hard time of it, what with her twins having to move back in, so it'll be nice to catch up and…"

"Right, James, I'm all ready. Shall we head?" As Oliver passed Lucy, he held her waist in his palm and kissed her on the head. Just as he pulled away, she pulled him in for a hug and ended up kissing his armpit.

"Have fun!"

"Okay then, Luce, we'll see you. Not sure when, but we'll see you!"

Lucy looked from James to Oliver and back again. "Well, tomorrow evening, I should hope?"

James looked up to Oliver. Oliver widened his eyes, which meant shut up. "Oh yeah, sorry, I meant I wasn't sure when we'd back tomorrow, so we'll see you tomorrow, just not sure when." He grinned.

Lucy gave a brief smile in return. Before Oliver could go around and get in to the passenger's side, Lucy reached up on her tip-toes to whisper in Oliver's ear, "Please remember, I'm not blind or stupid." She kissed his cheek and waved as she walked away.

A shuddering crash rumbled through the house just past four in the morning. Reenie emerged from her room, eyes unfocused, blinking away the dream she was having about a rabbit watching her while she tried to untie her shoelaces. The noise had come from Michael's room, and it wasn't like any of the usual bangs and clatters that came from him.

Reenie opened the door to Michael's room and was hit by a breeze and a full palette of morning light. As the room came into full view, she could see what had happened. Michael had fallen through the wall, mostly. His legs were crossed under him, as usual, but his top half had burst straight through and onto the grass that ran alongside their house. By the rise and fall of his cauldron belly and the low snufflings coming from his nose, Reenie could tell he was still asleep. She strode closer and had to climb over him to check his head and back. This wouldn't hurt him, as she'd had to clamber on him before, first as a fidgety toddler with him chuckling, then later, a few days ago, when she had to stand up on his legs to clean out his eyes after he'd got sauce in them. He hadn't liked that, so pulled the curtain down.

Reenie carefully stepped onto his tummy; felt it squash and tense as it worked with his breath. After a few careful and balanced steps, using the broken masonry as handholds, Reenie hopped through the hole and into the morning. She pulled her dressing gown around her and looked down into her granddad's face. Snoring, eyes closed, mouth slack. He was oblivious. Reenie smiled.

"What the fuck? Is this a joke?" Trina appeared at the hole in the wall, hair in a messy bun, cheeks puffy.

"He's okay, he's still sleeping."

"Fuck's sake. Look at this. Did you make sure he was propped up in the corner? Like I said?"

"Yes, of course I did, I–"

"Well how's he come through the side then?" Trina was tapping on the wall, figuring out prices in her head and turning around the room. "You insist on looking after him and look at this. We need someone else. You need to get to university. Such a dick, Reenie, aren't you? Honestly. Old enough and yet a bloody child still." The team came an hour later with the machine. They backed their truck up towards the house with the machine anchored to the back. White and boxy, the size of a caravan, the back door of the machine slid up and into its roof. Inside was padded and empty, except for the very back wall, which was a metal plate, punctured with fist size openings. A woman got out of the truck's cab and came around to Michael's head holding a remote control. A second woman got out and stood idly by the machine, fiddling with something at the back.

"Alright, folks? Won't take long. He's not as big as we thought he'd be. Miss, if you could stand back a bit." The operator fiddled with the remote and slender arms unwound from the depths of the padded room, from the holes in the metal plate. "We'll need just two, I reckon," she said to herself.

The arms, each with blunt metal grippers on the end, slithered under Michael's splayed arms and wound around them like tourniquets. He didn't even stir. The arms tensed, pushed upwards, and Michael rose at the waist as if waking. He was manhandled and manipulated back into the house, the arms twisting to get his body back in through the hole of his own making. Once his torso was back inside the house, the arms managed to shunt his entire body over into the corner.

"See?" Trina hissed into her daughter's ear.

After the arms had retracted and the machine's door had slid shut, the operator said "I'll give you the receipt later today, if that's okay? I'm back here this evening for those guys." She jerked her thumb over her shoulder at Georgia's house.

Row after row of pine trees huddled closer to the road the further they drove. The occasional deer was seen skittering away, but apart from that, the forest was empty. The car's radio mumbled quietly, and James played commentator under his breath.

"Go on, that's it, nicely, nicely, yep, there you go, there you GO, YES

HAVE IT YOU BEAUTY!" He slapped his palm on the wheel as the muffled crowd screamed. "She's bloody done it again!"

Chin in his hand, half listening, Oliver said, "Zielinski?". The sun bobbed and wobbled on top of the pines, making the branches look as if they were grasping for its rays.

"Course it was. Half volley from just inside the box. Hey, I was gonna get tickets to see United against Preston next weekend. Do you want to come?"

Oliver hadn't thought about how long they'd be gone. James' map said the grove was a two hour walk from where they needed to park up, and that was still another hour away yet. Moreover, Oliver didn't know what they'd find, or what he wanted to find, or how long they'd be gone and if they'd ever come back. "We'll see. Depends what happens."

"Well, you're right, but I'm not missing Zielinski on the pitch for much longer."

James had shown Oliver some grainy photos of the grove on his phone. Most of them were Loch Ness Monster-level tripe, but one seemed interesting. It had been a clearing and men sat in huddles, under awnings or by fires, all smiling at each other and all as huge as the lower branches of the trees. There was one even stood, chest puffed out, fists like boulders clenched by his sides. Oliver had said, "How are they still alive?" and James had replied "They're allowed to be, I reckon."

"He'll get cold," Reenie said, nailing the plastic tarp over the hole in Michael's wall.

Trina stood in the doorway picking the edge of her nail. "He'll be fine." Her voice was muted through the mask she was wearing. "He needs the fresh air anyway."

"He might get ill. Or an animal might come in." Reenie stepped down from the chair she was using as a ladder and looked at her mother.

Trina continued to dig into her nail. "Yeah, I reckon a fox might come in and steal his bollocks." She laughed at herself, then furrowed her brow and dug a bit harder.

Reenie looked over to Michael, propped in the corner. He was awake and silently looking from his granddaughter to his daughter-in-law. His hands rested in his lap, one over the other. Reenie smiled at him, but Michael just scrutinised her mouth.

"Anyway, it's for the best, saves us getting someone to come and, ow, too much, pulled too much off there." Trina sucked at her finger and vanished in search of a plaster.

Before Reenie could shout at her mother that Michael was *fine, just look at him for a second, he's fine, I'll do everything I can to look after him*, a gurgle erupted from her granddad's stomach, followed by a fart that almost walked across the floorboards towards her. Reenie put her mask on and said, "Right, I'll be back with your breakfast."

While her mother watched endless repeats of sitcoms on TV, Reenie split her time that Saturday afternoon tending to Michael, washing him, cleaning him out and feeding him, and looking out the window over to Georgia's house where she could see the top of the pyre that would burn that evening.

After lunch, Reenie sat in Michael's lap as he napped. No matter how thoroughly she mopped and hosed him, and no matter how many air fresheners she attached to the walls, Michael reeked, but Reenie loved being close to him. She let her head rise and fall with his belly and nestled into his elbow, using it like a hammock. In classic Granddad fashion, he used to "steal" her nose when she was small and pretend to eat it, chewing on and gulping it down dramatically. The first time he had done it, Reenie cried, terrified that her ability to smell was lost, but when he spat it back out and reattached it, she knew it was great fun.

A sharp flap from the plastic sheeting awoke her. She was still curled up next to Michael, who was still sleeping. With a yawn, Reenie clambered out from the shelter of Michael, stood up and stretched her back. Before leaving, she kissed her granddad's hand, tendons thick and sinuous, and walked into the kitchen.

Trina was there fussing with the crotch of her overalls, and she looked up when Reenie came in. "Are you not ready yet? We have to go in twenty minutes."

"Sorry, I fell asleep."

"Come on, hurry up. These haven't been this annoying before..." Trina continued to rejig herself. Reenie went to her room to change.

She pulled her overalls out from the back of her wardrobe. She'd got too close to the pyre at the last funeral (it was her uncle's) and a cinder had burnt a hole in the right knee. Other than that and a few smudges, these overalls looked barely worn, the collar still somewhat stiff.

Before they left, masks and goggles looped ready around their necks, hide gloves tucked into their belt loops, Reenie went to give Michael his dinner (salmon, whole, with three loaves of bread and a jug of oil) and say goodbye. He didn't even look at her when she came in with his food; he grabbed and sucked at the trolley, the salmon gone in moments, the oil slurped and licked out of the jug. Reenie smiled and made sure his blankets were in place.

The two men parked at the end of the road, tyres crunching over the gravel. They got out, stretched and looked around.

"This is it, Ollie. The bloody outside! Smell that?" James strode over to the nearest tree, bark dark and ridged, unzipped his fly and urinated against it.

"Smell *that*, yes. Which way do we go?"

James shook off, zipped up and pulled his map out of his back pocket. He stared hard, turned the map around, over, and then back to its original position. He stabbed finally at a point on the map and said "This way. That path over there." He pointed to a trail on Oliver's left. The grass was shorter, the ground clearly harder, but it was still overgrown.

They trekked onwards through the woods. "My car'll be okay there, won't it?"

"I don't see why not. I've not seen anyone for a while."

Nettles were abundant, jagged fronds jutting out over the path. James attempted to grab one to prove that if you did it right, you wouldn't be stung, but quickly went off to search for a dock leaf waving his hand in the air.

"That doesn't work, you know!" Oliver called after him.

"It does if you want it to, miserable get," James hollered back. He stumbled off into some bushes, ducking under a branch.

Oliver carried on down the path, shaking his head. He pulled out his phone.

Hi Lucy, we made it to the campsite. We're just setting up our tents and then we're going to go fishing at the lake. I'll send you some pictures. I hope you have a nice evening with Kathleen. See you! Xx

"FUCKING SHIT, OW."

Oliver put his phone away in his trouser pocket and whirled around. "James, what's wrong? Where are you?"

"Fuck. Ow. Ow ow ow." Oliver jogged, slowly, to where James was swearing, behind some brambles. He was sitting and holding his leg.

A hot wave spread from the back of Oliver's head and over his body. "What's happened? Are you okay?"

James tried to roll his trouser leg up, but it wouldn't go past the top of his shin. "It's my knee. Bloody hell, that grew a bit quick." He unbuckled his trousers, and before Oliver could give him some privacy, pulled them down to his ankles. There was no blood, no bruising, nothing wrong, except for its new bulk. James' thigh looked like it held a full bag of rocks under it, and then under that, his lower leg.

"Oof, that was a lot. It's not hurting so much anymore." He bent it to see if the joint still worked and it did. He looked at his knee, first the left side, then the right, then burst out laughing.

Oliver looked at his friend, his heart banging against the back of his eyes, his thumbs twitching. "What?"

James fell back and lay in the grass. "I've got a big knee! A big knee." He let out a few more chuckles.

"Why is that funny? Can you keep going or do we need to go home?" Oliver stood up and paced, avoiding looking at the knee.

James sat up, shrugged and pulled his trousers up. "I'm okay. How can you not find a big knee funny?"

The fuel from the bowl shimmered in the light from the house. It flecked the air, morphed into streaks and blobs, then hit the pyre. Reenie put her bowl in the growing stack on a trestle table when she was done. Trina threw her fuel without looking. The column that shifted slowly past the pyre, with Franklin draped on top of it, petered out into small groups of talking women and children.

Trina nudged Reenie with her elbow. "Martha's here. I'm surprised she came, with the state of her son and all." Reenie looked over at Martha, a tall woman in red overalls who was stood next to Georgia's mother. She clutched a pint of beer in one hand.

Alone in the corner of the garden, smoking, Georgia sat with her back to everything. Reenie left her mother to pay her respects to the family and went to sit with her friend.

She put a hand on her back and sat next to her, but faced the other way.

Georgia glanced over, dragged on her cigarette for a final time and stubbed it out. "Thanks for coming. I'm sure this is the highlight of your week." She flicked her butt away, careful to not let it fly near the pyre.

"Of course I came. Your dad was a lovely man and he–"

"Can you not? Please?" Georgia turned to Reenie, eyes bagged and jaw clenched. "All the neighbours have said the same thing, but I need you to not." She pulled out another cigarette from her back pocket.

"Sorry." Reenie let her eyes wander over the pyre, soaking ever more with the thrown fuel of the attendees. The timber and kindling were piled high, slotted together and balanced so Franklin didn't fall straight through. The operator that had come out to get Michael back into the house that morning was here, adjusting the pile with her crew and making sure it stayed stable.

Franklin had been laid out belly up, his hands crossed over his chest, his legs dangling down over the pyre, the soles of his feet hovering above the heads of his mourners. His head was bent back too far, his neck clearly not supported by the beam it was on, and it looked like he was looking behind him into next door's garden.

Reenie felt her forehead prickle with heat and her brain beat inside her skull. *Have I fed granddad enough? Was he too cold? Does he need me?*

Georgia nudged her. "What's wrong?"

"Nothing, I'm okay. Did you see that thing I sent you on–"

Georgia's mother clapped her hands together twice and the murmuring groups quietened down. Everyone gathered around the pyre and pulled their goggles and masks into place. "Hello all. Thank you for being here. I think we should make a start. Please take a torch as they come round." The operator and her crew handed round torches, and woman after woman lit hers from the torch before. "As before, as will be," she said and then said nothing more.

Reenie lit her torch and then Georgia lit hers, the soaked wadding going up and illuminating her eyes. Once all of the women and children had their torches, they all stepped together to the pyre and lowered their flames. The fuel lit and flames crawled with grasping arms all over the wood. Everyone stepped away from the heat and light and looked up at Franklin, the fire jumping up to his body. After a few moments of quiet, women, one after the other, put their torches in sand buckets dotted around and went back to talking quietly in their groups.

Reenie and Georgia stayed for a moment. Reenie couldn't help a tear fall from her right eye and down into the corner of her mouth. Georgia lit another cigarette. They both looked up at Franklin, the waves of heat warping his skin, making it look like it was moving, rippling. The fire had reached his arms, scorching the hair, darkening and tightening the skin.

Amongst the flitting cinders floating into the night, Reenie saw another movement, a flickering. Upside down, face looking away from it all, Franklin's eyes closed. Her forehead went hot again, and her toes dug into the ground. The eyes then opened. *It must be the heat, surely*, Reenie thought, looking hard at his face above. Again, the eyes closed, then opened, the mouth still slack. "Georgia, look," Reenie whispered, grabbing her by the arm.

Georgia saw, tilted her head and looked down again.

"Did you see? He's just blinking, he's awake, Georgia. Look."

Georgia eased her arm away from Reenie, looked around at the crowd and walked away.

A laugh issued above the quiet conversations, and it was Trina, laughing at something Georgia's mum had said. Reenie looked up again at Franklin, blinking slowly and looking away into the night.

Her breaths came shuddering out of her chest and she didn't know what to do with her hands. *This isn't okay, is it, no it's not* whizzed around her head. No one was looking at Franklin now, the fat of his belly melting from him and dripping through the timbers, his legs blackened logs. The operator and her crew were covering the ground in plastic sheets for when the pyre would start to collapse. Franklin blinked again and his eyes still shone.

Hands twitching, Reenie made her way through the crowd, past her mother who was finishing a pint, down the side of the house and into the street. She crouched, mouth twisted, and pounded her fists on the tarmac. All she could think about was Michael and how okay he was and how he was fine and that he needs looking after. She turned back towards Georgia's house and there she saw the crew's truck, machine hooked to the back.

Reenie's breathing slowed, remembered the arms snaking out and looping around her granddad. She walked over to the cab and looked in the window, where she saw the remote console attached to the dashboard.

"Can I help you, miss?" One of the operator's crew, removing her mask and goggles, came from the side of the house and over to the truck.

Tears still dripped from her eyes, but Reenie pushed them away with her hand. "I... yes. Please." She looked back to her own house, saw the flap of the plastic sheet over the hole in Michael's bedroom, and turned back to the concerned crew member. "My granddad. He's hurt his head, he fell through the wall, see? Can you help me take him to a hospital?"

The woman looked from Reenie to her machine and then scratched her nose. "You should really get an ambulance; I just came out to—"

"Please, please will you help? He's…bleeding and you're here. Could you?"

With a sigh and a look back to the house, the woman nodded. "Okay, let's see what I can do."

Reenie smiled through her tears and gripped her fingers into her fist. *You're okay, Granddad, we're going to be okay.*

Their journey dragged out into the night. James limped behind Oliver, who had a torch trained on the path ahead. Beyond the orb of light ahead of them, nothing. The moon struggled to push its way through the branches and no stars shone at all.

"I'm going to have to have a sit soon, Ollie, my knee's stiff." The *thump drag* of James' gait was getting more pronounced as the night wore on.

"We're surely nearly there. What does the map say?" Oliver kept walking, searching the path for any openings to the grove.

"Well if we stop, we can have a look. I need a shit as well."

Oliver rolled his eyes and stopped. "Okay, let's sit down. Just for a minute."

James dropped where he stood, using his pack as a cushion. "God, this hurts. Here," he said, pulling the map from his pocket.

Oliver studied it. "So we went that way, then up there and now…no, we're here, surely. So the grove is—"

"Wait, do you see that?" James was squinting past Oliver.

Oliver turned, not seeing anything.

"Turn your torch off a second."

With a click, the torch went off, pulling them into the dark. The forest felt so close.

"Look, there." A speck of light pricked the shadows and wavered in the distance.

"I thought we were close. That must be it. Come on."

"What about my shit, I'm busting here."

"For goodness' sake, James, let's go."

The men pushed and limped through the undergrowth guided by Oliver's erratic torch light. *This is it*, he thought, *we've found them. They can help.*

Thorns tore at their trousers, tree boughs knocked the top of their heads, gaps had to be squeezed through, all in pursuit of the growing light, which was a flicker, then a flame, then a fire pit.

The small flames made the faces of the huddled men orange. Their eyes were closed, heads bowed, sleeping. One man at the edge of the fire was leant against a tree, head nestled into a nook between two branches. Other masses, bigger, made lumpier by shadows, were further off.

"Shitting hell. We're here, mate. This shit's coming out, but we should get the tents set up after."

Oliver stood wide-eyed at the gathering. His lips curled into a smile.

The operator had manoeuvred the truck back towards Reenie's house, got out with the remote console, unwound the snaking arms and dragged Michael through the hole in the house and into the padded space in the machine, all before Reenie had properly decided what she needed to do. Once Michael was in the machine and the operator was putting the remote console away, only then did Reenie decide that she needed to pull the other woman from the cab, push her to the ground, jump into the truck and drive away somewhere. The operator had managed to grab onto the driver's side door, open it with a shout, but Reenie pulled the door back again, crunching the woman's fingers in the metal casing.

Trina had taught her daughter to drive when she was twelve and she passed her test two years later. The truck was more difficult and cumbersome than her family's car, but she moved through the gears and put her foot down nonetheless.

Amongst the dotted lights of lampposts and flashes of televisions behind curtains, other pyres burned. She could tell by the curling sparks, smoke in the air and enlarged shadows writhing in the glowing flames.

She stopped at a red light on the other side of town and looked left. A huge metal sign read

MIGHT FAMILY FUNERAL HOME AND CREMATORIUM – DIGNITY, FAMILY, ETERNITY

Behind it loomed the incinerator, designed to blend into the town with muted beiges and greys.

A car beeped behind Reenie, and she glanced at the green light above her. She drove on.

The sun's heat burned through the morning dew and brought out the stink of the grove. Loamy whiffs drifted up from the ground, mixed with the sweetness of rot and decay. Oliver couldn't bring himself to look at them.

He'd been too excited to sleep, turning fitfully and wondering what to say to them. He had so many questions to ask and so many answers he needed. Before sunrise, he'd sat up and scribbled his ideas in his notepad by torchlight and written down questions with follow-up questions.

When the sun rose and made the inside of his tent glow, Oliver emerged from his tent, fingers scrabbling at the zip. They'd pitched up on the outskirts of the camp, so as not to disturb the men, but Oliver could see their fire still burning. He quickly urinated against a tree and walked softly towards the fire. Between the trees, the sloping, boulder-like shoulders of the men could be seen, craggy and worn. Oliver fidgeted with the flap of his notebook in his hands.

He dropped it, however, when he saw them.

One close to him, sitting cross-legged and facing the fire, was graffitied and tagged in streaks of blues, yellows, reds, greens.

FAT CUNT
DIE FUCKER
FEE FI FO FUM
LAUREN 4 ZARA

The one by the tree, the one whose head was nestled into a nook, had been peppered with missiles: stones, sticks, shards of metal, a sole bolt from a crossbow. A crude red target had been painted on his pocked belly.

A blackbird landed on one at the far edge of the site. It twittered a high, curious song and disappeared into a nest it had made in the temple of a man's skull.

Oliver dropped his notepad on the ground through his slack fingers. His shoulder strained against the fabric of his shirt. With numb steps, he picked his way through the camp, around the still-blazing fire, and further into the grove. More of them sat slumped against trees, lay on the ground, face up and down. One was incredibly young, perhaps only twenty, his torso proportionate and vital, but his legs had ballooned into knots and knobbles, elephantine in size and near bursting. He blinked when Oliver passed him.

Scraps of something hung in the trees ahead, blocking the sun. Oliver passed under it, shirt ripped now, mouth dry. It looked like the trees had lifted the remains of a man high up off the ground and torn him. His colossal white snake of a spine, still attached to a skull, was wound around the upper branches. Parchment strips of skin mouldered in rags masquerading as leaves. It took ten minutes to walk under his life.

At the end of the grove, sat next to a brook, were two men. One had his head in the other's lap; the other was stroking the hair of his companion. They both stared wet-eyed at Oliver, or at least at the way he had come.

Oliver pulled the torn shirt from his chest and dropped it onto the ground. He approached the two men, whose eyes didn't move. He sat next to them both and looked back at what he'd left behind.

The truck ran out of petrol on the ridge of a fell overlooking a lake. Reenie had never been here before, had never seen the world like this for real. The lake came alive in the morning sun, dazzling up at her in a dance of jewels that came and went as the waves pushed to the shore. *Granddad won't* *want to miss thi*s, she thought.

After some missteps and swearing, Reenie managed to slide the machine's door open. Michael sat dazed and floppy on his side in the padded unit, but he swivelled his head to look at her. Reenie smiled at him. "Look, can you see? Isn't it—"

Michael cut her off with a groan. His eyes roamed over her, looking for food.

A coolness spread over Reenie, and she closed her eyes. *Food. He needs food. How is he going to live without food? He needs food. I need to give him food.*

"I'll find something for you, hold on." Making sure Michael was comfortable, Reenie walked up into some scrubland across from the road.

There's got to be berries, nuts, all sorts of those things, surely. I need to give him food.

Reenie returned an hour later with several nettle stings and a sprained wrist she got from a broken fall.

She sat in front of her granddad, shuddering from heaving sobs. "I'm so sorry, I don't know what I was thinking, I can't look after you here. I have nothing. Too fucking stupid and too quick to 'save you', but you didn't need saving because you're fine. You're okay."

Michael whined and groaned at her, almost falling out of the machine to implore her to give him something, anything he could eat.

Reenie reached out to stroke his face. "Granddad, I'm sorry, I'll look again for something, or we can wait for someone to—"

His mouth moved round, and his jaw opened wide around her hand; just after Reenie jerked away, his teeth clacked shut. He whined again and stared at her.

Reenie skittered away on her backside, away from Michael. She held her wrist as if he had hurt her.

The evening fell away, and the night drew in. The lake in the valley became an inky patch, no moon out to brood on its surface. An occasional owl hooted somewhere around her, masking Michael's cries.

Reenie thought about how he used to bring her sweets every Saturday, and how he used to read to her in a swing in their garden.

She thought about how when he started to show signs, he tried harder to show her he loved her. He bought her toys and pet fish and chocolate.

About the time he lost his voice, and that the last thing he said was that he was sorry.

About the bedroom her dad was locked in and about the key her mum had hidden somewhere high up in the kitchen.

About the strip of her dress she was tying tight around her forearm, enough to feel the pulse of her heart there.

About how her skin had split in his desperate mouth, the tendons twitching and rending in the bite; the coming loose and the loss; the spasm at her wrist and the squall that erupted out of her mouth; the tears running into her upturned smile; the eyes that trembled open to let her granddad know that she loved him.

The Schrickx Lineage

Joshua Spiller

Fuck (v.)
   1. To copulate with (aggressively or unemotionally)
   2. To ruin

He was led into the room. It was simple, unadorned: two chairs and a table. Lights embedded in the ceiling lit the room's heart, but left a penumbra of gloom, rendering the off-white walls grey.

The woman stepped into the light, placed the metal safety deposit box on the table, and left.

He didn't bother to sit. The box responded to his touch, and opened.

There it was. The clean white envelope he'd first held all those years ago. And he was in the private room he'd been told it must be read in.

He extended a hand. Guilt trembled his fingers, irritating him. Withdrawing the envelope, he carefully unsealed it, and began to read the page-long message:

o Y u

Ia htyucl orY aet Iett aigavne ok ifrnl mn ykn h ot acrt emIcngv o o yeʃı e Alg Ɣ Ɩlrɑ
       Yu r eest sa yebig I rt eaehmn rmyu uue
          eeiti a ol ʃsai ti da n a enti a o ilni hsi hty uprev sasrwig aiaepatm Ti stetm oefo hog y

Like this, on and on, the message went. Gibberish. Utter, meaningless gibberish.

He felt his anger rise, that he'd betrayed his word, given in to his baser urges, for nothing.

Wertand Schrickx stood in the small bedroom of his apartment, his dark-mahogany-coloured shirt lined with creases, and—in dishevelled fashion—only half tucked into his grey trousers; stood in the narrow space between his single bed, pressed against one wall, and his desk, pressed against the opposite one. Above his desk hung a wide shelf of books, most owned for years, most unread.

He breathed. Every day felt hard, but this one, at least, was flavoured with a dim uniqueness.

Leaving his bedroom, he passed through his living room / kitchen, with its mound of dirty plates by the sink; its worn and faded leather sofa, sprinkled with unnoticed and unintentional crumbs; its 3DV in standby mode, a projector for immersive holographic home experiences.

The lift. The short walk to the building's entrance, semi-grimy windows reflecting back at him his floppy black hair; his unusually pale skin, considering his Asian-European descent. Then out.

Late morning. The city, a web of roads made by a senile spider, felt like it was still groping itself into being. Red and saturnine, the tumefied, low-hanging sky domed his awareness. Not much light got through the atmosphere anymore.

On the street, an elderly man, with an italicised back, passed Schrickx. Moles on bald scalp; decay. Schrickx dismissed the thought, and walked on. He had nowhere particular to be. His sustainment income kept him afloat, and he had no job, apart from his obligatory weekly community work. That was all most people had these days. Aimlessness permeated his outlook: performed itself in every step that he took.

Hovering atop a distant skyscraper, he glimpsed a tiny, humanoid speck, of pure blue and white energy: a hyperbeing. Its lower third was concealed behind the roof's stone parapet, so that Schrickx couldn't tell for sure if it was levitating; but they always were. And its arms seemed to be grasping the parapet's metal railing. A strangely human-like, empowered pose for a hyperbeing to strike. However, Schrickx was squinting. Maybe it was just a trick of his eyes.

The hyperbeings had arrived, seemingly out of nowhere, six years ago. Since then, they had been utterly peaceful, if intransigently cryptic. Various speculations circulated about them. A vocal minority posited they were from the future. But the received wisdom, by far, was that they were aliens, of an unknown magnitude and order far beyond the ken of human beings.

They had come with a message. They had said that the end loomed: that the only hope of escape lay with them, and the process they espoused. Apocalypse-averters. Yet no one knew what form this supposed apocalypse was meant to take, nor understood the point of the hyperbeings' disconcerting proposal. It all had to be done on trust.

Yet this imminent apocalypse *felt* true. To Schrickx, at least, and, he was sure, to many others besides.

A familiar saying flitted through his mind: "If you make an impact, you make an enemy." But the hyperbeings hadn't done that. They were accepted, if queasily, like a shard of honesty that was vital, but could wound. They couldn't even speak in anything approaching conventional language. As such, press, visual-media communiqués, were largely beyond them. But they had brought new technology with them. And this technology, among avant-garde thinkers, was providing new, lived metaphors through which to understand reality; like the computer, and coding, had opened up the idea that reality was a simulation; like electricity had opened up the idea that secular invisible powers could animate our existence.

With muted interest, Schrickx dropped his gaze from the hyperbeing, and walked on.

Of more concern was the city's ambience. There were few people on the streets these days, and today, fewer than usual. A deep unease, a low-level panic gripped the populace. You could feel it in the air.

This subdued, somewhat unspeakable terror was due to the mass of recent suicides which had, it seemed, viralled through the city like a plague. The spate had occurred over the past month or so, an initial ripple of public sympathy and token sadness morphing into a tenor much more profound and disturbing. The number and frequency of suicides had intensified, pretty much all of them lacking any obvious motive; any straightforward and basically understandable impetus that would precipitate such an extreme and final decision, which would mark off those individuals as a tragic but relatively self-contained social event, and which could serve as a warning signal to avert any similar future bereavements. Instead, amorphous and beyond comprehension, the threat was much more unsettling. It could snatch away any of your loved ones next. It could—a small voice at the back of your mind feared—in the dead of night, snatch away you.

And while a fair number of the suicides had been around thirty years old, along with much older outliers, the vast majority had been teenagers and people in their early-to-mid-twenties, with a particular slant towards those in higher education, and those who had found precocious success. It implied, deep down to people, that humanity might not have a future; or at least, if you stared cold and hard at what lay ahead—as perhaps those suicides had done in their last moments—not one worth pursuing.

This was something Schrickx had been thinking about more and more.

He thought of all the film posters he had seen in his life, that tried to sell their subject with a quote that claimed, grandiloquently, that the movie was "life-affirming". Never had such spiel felt more desperate, as, around him, the project that was society seemed to be unravelling at the seams.

His thoughts drifted skyward, and higher, into the broken infinitude above. Although no one knew the cause of the suicides, to Schrickx's gut instinct, their connection with the Edge of Universe Discovery was almost inarguable. This cosmic revelation had occurred around eight years ago, when Schrickx was twenty-five. For nearly a quarter of his life, he'd lived with it.

Space wasn't endless. What lay beyond had been encountered, scissioning certitudes and false consolations. Even its periphery, in astro-normality, had bequeathed traumas to the human worldview. In an asteroid belt, an event that was like chaos mutants, born in blood and thunder, and boiled up from the unconscious into atoms and intent. A mulch of banished intuitions.

Since then, givens, institutions, and even human psychology had undergone throes, either of death or rebirth, as the implications of the EOUD had been further unpacked and absorbed. The universe changing, and it was only becoming harder to fathom.

It was against this backdrop that the more recent hyperbeings had made their relatively trivial impression. The interest in them, for most people, couldn't energise existence with meaning. It was as if the scale of the previous discovery had numbed humanity to lesser, more minor shocks. Everything felt so uncertain, the future so full of hazard; treacherous with despair.

Along a cracked inner-city pavement, Schrickx passed two careworn children. It seemed a common sight these days. Then, one of the children—a little boy—for the briefest moment, shook his head violently, as if dispelling a horrid, scuttling thought from his mind.

So, Schrickx mused, taking some comfort. *He's a TT too.*

They also seemed increasingly common these days. But perhaps Schrickx, because of the choice he had to make, had just become more attuned to spotting them. The oldest TTs, now, could only be about five years old. And that's roughly how old this little boy looked. The man escorting them, presumably the children's Y-parent, must have been one of the first "maters".

Schrickx looked at him, a wisp of hope curling within himself. The man, understandably perturbed by this attention from a stranger, deliberately avoided Schrickx's gaze, and unobtrusively hurried the children along.

But maybe Schrickx had been wrong. Perhaps that man had been the children's X-parent, and bore the scar that Schrickx would soon have. The Caesarian cut, statistically possessed by numerous men in the city, although, with it hidden beneath their clothes, Schrickx had never knowingly met such a progenitor. He'd had his own womb, and other necessary systems, implanted a year ago. Now, after waiting for his tissue to regrow around those artificial expansions of his being, they were finally ready to use.

He thought about how natural births had once been the norm, before C-sections became the default, for men and women. It must have been so vulgar. All that ripped flesh. So messy and primitive. Human childbirth had been an odd quirk of fate, the enlarged cranium necessary for human evolution, but too much for nature to handle. That was why there had been a high X-parent mortality rate. But science and technology had remedied that, as was always meant to be the case.

The intimacy of feeling the child grow inside you, and of skin-to-skin contact at the end—that was all you needed. The rest... well, it just made him glad he was alive when he was. The past always seemed so barbaric; he was amazed any human had had the strength to get through it.

He'd thought having a baby might bring some purpose back to his life. But now the hour was almost upon him, he wasn't sure he wanted to go through with it. What sort of world was this to bring a child into?

He rounded a corner, coming off Delahmé Street, into a wide-open concrete plaza, with expressionist skyscrapers—trillionaire egos writ large, clad in faux-visionary facades—hemming it in on all sides.

Protestors clustered in the square—maybe about fifty or so. It had been a few days since the Sixth Consortium, and the protestors were all wearing haute couture *Unify!* clothing. The slogan had been a political youth banner for decades, ever since half of humanity—sore at disagreement—had voyaged away in their ships, and disappeared into an unknown realm.

The rebellious crowd was chatting amongst itself, no doubt preparing for the chanting and rousing marches to come. One woman in it, her head shaved, made eye contact with Schrickx, as if aware of his general gaze upon the group, and inviting him to join it. He immediately looked away, belatedly realising this was an echo of what the TT parent, moments before, had done to him.

Then, a new colour on the scene drew back Schrickx's sight. A mass of figures in black outfits, their faces half-concealed by black ristos, were crossing the plaza towards the protestors. They squared up to the *Unify!* group, pressing in close upon them. From the way some of the aggressors' hands were bunched up and shoved deep in their pockets, Schrickx had the impression they were armed with weapons. Maybe knuckledusters. Maybe worse.

Defensively, defiantly, the protestors closed ranks. Inaudible-to-Schrickx hostilities were fired between the two factions.

A taut, brewing sense of civil violence hung in the air.

Moments like these, Schrickx thought, were tenacula picking away at the city, lifting its innards into view.

Perhaps he should intervene. Call the authorities. What if people were seriously hurt? But what if that dragged him into it? His face was exposed. And although, socially, he'd always had the baseless paranoia that he possessed an utterly forgettable face—that whenever he met someone again after an interval of two weeks or more,they'd have no recollection of ever having encountered him—he now felt certain that at least one of the blackly dressed figures had glanced at his onlooking visage, and that his anxious, diffident features were seared indelibly into their memory.

And perhaps... perhaps even if he left, nothing would happen. There would be no violence. Perhaps those knuckledusters and concealed weapons, which he'd imagined, didn't even exist. In that case, he'd be drawing their attention upon him, putting himself in the crossfire, for nothing. And who knew what amount of trouble could hound him for that?

He could walk away, and never know. Never know what happened.

For a long moment, he just stood and watched, caught between what he felt was right, and what he felt was safe.

He mooched along the path that lay parallel to the barren riverbed.

"You ain't should do that! You ain't should do that!" a mechanical voice kept repeating. Schrickx lifted up his downcast face. It was a robot, teal and rubiginous, whirring and waddling towards him in the tow of its patently uninterested owner. "You ain't should do that!"

The robot reminded Schrickx of some lines from a poem he'd recently read, about a robot manufacturer who created his own, personal female automaton. Though surprisingly sexually arousing, it turned out the robot displayed these suggestive traits for a nefarious purpose of its own.

The lines were:

"On some level, she triggered my sexual drive
I could see the apocalypse in her beautiful eyes
Made of silicon and soul combined..."

The twist had been that that last line referred not to her eyes, but to the apocalypse.

His friend Shsedo had shown him that poem (Schrickx had actually known Shsedo's older brother, sSalerio, first, but he was closer to the younger sibling now) posted online by the poet in the form of a photograph of a tacitly real diary entry. Very contrived, but it seemed to work in terms of garnering attention. Schrickx thought about how there was a certain psychology of form: how certain mediums (text messages, handwritten diary entries, etc) tended to innately draw readers in. Probably, any form that connoted privacy. The thrill of glimpsing what should be secret. In that sense, the poet had exhibited businesslike smarts.

Still, as usual, Schrickx had wanted to like the poem more than he actually did. It was the same with classical music, which he'd idly read *about* far more than he'd listened to. They just didn't connect with him, even though he wished he was the sort of person who was receptive to that stuff.

But, for some reason, those lines had stuck in his head.

He walked past skeletons of light glowing dimly on riverine trees. Such lights glowed even for much of the daytime now. The ostinato of the seasons, similarly, had been dulled.

Pedestrians passed by. North Acton-bound amblers. Runners. Each individual or tiny group wrapped up in its own small world. An atomised collective, with every fragment obsessed with elevating its own status, or seeking a leader, someone *else*, to lead their society out of its mess. An appalling rabble. Centuries after anarchism's creation, still hardwired on pyramid geometries.

An attractive woman with brown skin jogged by. Schrickx heard the faintest, tinniest of audio coming from her ears. Which meant her ynyx was blaring. She'd had the zoned-out gaze of someone oblivious to all around her; the metal stud, embedded in the between-bone hollow next to her ear lobe, that felt like it vented sound straight into your psyche. Traded thoughts for music, for endless chats with others, and for illimitable AR entertainment.

When does she have time to think? Schrickx wondered, his criticism of this stranger's life based on almost nothing. *When did she last hear the noise of her own thoughts?*

Nearly everyone in the city had such a device. You immediately seemed a bizarre curiosity if someone noticed you were an exception. And people used them obsessively; incessantly; frequently, people didn't even hear each other anymore.

Schrickx felt the cold metal nestled behind his own ear lobe. In the last, depressed weeks, he'd barely switched it on. Everything he listened to felt meaningless and hollow, as if everyone was missing the point, although if you'd asked him, even he couldn't have articulated what that point was.

Away from the riverbed. Down a visually enticing boulevard, populated with casual leisure-seekers. Giant adverts on behemoth screens covered each side of the passage; parallel walls of blazing, screen-bright desire, with adverts constantly phasing in and out like colours on chameleon flesh.

A dating advert, stylishly and silkily promoting a program that connected users exclusively with friends of friends, based on the assumption that nature's social filter system was the surest way of finding your ideal partner:

Yeah, there's more social risk.

But there's more chance of finding love.

So F it...

Download Fit today.

Such needy marketing pronouncements glazed hazily off Schrickx's abstracted mind. Scant weeks ago, he had read the start of an in-depth – read little more than a shorticle's worth of it, truth be told, before it had felt too heavy-going for that late time of night—but its main fascinating idea had been up top. The important, most impactful thing about adverts wasn't the message. It was the meta-message that you were being bombarded with; the message that, collectively, the advertisers and media-makers were conveying, almost certainly without intending to do so; and which was so powerful because so many of these marketers—with no conscious collaboration—were drilling the same notion into your subconscious. *Materialism is important. Put this type of sexual partner on a pedestal—that'll give you social unwhot. Keep your head down, and life will go as you want it to.*

"The subtext is more important than the text"—that had been part of the in-depth's subhead. And right now, Schrickx felt like he was sea-walking through subtext. Since he'd been a philosophy-gorging teenager—an aspirational habit he'd regrettably lost—he'd believed that, in the glowing maze of advertising which he and everyone he knew, guinea-pig-like, was forced to live, insecurities will cost you a lot of money. So, as much as he could, he'd long ignored the nagging commercial frenzy, and soothed his occasional disquiet, of being an oddball loner in this regard, by donating to worthy scientific causes instead.

The advertising screens gradually bled away, replaced by outlandish building-sized murals. Dressing banality in city-sanctioned, "outsider", yet—on an intellectual level, at least—appealing imagination.

Schrickx passed a block of whitewashed concrete with a slanted surface. Upon it, ants scurried in a mesmeric tangle of random patterns, each leaving a coloured trail of graffiti in its wake. A hypnotic, constantly unfolding installation piece.

A sign he was entering the art district of the city.

The murals funnelled him to a more ornate edifice, with a classically clean facade. Arched over top of the entrance, in tarnished gilt letters, was the phrase:

You can't ensure success
But you can ensure honourable failure

Schrickx entered, glad to get away from the few remaining, milling canaille outside.

The building was a gallery/museum, historical curios mingled with elegantly displayed contemporary art. Schrickx melancholically studied a vibrant, textured 3D painting, of psychedelic tie-die swirls embossed with dark, gleaming gems. It was entitled: *Octopoid Deliquescence in a Sea of Jewels*.

He studied an ancient crest, hung up about a foot above his own head, which depicted a jagged lightning bolt cleaving an oak tree. It symbolised how a powerful and long-built-up life/institution/dynasty could be destroyed in a single moment of God's wrath; the need for sustained humility. At least, that's what the explanatory card beneath it said. After the havoc of advertising outside, Schrickx appreciated this relic, this hub of raw, centred meaning. It helped to clear his mind.

And, near the far corner of the building's spacious and sole viewing room, he studied the monolith of hewn stone propped against the wall; studied the prehistoric drawing preserved upon it. Against a background of mottled grey-and-white rock, a simple human figure—little more than a stick man—had been inscribed, in profile, in twilight-blue chalk. Its legs, if it ever had any, had been rubbed away into a blur at its base. Though weaponless, the figure somehow looked proud; battle-ready. It had the aura of an abstract ideal.

Gazing up at it, Schrickx let himself feel its dreamvague meaning; its hum of lost-to-memory significance. Did it depict a god? A primitive human? Or even, perhaps—if they secretly visited the planet long ago—a hyperbeing? Schrickx couldn't tell. It could've been any of them.

He thought about the image in relation to his own life, and it became more profound, like two shadows overlapping.

He thought of the not-far-away, 500-year-old derelict porn studio—said to be haunted with violence. A hangover from the Age of Identity, where, Schrickx speculated, had been all the seeds of now.

Thought of the sort of person his child could become.

Stretching out his hand—there was less reverence for the past than there used to be—he touched the grit and grain of this epoch-surviving art, as if it were his own child hidden behind the veil.

Schrickx sat on a park bench. It was now late afternoon.

Snatches of subdued conversation perambulated by him, before fading back—like restless, mumbling infants—into the enveloping, parent-like silence. Beside him, an alabaster statue towered, facing in the same direction as him: the Veiled Butcher. A meditation on the grace of the grave.

The walk had helped clear his mind, and confirm his decision. But, in a way, he'd always known what he would do.

Standing up, he let go of the dark uncertainty that clouded his mind... released it in a downpour of doubt that sank into the mud of his being, and nourished floriferous, tentative hope... and headed to the destination that his day, his very life, now orbited around.

The building was vast, its exterior a mingling of blackness and glass. A perfectly mundane skyscraper. Schrickx entered the lobby, the park he'd just left only a few minutes' walk away.

The skyscraper had been gifted by the humans to the hyperbeings, as a base of operations; a place to carry out their enigmatic, apocalypse-averting plan.

Schrickx went up to the man on the front desk.

"Hi. I've—got an appointment."

"Name?"

"Schrickx. Uh, Wertand."

"Right." Pressed button. "Head on up."

Schrickx had noticed the receptionist glance contemptuously at his unkempt appearance; his half tucked-in shirt. He ignored it; or at least, tried to, feeling bitter and resentful at this superficial snap-judgement.

He took the elevator up. His heart, like that of a foetus on an ultrasound scan, pounded.

He was going to meet one for the first time.

He knocked. And felt his first psychic bidding. He entered.

The room was a converted, conventional, large office. Completely at odds with the luminous, up-close-impossibility in its midst.

Time dilated; rubatoed, to contain the swell of emotion Schrickx felt inside. The hyperbeing—the simmering blue-white radiance levitating, in humanoid form, before Schrickx—felt like pure, unadulterated energy. Or the pure, active *absence* of energy.

Schrickx was a short man. The seven-foot entity dwarfed him.

He didn't know what to say. Then a foreign thought impression blossomed—like an infinitesimal and silent nuclear explosion—in his mind.

The thought was not words, or image, or sound or scent. It was just thought; undefined. An impression. But, verbalised, it was:

Are you ready?

Schrickx nodded. Then said, "Yes". Then, confused, furrowed his brow and thought, *Yes*. He felt foolish; out of his depth.

The hyperbeing turned –

Follow me.

– and drifted, as if with fused and nebulous legs—form itself seeming to softly rot away in the creature's lower third—into the next room. Schrickx did as he'd been told.

The room was brighter; sterile and lab-like. Presumably, a more thorough conversion.

The hyperbeing faced Schrickx with its featureless face. Partially excepting the "legs", there was a solidity to its energy that made Schrickx feel like you could touch it, and maybe your hand wouldn't pass through, but press on raw, thrumming power.

Remove your upper-body clothes.

Schrickx did.

Lie down.

Intuitively, Schrickx sensed there was something neurologically intricate about the hyperbeing's brain—if indeed they had such a thing. He lay back on the comfy, padded dark-blue operating table.

The hyperbeing grasped a frighteningly large needle. Then insertion. Insemination. With the hyperbeing as the Y-parent, its ampoule-housed DNA released into the X-parent: into Schrickx's womb.

A clinical conception. The mating of two strangers; surely, two species.

Such procreations were the hyperbeings' enigmatic, apocalypse-averting plan. It had been running for years. Schrickx was far from the first. And although the majority of people dismissed the project as a ludicrously abstruse, pointless exercise, for others, it offered—for the future—a mysterious, delicate hope.

Schrickx had wanted a sense of purpose in his life. An end to the meaningless drag of depression. He hoped the child would bring it.

At the converted office-room's exit.

The looming hyperbeing handed Schrickx a clean, white envelope.

Deposit this at Bedlon's Bank. It will be the child's inheritance. On their nineteenth birthday, give them access to it. It must be read in room 5F.

An unyielding, examinatory pause. Schrickx nodded at the eyeless entity, expressing comprehension, and a solemn will to retention.

Then, more un-words:

It is not for your eyes.

Scrickx left, with the forbidden, mystifying note and newspawned life.

With the forbidden, mystifying note.

With the forbidden.

The Caesarian cut. Putrid blood; bone and muscle-meat. The horror of what's inside us. And yet it is a marvel.

Then, from this filth, a screaming wonder is born.

Eleven years later:

Schrickx was led to the room...

... and felt his anger rise, that he'd betrayed his word, given in to his baser urges, for nothing.

Alannah slipped on her shimmery blue kurta, its colour fondly reminding her of her Y-parent. Today was the big day: her birthday. She could hardly wait.

Apple-red, morning sunlight streamed through the dust-decked window of her small, first-storey bedroom, illuminating her tall, slim figure, and casting the rear of her body—by contrast—in soft gloom. Beyond the window, two immense skyscrapers loomed on the opposite side of the street, their bulk, from her perspective, filling up most of the frame; with, visible between them in the mid-distance, a strip of familiar parkland, bathed the shade of a crimson, solar rose.

This was the physical world. But a ghostly overlay intruded upon Alannah's vision of it. Bleeding through solidity, it depicted, to the left of Alannah's window, in her own room, a frozen starburst of motes that, when she'd previously peered close at them, appeared to be microscopic apparitions of feathers; while, beyond her window, three spectral hyperbeings soared *through* the upper echelons of the skyscrapers, singly, but somehow—in their typical fashion—as if a deliberately unpatterned unit; and, at street level, a panoramic, ethereal grid was superimposed over existence, as though the earth itself were reduced to the lines on graph paper, with, beneath this wraith cage, an equally wraithlike jailed and quiescent sea.

Shaking her head, she dispelled the ghost vision, at least for a time. Apart from the mobile hyperbeings, the vision, from her room, was always the same, like a moment suspended in time. If the putative sea was what it seemed to be, she'd never seen it move.

154

She remembered, as a baby, that the world had been black and white. Then colour came. But the ghost world had stayed monochrome. This personal development of colour vision was something that many other TTs, unlike regular people, recollected as well.

Thick, jet hair still faintly wet from the shower, she put it in a ponytail, drawing the strands taut at her scalp, while letting the rest cascade in a mess of tight waves down her back. Then she hurried across the room's faded-cream carpet, and raced downstairs, her hand sliding on the petite spiral staircase's black metal banister.

The warm, fragrant scent of the goti she'd cooked for breakfast still lingered in the combined and open-plan kitchen/dining-area/living-room of the house's compact ground floor. Nipping across the room, she knelt down, slid open the concealed compartment-in-the-wall beside the front door, and withdrew her shoes. As she was putting them on, she glanced over her right shoulder, and saw, on the grotty and old dark-olive armchair in the room's cramped living area, the man she'd stirred awake to share that traditional birthday breakfast with. Her X-parent. Her womb father.

He sat, facing the wall only a few feet from him. Already, a beer can was in his hand, perched on the chair's arm and besides the accompanying, bloated belly that years of such drinking had produced. His floppy hair, despite him being in his early fifties, was still black. But his face hadn't been shaved for days. He looked rough.

Her shoes on, Alannah walked over to him. He continued to stare dead ahead, as if zoned out to the world. Then she bent down—her six-foot height towering over his own, comparatively diminutive one; her skin tone, a pale Asian-European like his, nonetheless having a subtly darker, healthier hue, while his had acquired the added pallor of ill health—and kissed him on the head. As she did so, she heard the tinny noise of his ynyx; of the entertainment he was lost in.

"I'll be back soon," she said. "Probably around two-ish."

He only, briefly and inarticulately, grumbled.

Then she left the house.

"It's just gibberish!" her X-parent shouted after her. "Meaningless gibberi—!"

She closed the door behind her. He was ranting again. She loved him, and it was with love she understood that he was someone whom life's shocks had worn down into a miserable and self-defeating coward.

Nonetheless, in this instance, he was probably right. Still, that didn't mean she wasn't excited to finally see it.

Beneath her knee-length kurta and black leggings that left her ankles exposed, her feet—in scuffed, inexpensive, plimsoll-like trainers that were laceless and had a thick tread—paced down the street. She wasn't seeing anyone today. She didn't have any friends; just familiar faces. She was happy in her own skin. Just her, and the visions.

The city buzzed with activity, an expansive urban marvel distilled out of technology and complexity, sun-blushed with the new day, with the aged dawn's dying ascension, and wreathed, for Alannah, in spectral non-existences that decorated it with endless private pleasures and mysteries.

Over the years since her birth, the presence of actual hyperbeings had lessened significantly, although they still visited intermittently. As a TT, the result of a union between a hyperbeing and a human, Alannah felt this absence. Thinking of her X-parent in labour, nineteen years ago to the day, she couldn't imagine having a child herself yet.

"White City is massive," said a teenager ahead of Alannah in the queue. His voice went up at the end of the sentence in a funny way. But this is prose, so you can't get that enjoyment.

"Passes please. Passes please," the rotund conductor with the white walrus moustache refrained (in the musical sense) at the top of the ramp.

Alannah showed hers, eliciting from him a polite, perfunctory nod.

"Thanks," she smiled back, with genuine warmth.

The vehicle she was boarding was an old underground carriage, kitted out to merely be the torso of a four-footed, mechanical, folkloric monster: a hulking industrial beast, daubed with sickly topaz-coloured eyes, its wolfish snout baring predatory steel teeth the size of small children, like a grungy cinematic menace. Part of the Opulent Line, the carriage had been grotesqued thus to make it more tourist-friendly; a more appealing way for parents and their kids to travel.

The ramp led into the creature's rear, which Alannah thought less than ideal.

Inside, she spotted an old lady spraying caramel aerosol into a mouth of already rotten teeth. Then, as was its wont, the seemingly airless, eternal geography of the ghost world began to encloud too much of her peripheral vision. She shook her head violently, and when she looked round again, she noticed some passengers staring at her, while she could tell that others were considerately very much not-staring at her. She was used to this reaction. Now, they knew what she was, and her kind were relatively rare.

Along with everyone else, she buckled herself into a seat, absent-mindedly grabbing on to the yellow plastic ring-strap above her as a safety precaution. Then, there was a juddery downward lurch, mixed with, from outside, a piston-hiss of escaping air; a pause; then a vertical blasting leg-launch into G-force pressures, as the monster, with demented serenity, sailed into the sky.

TTs were widely believed to be deformed—that's why some of the surrounding passengers had reacted so visibly and disparately to her presence. The headshakes unnerved people. In fact, this stigma was so pervasive that TT mutual-support groups had even been set up, one of which Alannah had briefly attended. She'd quickly found the group to be, for her, unnecessary and a tad depressing, especially when there was so much joy to life, but it had taught her one interesting thing: although all TTs possessed the ghost vision, their perceptions differed. They all saw the same pristine, strange otherworld, with its crawling bow-light, its blank-canvas ether, time-stripped as devoid of all celestial bodies. But details changed; and reports concerning mobile entities, like hyperbeings, never added up. Where one person saw three hyperbeings flying through the sky, another saw none, and another saw seven, but far away, and flying in the opposite direction. Although there was a lot of overlap, fundamentally, the visions didn't agree. It was another lingering mystery for her about the ghost world, one nestled among many.

And even the term "TT" didn't help with the stigma. Dreamt up by the sensationalist strand of the media, it stood for "Tolemy's Tykes", referring to the politician who first brokered the unique procreative scheme with the hyperbeings. It had, from the get-go, pitched those newborns as a bizarre subsection of society.

Then again, maybe the passengers didn't look at her because they realised she was a TT. Maybe they just noticed she wasn't wearing any make-up. Even men always wore at least some discreet form of make-up. She smiled gently to herself. It was enough for a minor scandal.

Contemplating her origins, she also thought about the era she was born out of. The Suicide Panic that had blighted it. That dismal black wave had taken about three years to crash through society, if her memory was correct. Thousands died. Then, slowly, and with no one being quite sure why, the number of fatalities had subsided. But some speculated it had been due to the growing understanding of, and meaning derived from, the potential of anti-matter in the universe. A public fascination that continued to this day...

Bang! The monster rocked wildly on impact, despite the crash absorbers. Then, swiftly, the G-force dissipated, and Alannah's face resettled. It had been only thirty seconds since they precision-jumped into the sky. So much thought in so little time.

Descending the vehicle's ramp, her feet touched the almost impossibly solid, concrete-like landing pad.

And five minutes later, she reached her destination.

Bedlon's Bank. At last—she was here. Alannah started to feel giddy with anticipation.

Through the stately building's desultory swirl of perplexed customers and fussy, busybody employees, she approached an enquiries counter.

The woman behind it did the ID test.

"Nineteen today?" the woman chit-chatted, knowing the answer full well from the data in front of her.

"Yep," Alannah smiled and nodded. "Today."

"Happy birthday."

Before Alannah even mentioned that the item had to be opened in Room 5F, the woman said the same. Then she led Alannah downstairs, to the subterranean levels. They collected the safety deposit box, which Alannah knew had been paid for, all these years, by the government; another intriguing facet of the hyperbeing scheme. Then the woman escorted her to 5F.

It was simple, unadorned; two chairs and a table. But in her ghost vision, Alannah stood on a low, rugged stretch of rock; a winding path that skirted the base of a much bigger cliff. And to her right, astonishingly, the dead and smooth ocean towered above her, a frozen, vertical wall. Sea above land. She'd never been this close to the ghost sea before; it had always been below street level. But now, looking at it, she was less and less sure that a sea was what it was.

And on that rocky path, just off to the right of the room, was a frame.

"Shall I leave you now?" the woman asked, having put the metal safety deposit box on the table.

"Sure. If that's okay?"

"Of course. Just press that buzzer when you need me."

A few seconds later, the room's door swung shut.

Alannah stepped forward, her plimsoll-like black trainers occasionally gliding through ghostly rock, as she traversed the uneven, insubstantial ground. She could've buried her hand in the sea. Maybe, in a moment, she would, just to experience it. But not before she'd witnessed what she came for.

She entered the light at the room's heart. The box responded to her touch, and opened.

There. The clean, white envelope her X-parent had told her about. She reached out; her fingers almost trembling. Stupid—she knew meaningless disappointment lay within. But this was her long-awaited inheritance.

Unsurprisingly, the envelope had already been opened. Her X-parent's doing. She pulled out the letter:

o Y u

*I a h t y u c l o r Y a e t I e t t a i g a v n e o k i f r n l m n y k n h
o t a c r t e m I c n g v o o y e f i e A l g Q Z l r a*
    Y u r e e s t s a y e b i g I r t e a e h m n r m y u u u e
    *e e i t i a o l f s a i t i d a n a e n t i a o i l n i h s i h t y
u p r e v s a s r w i g a i a e p a t m T i s t e t m o e f o h o g y*

All of it was in the same, incomprehensible vein. He'd been right. It was gibberish, just like her X-parent had said.

She felt her heart sink, that this clue to her origins and being had proved so fruitless. And there was nothing more to come. She may never learn more about herself.

Then, as if piloted by some deeper instinct, or possessed by some beyond-words hunch that she couldn't have explained, even to herself, she walked back to the frame that had caught her eye.

Within the ghost realm, it appeared to be made of wood. It was a large, vertical rectangle, going some feet above Alannah's head, its centre at roughly the height of Alannah's dimpled chin. An upright post—an extension of the frame—supported it from the ground, and rose to Alannah's waist, while, like a mirror reflection, a wooden post also aspired from the frame's upper horizontal beam, seemingly redundant save for aesthetic purposes. And, hanging in the empty frame's midst, as though in a much smaller and invisible vertical rectangle, was a dully luminous script, the suspended letters seemingly emitted from secret projectors that had been expertly concealed inside the frame itself. These alphabetic characters had a sharper definition than most of the ghost world, and, unusually, a muted pale-blue sheen, perhaps reflecting their super-vivid colouring in that alternative and dubious reality.

Alannah had only half-noticed this script when she entered the room. But, gazing at the frame now, she realised it both resembled a primitive sylvan artefact, and eerily spoke of an almost human way of being. She had never seen its like in the ghost world before.

The blue-hued script appeared to be written in the same impenetrable language as her inheritance:

T o ,

m w a o a l y u -p r n . d n i y, h v n d a c d, w r s d f e e t y a o g m i d.
T e m s c u a e t r a i e y u f r m s l s X m/ l a e/ o/ a e i h.
   o r e a r f r o u s h p r e n s. n t u h, w r u a s f o o r f t r.
      W x s n a w r d o t s s. I s i e l, a d h s b e h s w y f r m l e n a. T i s
w a o e e v s a p a l n, n m t h n o. h s i h i e I c m r m. T r u h m

160

And so, on, it went.

Then Alannah raised the letter in her hand and, holding it flat and parallel with her face, immersed it in the ghost text.

The merging of ethereal and actual was perfect, like a long-searched-for cable clicking into a slot. Ink letters and translucent ghost letters lay beside one another, like old and snug bedfellows. The vertical rectangle of floating script, in size, matched exactly with the paper rectangle in Alannah's grip.

She stared at the fused dyad of messages, with their emergent, estranging names; stared at the letters and characters.

And read...

To You,

I am what you call your Y-parent. Identity, having advanced, works differently among my kind. The most accurate term I can give you for myself is Xem/Allage/Qo/Zaleriah.

Your era refers to us as hyperbeings. In truth, we are humans from your future.

We exist in a world of stasis. It is ideal, and has been this way for millennia. This is what you perceive as a sprawling, animate phantom. This is the time I come from. Through my interbreeding with your X-parent, you were born with two time-genes, each operating on a distinct frequency. This is why you grasp two sections of the timestream simultaneously; but your perceptions are grounded in the historical period in which you mature. It is not until you are nineteen that your base reality concretises; that your brain hardens into a stable, durable outlook. That is why you are only receiving this message now.

You are a product of miscegenation. And miscegenation is the means to elevation.

We hyperbeings are not merely confined to your era. We have manifested all along the timestream, solely targeting apocalypse-laden zones: which is most of them. We say escape from the end is only possible through us. We allow you to misunderstand. And this makes you more susceptible to our requests. Yet our reasons are benign; I want you to have a dispelled view of this mirage.

In our era, linear evolution has reached its end. Hyperbeings are its summit. But we have glimpsed higher-plane entities, seemingly ascended from humans. Upper Beings. However, they exist nowhere in the timestream. We have looked. That's why we must search beyond. Miscegenation—cross-temporal procreation—is the way for humans to break through the wall of time. It's the next, eugenic step in humanity's evolution.

That is why we have turned vast swathes of the past into our breeding ground. Centurion helmets fade from existence like blooded ghosts; lonely frescoing labourers are whisked into a crowded and undreamt-of futurity; pilgrims' rags, and internet addicts. All like you. All possessed of double sight. There, they will mate. Their offspring's genes will allow the perception of four times simultaneously. The next generation, eight. On and on, overloading the time gene, until we reach beings for whom the perception of time collapses. Until the Grand Plan is complete. All humanity's journey, we now realise, has been to evolve and stretch through time until this programme was mathematically possible.

We don't know what awaits our aim's conclusion. But we know this is what must be done for humanity to evolve into Upper Beings. Your X-parent didn't know why he did what he did. We don't know why we do what we do. But we trust revelations lie ahead.

Your spot of existence, benighted now, only becomes far stranger than you can imagine.

You can be part of this Plan. Lifted from your time and, safely, under our stewardship, mated with another person like you, from elsewhen. You would then be returned to your era, to bear the child, birth it, and raise it. This would be your contribution to the creation of an Upper Being; to our great lineage-mosaic of time. But only if you want this.

If your consent comes freely, be outside the entrance of the building of your conception, at 3am, in three days' time.

No one else can read this message. No other eyes can perceive its truth.

Your child can be what all humanity has been building towards.

The Loophole

Laura Roklicer

The only destiny is eternity.

H e could hear the stillness of the water playing with his mind. He could see the silence passing through his chest. On the edge of his sanity, Emrys looked over the boundless ocean, matching the carpet of blinding clouds, becoming one with infinity. The seeming bliss of this uninterrupted coastline drowned him; these fruits of utopia did not sit well with him.

His footsteps left no trace in the soft white sand behind him. Looking for reasons, Emrys noticed an unpleasant but relieving warmth in his abdomen. He glanced down to see his hand shaking over a bleeding wound; red bandages drying around badly sewn stitches. He looked down, taken by surprise—as much as a man can ever be surprised. Looking down the path he must have walked around a thousand times, Emrys recognized a childishly painted blue wooden bench that would rest his soul for at least a moment or two.

The air was to blame for the fact that he couldn't breathe, even though it was purer than the child's laughter that he could still hear in the far, far distance. Choking on the irony of transience, he let out a deep sigh, almost as deep as his voice was getting by the minute. Stretched in this space-time, his mind was trying to connect the dots, but his head had become too heavy to care. There was no time in this space, and there was no space in this time. He realised that he was yet to feel, but that he had already felt it all.

Before he knew it, his surroundings had grown darker than loneliness. A few light particles danced before him, in all their madness, and he stared at each of them as though they had mercifully come to take him away. Soon, the particles lit the coast, and then he couldn't tell the sea from the sky; couldn't tell the stars from their reflections, and couldn't tell his face from its silhouette. He liked this undefining view better than daylight. He liked the excuse of blindness. And all his comfort slipped through his fingers and spilled over the water like an oil stain.

He glanced at his plastic boat, steadily waiting for him just a few feet farther. That was the only thing that kept him going; knowing that he had a way out. He decided to sit there for just another moment or two, just to gather enough strength to get to his boat. Then, he would leave at last. At last.

As he was about to grunt one more time and throw his body to the mercy of his swollen feet, he heard a scream. Not a high-pitched one; no, he heard a roar for help. A young man was drowning in the swirl of the ocean, which was rapidly sucking in every wave, every light particle, every atom he could perceive. He could have sworn he saw a black hole taking back all the Earthly life-forms, mercilessly, as the voice of the unintentional universe. The young man was drifting farther away.

Emrys knew nothing about saving a life. He had been on this journey long enough to be sure of that. Still, he felt unsettled sitting so still while all this madness was playing out in front of him. He glanced at his boat again, hating the thought that came to him. He wanted ignorance to wrap around him so badly, and he almost succeeded in cheating his own conscience: if he sailed to the young man, they would both get sucked away, stretching and screaming for eternity trapped inside timelessness and spacelessness. He hated the next thought that came to him even more.

Grunting one more time, he got to his feet. Swallowing the last of his bile, he untied the rope holding his boat so still against the swirling ocean. Through agony more than anything else, he watched his way out get taken away at the speed of light. He didn't even have time to feel sorry for himself. Accepting the inevitable, he swung the rope behind him, forgetting to bleed, and threw it over to the young man, who grabbed onto it for dear life. Pulling the young man out of the water, Emrys watched the world become still again. Typical, he thought to himself.

Something strange happened when the two looked each other in the eyes, and even stranger when they realised they were still holding each other. Was it remorse? Desire? Hate? He couldn't tell. The young man shook off his hand and walked away, down the longest coast, without a single word. Emrys stood confused, watching the young man get swallowed by the dark. Losing the blue bench from his sight, he decided to follow the young man.

Focused only on the echo of the young man's steps, he had not noticed that he had found himself in a dark, wet alley of flickering lights and worn-out souls. Bargains for anything that makes one feel alive were forming a dense smog in the air. He felt he could breathe better over here. He felt a part of him belonged to the corners of depraved morals. Every time he'd turn around—to the left, then the right—he'd see a child weeping through his violin, a woman asking for a second chance, a man with his eyeballs in his hands, then another child stealing someone else's pride, then a woman sucking on the neck of her abuser, then a man painting the rest of the alley that the young man will walk down.

We are all creators, and we are all destroyers, he thought to himself.

And as he walked past all these characters he had once written, each would rip a part of themselves and hand it to him, to either add another stitch or another cut to the old hole in his abdomen. He started every time his body received another stitch or cut, thinking the mere attention given was the proof of gain. He almost slipped on his own blood, but he did not feel weaker the more he bled; he might have just reached the promised indifference.

As the alley became narrower with every step taken, his choices became thinner as well. The young man did not turn around nor did he pay any attention to the traded world around him, yet he must have known that he was being followed. Emrys could not figure out whether he was a welcome stranger or if the young man was purposefully leading him deeper into the place he'd been trying to leave. He followed him anyway. He did not have the strength to find another boat, nor had he had anything to bargain with.

Watching the young man walk down the stone steps, past the neon sign and into a basement full of laughing hyenas, the painful realisation dawned on him: he was yet to master the bliss of indifference. Pressing the spreading wound of his decaying body on the cold steel rail, he entered a bar that seemed painfully familiar to him. Emrys took in the scene: the stop-start ceiling fan; the broken glass of the toilet with no doors; the stale smell of beer and piss mixed to form the stickiness that would trap his shoes… The bartender looked at him with an expression of profound pity; more sorrow than disappointment.

He left his shoes at the neon sign that would not let him pass unless barefoot, and walked toward the bar. He sat down next to the young man, then stared into his eyes, trying to unravel the intrigue. The young man wasted no words on him, and returned no favours, sucking on his cold beer.

"Have we met before?" Emrys asked, his hoarse voice sounding as if he were asking for forgiveness.

The young man smirked with a hint of annoyance. The bartender, catching his own tail, slid Emrys a cold one.

"At least the beer's good around here, eh?" The slave of the capitalistic hierarchy tried to grab his attention. "Is that why you keep coming back here?"

"Back here?" He shifted his focus to the bartender.

"This one's on the house, but then you've exhausted your credit."

He looked up at a white clock above the whiskey selection. Three was in the place of eight; nine was where seven should be, the other numbers might have made sense, but the clock was rusty and had no hands. For a moment there, he forgot how to speak. And for that brief moment, he understood the young man. But then he made another loop through his consciousness and embraced the notion of time.

"Every time you take me here, we earn ourselves some new scars," the young man spoke. He did not have the voice that was expected of him; he sounded much too wise, and his face suddenly became much too old for such a young man.

"What do you mean, every time?"

"You are so forgetful these days. But the memory's not the only thing you lost today, is it? You let that boat get away from you again."

Emrys looked at the young man through nerve-wracking agony, yet he felt that he would only harm himself if he were to hurt the young man.

"It seems that you just can't escape this place, no matter how hard you try." The young man finished his beer and decisively looked him in the eyes.

Trying to catch up, Emrys swallowed his beer and a bit of lost pride. "So, what are you doing here?" he asked. With not much to give, he tried to get whatever he could out of the young man.

"Well, you called me."

"I did? Why? What did I want?"

"The same thing you always want."

"What's that?"

"Drink another one, maybe it'll come back to you."

The lizard of his memories slid him another cold one. Looking around the dust of the seemingly abandoned bar, he realised the space had become much smaller than it was when he came in. The young man, noticing the confusion in his eyes, stood and walked over to the middle table.

"It's closing in on us."

"What is?"

"You still don't know where you are, do you?" The young man paused and sighed. "You better go and find yourself another boat."

The young man sat on top of the creaking table and softly giggled, watching him lose all his sense all over again.

"If I find another boat, will you come with me?"

"Where would we go?" The young man asked, entertaining the ridiculous proposition.

Emrys looked over to the door behind the bar that opened for a split second; long enough for him to grab onto another longing. The blinding brightness came forward and trapped his eyes. He had never seen such whiteness in all existence.

"You don't want to go there." The young man stepped forward.

"Why not?"

"It never ends well."

"Oh, you are so wise, aren't you, boy?"

"Suit yourself."

Emrys mumbled something to his chin and looked over the young man suspiciously, yet he felt he had never trusted anyone more than him.

"So what, am I supposed to just stay here, in the dirt of this basement, forever?"

"If you think you can stay here forever, you are a fool."

"A fool?"

"Yes, a fool! You don't need another door; you need a boat."

"I lost my boat because of you!"

"Oh, the blame game has started. Don't you know which one of us always wins at that game?"

Emrys grunted again, remembering to support his wound, although his hands had started to bleed all the same. Walking over to the back door, he slowly started to open the place of no commands and no will. The light killed his pupils as he walked out straight into it.

Dissolving in time, he could not feel the weight of his own body, and even more so the weight of his mind. He was rid of consequences just as he was rid of decisions. What a blissful place! There were no dimensions, no directions; nowhere to go. Just a white space and the mere awareness. He smiled through the lightness of his thoughts, touching the ultimate pleasure of solitude and peace, though the tingling sensation on his estranged skin soon started to feel intruding.

It seemed like it had been years that he had been in that place now. The initial bliss turned into a haunting monotony. He understood that he could not escape the whiteness as he had no eyes to close. Unsettled in his own presence, he started to hate the only company he had—himself. He looked at the far distance and felt his heart again when he saw the young man somewhere in the haze. Crippled but willing, he made his way toward the young man. It became clearer that the young man was crucified, staring at him with bloodshot eyes. He rushed to him, only to find a white crow on each of his shoulders. Even as fast as he went, he soon realised that he was not getting any closer to the young man—a mirage of his loneliness. Eventually, he gave up the chase and curled up in a ball of self-pity, getting lost in himself. The young man touched him.

"Told you."

"What is this? It's so empty!" Emrys whispered in between sobs.

"It's a place of peace."

"But… this is no peace, this is horror!"

"Yeah, you always say that."

"How do I get out of here?"

The young man made himself comfortable and lit a cigarette, just to show him he was no better.

"Why does it matter?" He blew out the whitest smoke.

"What do you mean? I've got to get out of here!"

"Wherever you come, no matter how full or empty it is, you always try to get out. Haven't you learned already? There is no out."

"What?"

"There is only here... and there."

"There must be a way!" Emrys started chasing his own thoughts, running *through* and *in*, getting nowhere but back to where he'd always been.

"Fine." The young man sighed. "You want to get out of here?"

"Yes! Please!"

The fall was harsh. Dropped from an unmeasurable height, Emrys did not feel the turbulence he had caused as he fell to the ground. He found himself face down in long, fresh grass. Even the warmth of the muddy earth seemed friendly here, where the sun shone through every blade of grass and on every creature that dared to exist. He smiled, then he started to laugh, turning on his back and facing the sun.

Closing his eyes to breathe in the momentary weakness of the inevitable, he felt a warm drop on his face and the darkness behind his black mirror suddenly became darker. He opened his eyes to see a line of clouds crashing into each other. Drop by drop, they started falling faster and faster. He quickly stood up, still smiling, running through the long grass, and touching every colour he found. Stopping before an abyss so deep that he could not see its end, he turned to his left to find a small wooden cabin on the very edge of the field. Though it was leaning toward the abyss, it gave him a sense of protection and the illusion of belonging. He ran through the grass, ignoring the thunder and the strong wind trying to knock him over the edge of the abyss, and burst into the cabin.

The young man was standing by the fireplace, pouring two glasses of whiskey, one on the rocks and one straight. Giving the one on the rocks to Emrys, the young man sat down on a carpet right next to the fire.

"Even the way you have your whiskey frustrates me."

"Why?" Emrys sat at the other end of the fire.

"You have to mellow everything down."

Emrys ignored the perceived slight and looked around the cabin. It felt right.

"It feels like a home away," he said, observing every detail of the simple hideout.

"Away from what?"

The harsh wind breaking one of the windows interrupted his contemplation.

"It's always nice at first. But it's closing in on us," the young man said, leaning against the fireplace.

"What is? What are you talking about?"

The young man raised his glass.

"We are all stuck in our own matrix."

Emrys gave him a pleading look. Of all the things he didn't want to be, stuck was the deadliest one; paralysed minds of certainties only *think* they can think, he thought.

"Don't worry, it won't kill you. The wind will learn to live with you."

"But will I? Learn to live with it?"

"Well… it will break all your windows. It will knock down the walls. Take out the fire. It might even break some of your bones. But whether it breaks you or not is up to you."

"What good am I in the broken place? I might as well break too, then!"

Hearing this sentence he gave himself for the countless time, the young man frowned.

"Aren't you sick of this?"

The young man stood, throwing his glass into the fire, and got in Emrys' face. He startled.

"Why are we here, old man?"

"You brought me here!"

"Make up your mind already!"

Emrys retreated in fright, but the young man only got more and more decisive that he was not going to have it. After the wind broke another window, heavy rain started to fill up the cabin.

"Which way are you going? Which way?"

"I don't know!"

"Which way?!"

"Out! Out of here!"

"Oh yeah? You always say that, yet you always leave your boat at the last minute!"

The rain had now filled most of the cabin and was rising up to their throats. Struggling to breathe, Emrys grabbed the young man by his shirt.

"We have to get out of here!"

The young man started hysterically laughing as they had both started to choke.

"You want out of here? You want out?"

"Yes!"

"All right then."

Laughing his eyes out, the young man waited for Emrys to close his under the water that had now reached the ceiling.

Opening his eyes, Emrys found himself hearing the stillness of the water playing with his mind and seeing the silence passing through his chest. On the edge of his sanity, he looked over the ocean with no ends, becoming one with eternity. The young man was standing right beside him, focusing on that line in the distance.

"It's a very thin line, you know? Between sanity and reality."

"Why won't you help me? I saved your life."

"You? Saved me?" The young man burst out laughing again. "Don't you remember? You were the one who left me in the water in the first place. But don't worry. Tomorrow, we will have our adventure all over again. Maybe this time you get in your boat before the water sucks you in."

Then the young man looked at his old reflection and sighed mercifully.

"Well, you won't. But you know that's not the point anyway, right?"

Through a bitter smile, the young man turned into a light particle, disintegrating into the sand under his feet. Emrys broke down, desperately trying to count all the sand grains.

"I know. It's the search, the constant search…"

Looking up, he saw a shiny plastic boat tied to the mooring. He gasped and ran toward it. Walking slower and slower, he felt a strange warmth on his abdomen. He looked down, taken by surprise, as much as such man can ever be surprised. Looking around the blissfully still coast, he recognized an old blue bench. Maybe I'll just rest for a moment, he thought to himself, watching a swirl form in the vastness of the ocean.

– THE BEGINNING –

Emissary of Earth

Cavan McLaughlin

Rikki loved needles. An odd thing to love, no question, so it wasn't exactly something that she shouted from the rooftops. She loved needles because she loved extreme experiences. It was probably fair to say that she was an experience junkie. It's not that she liked pain exactly, more that she was fascinated by it. And not in some sort of sadomasochistic, kinky way (well, no more than the average non-vanilla person) but in an exploratory, curious way. She didn't look forward to the pain itself, but the rich array of experiential data that encompassed the whole event. Nerves, the fluttering of the belly and the tingling of excitement, of expectation—adrenaline beginning to course through her body. The shift from awareness to hyperawareness as she focused on and steadied her breathing. The fact that, though she had done this many hundreds of times, the thrill and the desire to abort never lessened. The quiet moment of acceptance and stillness as one acquiesces to the inevitability of what was to come. Then the piercing, and with it such a bizarre complex of entangled opposites: the pleasure and the pain, the soft warm flesh giving way to the cold hard metal, and the sudden tension that gripped her body followed by the almost immediate rush of euphoric release. Those heavenly endorphins: the human body really was a marvel. It never failed to intrigue her that throughout it all she could both be utterly absorbed by the intensity of her bodily sensations, and yet, somehow, detached and dissociated in that way that had always served her scientific mind so well. She loved everything about it. Which, had she discussed it with anyone, went a long way to explain

173

the few body-piercings she still kept. If only her colleagues had seen her in her renegade youth, high as a kite on acid, forcing lighter-flame sterilised safety pins through her poor ears over and over again. The LSD took the experience to a whole new level. Rikki wondered for a fleeting moment if she would hold such a prestigious position if her colleagues could have seen her back then. Probably, she would, all things considered she was long past the contrivance of a professional persona. Then, just a few seconds after settling back into her chair, it was done.

"Your IV is in now Dr Devlin," the new young staff nurse, Jacob, announced.

"You're good at that." Rikki beamed. Partly because of how much she secretly enjoyed it, and partly to ever so slightly flirt with her younger colleague. Flirting helped her deal with stress, and Jacob was cute.

Jacob was a little flustered, she knew that he held her in high esteem, everyone on her team did.

"Thanks," he managed.

A flurry of activity broke out around Rikki as nurses and lab assistants took blood samples, attached the various probes and monitoring systems, and scribbled furiously on their clipboards. Rikki mechanically held out her other arm for her blood pressure to be taken. She looked up at the one person not otherwise occupied.

"I think it's your blood pressure we should be checking, Larry."

She wasn't wrong. He looked like a nervous wreck. Larry was gangly and unkempt with a closely shaved bald head. His baldness only served to emphasise how profusely he was sweating as he awkwardly, and repeatedly, folded and unfolded his arms. His eyebrows rippled and twitched in disbelief.

"Are you serious? Do you have any idea how much is riding on this?" Larry asked.

"My sanity?" Rikki replied flatly, fixing Larry with an unimpressed stare.

Larry changed tack. "Listen, your safety and wellbeing is of the upmost importance to us..." No more words came, just more twitching.

"Man. You want to say 'but' now so much, don't you?"

"No! Of course not."

"Uh huh."

"Look. See. The thing is—"

"That means 'but'."

Larry let out an exasperated sigh and gave up. "I am concerned for you. Deeply. I'm concerned for all of us. *Every ... single ... one of us.*"

Rikki softened again, and let her famously infectious smile creep back. "I know you are. I know. I've done this countless times before; everything will be fine."

"Not like this. Not for this long. Not since..." Larry struggled for words again. "You know." It was the best he could do.

Not since you broke every rule there was and risked everything we worked for and your own life to boot. Not since you were under so long that you emerged a total gibbering wreck. Not since you nearly lost your mind. That's what you can't say.

Larry was a reluctant psychonaut, unlike Rikki. Neither was he an accomplished neuroscientist and clinician like she was. He was a programmer and a data analyst. He crunched numbers and wrote code. He wasn't good with anything else; he certainly wasn't good with people. He had made entity contact, though, in his years as an undergrad. It was peer pressure that did it, of course, trying to fit in. He was desperate to be seen as anything but who he really was. He'd been offered a fairly innocuous looking vape pen... In hindsight he realised it had probably been a set up so he could be the butt of even more jokes. Youthful exuberance, folly and naivety have their uses though; he would show them how it was done and to everyone's surprise—including his own—he took a monumental and utterly heroic inhalation. Not knowing what to expect he held out the vape pen to return it before looking at it quizzically, wondering what on Earth he was holding in his hand. He then had the same confusion about what he had previously recognised to be his hand.

After that night, Larry never had the courage to try it again, but he became devoted to psychedelic research. When the quite brilliant Dr Rikki Devlin made shockwaves through the research community with her plans for intravenous infusion and prolonged immersion he was intrigued. Off the record, and off the clock, she would regale him with tales of hyperbolic, geometric, self-transforming, hieroglyphic entities cavorting under impossible bejewelled domes. He was smitten with her. Almost everybody was.

"It's real," she would tell him. *'More* real than real. Not just meaningless shapes and symbols. It's a code. A language. I've stood right there and known—known as much as I've known anything in my life, that if only I really understood it, I could shape existence like putty."

They had got funding and ethical approval to run preliminary trials. Collecting data for patients being immersed for a half an hour, then an hour. Progress was good, if a little slow, but Rikki had far grander ideas. Following a long tradition of scientists for utterly disregarding their own personal safety in the pursuit of knowledge, she made herself the test subject as no institution would ever have let her be. After that experiment, everything changed.

She waited until Christmas break when everyone was otherwise engaged with seasonal merriment and hooked herself up to her own machine. The intravenous catheter in her forearm and its machine-operated drip would deliver a continuous, steady dose along with a nutrient formula that meant, theoretically, patients could be kept physically healthy, and at a maximum level of absorption, for days.

She was found after nearly two weeks.

To begin with, it had been blissful. She passed through the veil and exploded into hyperspace, hurtling through a vortex of impossible beauty. The instant she arrived she felt nothing but love and acceptance.

Welcome back. We've been waiting for you.

The entities didn't speak exactly. Somehow their words, their thoughts, were already coexistent with your own thoughts, but utterly different and distinct. Like telepathy, for want of a better word, although that word didn't really do it justice. None of our words ever did justice to anything that happened in that place.

As the vortex swirled, more and more of the little rascals flowed out from its centre and spread their arms, washing over and through her and bathing her in love. She fell, and fell, and fell, until she began to forget who she was. She fell further and faster into a vast abyss of nothingness and bliss gave way to terror. There was no going back now, and everything that she was, and knew, began to fold in on itself. In her panic she tried to think what to do, how to escape, but her thoughts betrayed her too. There were no thoughts any more, there were no words, at least, nothing she could ever recognise as words. Everything was utterly alien.

After what seemed like aeons of falling, collapsing in on herself in an infinite regress, plummeting into the very source of her despair, he came to her. For the longest time she was sure that he was literally her Holy Guardian Angel. She wasn't a religious or spiritual person but what else do you call your own personal ultraterrestrial protector? Whatever he was, without his interjection she knew for a fact that she wouldn't be here. Her body might well be, but her mind would still be lost, perhaps forever. She could not see him, only sense him. All she knew was that she was utterly alone and then he was with her. His presence protected, bathed and enveloped her liked amniotic fluid. Although everything was still utterly alien, somehow, with his presence, she could finally make sense of it.

Be calm. Relax. Play. It's just a game.

And somehow there was a game. As she folded into herself, inward and inward, it was as though she was like a supernal puck striking an ever-moving target.

Just keep playing ... and you will make it through this.

Fear began to give way to single-minded attention. Focus. The will to be on target, and eventually, nothing existed but her angel, the game—and play.

When she finally emerged from her drug-addled odyssey the vastness and the gravity of her experience began to rapidly fade like a dream dissolving under the weight of waking consciousness. She remembered her horror, and she remembered her angel, but the fine details were lost. It was impossible to bring it all back. As she pieced herself back together, she recalled that in the presence of her protector she fully understood the totally of the alien language as though it were her own native tongue, now both were gone.

No, not gone. There was a word. One word. She did bring something back. She brought back one single word. A name. Their name. In their own language. A language not of this world.

Later, when she had a far better command of her faculties, she reflected that she ought not to have explained it like that to a group of research scientists. After a course of antipsychotics and psychotherapy, she gave up trying.

Rikki was wild and unpredictable, but she wasn't the crackpot that she knew she was being painted as behind the closed doors of her now former colleagues. She had a plan. She was going to talk to her detractors in a language she knew they would understand.

It was not long after that the published works of Dimitri Putin set the field of mathematics on fire. Paper after paper began to emerge resolving some of the greatest long-standing unsolved maths problems ever conceived at a rate so scandalous it was like Putin was absentmindedly ticking off a shopping list. That fire was stoked into an inferno when the Abel Prize committee tried to track Putin down to bestow their honour. It was the story of the century when it was finally verified that Dimitri Putin was a pseudonym for a little known and highly discredited psychedelic research scientist. Rikki had been particularly pleased with the choice of surname not only because it means "one who travels along the road", which she found particularly fitting, but also because Vladimir Putin had always been her weirdest celebrity crush. All of that paled in comparison to the pandemonium that ensued when Rikki chose to execute the nuclear option: an official statement on receiving her prize that she could not take credit for the work because she had, in fact, outsourced the problem-solving to hyperdimensional entities whilst under the influence. At first, it was decried as a gargantuan and tasteless prank, but then she went on record that she would invest a chunk of her newly awarded Norwegian Kroner on a public demonstration.

Now everybody was listening.

Of course, die-hard sceptics remained insistent that she was a savant engaged in a preposterously elaborate and bizarre hoax; that people should enjoy the fruits of her labour and the technological and economic advances they afforded but ignore the obviously lunatic rantings that accompanied them. Those warnings were drowned out though, en masse, by a single four-word meme: I want to believe.

Larry was the only member of her original team that she had reinstated. They had spent months now carrying out what Rikki playfully referred to as her "day-tripper excursions", bringing him and his legions of minions back enough transformative data to mine for a lifetime. So far as Larry could see things could not be more perfect; he really should have known that would not satisfy Rikki.

"No. I DON'T understand." he had cried at her in bemusement. "You want me to agree to putting you under for a whole month?! I mean, what? Why? Why would you even think about asking me that? Doing that? You have it all. You've done it. You have the world in the palm of your hand."

"This world."

"Really?"

"They explained. It's a liminal space. Like a waiting room. A holding cell. The dome, didn't you ever wonder what was beyond it?"

"No."

"When beings break through, that's where they end up. For their own safety. That's why we meet other entities in there, not just the elves, the others. They've been, I don't know, quarantined there too."

"Rikki, it's not a fucking airport lounge."

"It kinda is."

"Oh, sweet Jesus."

"I'm oriented now. Well, sort of, as much as anyone can be. I think–"

"You think?!"

"They think so. They think I'm ready, that we're ready." Her eyes were aflame. "They've said they will take me with them and show me what's beyond."

"What is beyond?"

"Well, I don't know. That's the whole point, isn't it?"

"Look, Rikki, when a stranger offers you a sweet and then suggests you follow them to an undisclosed destination—YOU DO NOT FUCKING GO!"

They both let the dust settle for a few moments.

"Larry."

"And that's when it's a stranger Rikki, a good old-fashioned raincoat-wearing school-playground-visiting human stranger."

"Larry."

"Fuck."

"You know I have to go."

"Fuck."

"I have to know."

He hadn't agreed to it that night, but she knew she already had him. Still, it was only after the press conferences had been and gone, when months of preparation meant everything was in place and the streets were lined with True Believers holding their "I want to believe" placards with bated breath that she told him the truth. Until now, no human had made it out of the Waiting Room. Other entities had seen us. The one's that had broken through into that space, just like we had, but that was it. If she did this, if she went beyond, that would put us on the interdimensional map, so to speak.

Rikki lay back on the bed, she looked back down at her IV and smiled. The nerves were building again, the fluttering in her belly and the tingling of excitement, of expectation—adrenaline coursing through her body. She closed her eyes, for a short spell, as she focused on and steadied her breathing. Even though she had taken the drug many hundreds of times she respected and feared it as much as she ever had. It never got easy. She needed to take a moment. A quiet moment of acceptance and stillness as she acquiesced to the inevitability of what was to come. Colours brightened; edges sharpened. It was not lost on her that everyone had framed this as though she were some kind of dignitary: an ambassador or diplomat. "Emissary of Earth" they had called her in the newspapers. But here she was, recapitulating her adolescence. She let out a delighted chuckle, and everything changed.

Colonel Cumberland Smith Kills Hitler

James Milton

The river narrowed as the boat rounded the bend against the current. The ruined skyline of Arnhem lay due east and was visible over the trees that lined this section of the waterway. Colonel Cumberland Smith navigated from the stern reading scrawled maps on a rain-sodden piece of paper. His orders had been received in pieces, in secret and from multiple confusing sources, forcing him to construct his briefing like a puzzle as he went.

Eventually, Cumberland spotted the tree formation he was looking for; he tossed the paper into the river and awkwardly piloted the craft through an invisible gap in the undergrowth that he had been told was there. He continued through a tunnel of branches that had been created over the water. The canopy got thicker and thicker making the tunnel darker and darker, and before he knew it, he was proceeding forward in complete and total darkness. Cumberland swore under his breath as the skiff crashed into the bank and he had to push off with his hand. Expecting to feel branches, Cumberland's hand pushed up against wet slimy stone and he almost jerked his hand back in fright. He strained to make out any scrap of light in the void in front of him, but there was none. Neither light nor sound penetrated this place. He could have been anywhere, nowhere, or everywhere. Periodically he put his hand out to test the walls, the stone changed to brick then to earth and finally to a substance Cumberland did not recognise.

He had been sent on his own through occupied Europe to find a Professor in Arnhem who could help him kill Adolf Hitler. He was prepared for a tough, gruelling and violent one-way trip through the madness of the war. He had been sent on this journey into the dark heart of Nazi-occupied Europe a month ago. He was tired, malnourished and had seen things people wouldn't have believed. Whether all those things had been real he could not say as he had seen his mother appear to him two nights ago and she had been dead for 10 years. He felt as if this journey spiralling towards the centre of the earth were interminable, and yet it was nearly at an end. Perhaps he should turn around and go back? He knew that was not possible, the only way out was through. But through to what? The instructions that he had divined from the disparate runes of seemingly random orders had worked out so far to the finest detail, which must mean he had followed them correctly. This was where he was meant to be, he was in the correct place at the correct time, and he would find this Professor Gek Wetenschapper at the end of the warren before him, and he would get his answers. Cumberland exhaled, clearing the anxious chaos swirling in his mind and as suddenly as the darkness had descended at the start of the tunnel so the front of the boat abruptly went through a wall of hanging plants thick enough to block out the light and emerged through the wet fleshy curtain of foliage to the room on the other side.

The light was blinding. Cumberland shielded his eyes and tried to make out the shapes in front of him which took several seconds to coalesce into anything he could reliably use to gather information about his surroundings. The waterway had widened back out again. As far as he could tell he was in a vast underground cavern. Huge, glistening rock walls rose tens of feet into the air, but he couldn't make out the ceiling as suspended from it were rows of high-powered lights illuminating the vastness of the cave. But even the many lumens worth of artificial light couldn't light the lateral extremities of the space. The boat continued forward, and his eyes adjusted enough for him to take his hand away from his eyes. Across the cave was a long row of rafts strung together; upon the rafts were dozens of naked people of a variety of sizes. As Cumberland got closer, he realised they were of a variety of ages from a child of no more than ten all the way up to a wizened old man of, by Cumberland's estimation, 80 years of age. The Old Man was stood in the direct centre of the platforms. The faces of the people were difficult to make out as white paint had been daubed on them obscuring their features. The closer Cumberland got to the flotilla he realised The OldMan had three distinct scratch marks across his face and was smiling as if in recognition as Cumberland approached. The rafts were not permanently attached, and they parted smoothly and soundlessly as Cumberland approached and began to let his boat through; however, as he passed, The Old Man stepped deftly into Cumberland's smaller boat and indicated he was to continue going forward.

"I'm here to kill Hitler," Cumberland said.

The huge crowd of white-faced ghouls began to chatter and laugh. One began singing, "Strasser Has Only Got One Ball" another shouted, "Heil der neue Führer" and voices chanted, "Gregor Strasser will rise."

"This way."

Cumberland saw there was a sandy shore at the back of the cavern and upon it was a tunnel with another cave beyond. He did as he was bid and headed to land on the beach. The Old Man had stayed silent, and Cumberland was fascinated by his facial scars as they had clearly been inflicted a long time ago, but the wound had remained open and had seemingly been very badly stitched and treated. It was almost as if The Old Man had deliberately allowed them to scar as a permanent mark or reminder of something.

"How did you get those scars?" Cumberland asked.

"His mother gave them to me." The reply came in the same crisp Home Counties accent that Cumberland himself shared.

"You're English!" Cumberland was surprised but felt reassured that at least there was a point of familiarity in all this madness.

"I am English because you are English."

Confused by the reply, Colonel Cumberland Smith stood straight and arranged his fatigues in as presentable a way as possible focusing on the only fixed point he could, while the boat gently touched and slid up the beach. As the vessel came to a stop there was movement and a figure emerged from a tunnel ahead of them. It was another naked man. This one had a white rabbit mask over his face and stood motionless with his arms crossed as Cumberland disembarked. The Old Man stayed where he was.

"Are you coming?"

"To return to this moment you must go with The Gek, and he will show you the way."

Cumberland nodded not really understanding anything that had been said.

The Gek gestured for Cumberland to go through the tunnel; he clambered through and emerged into another cave. This one looked exactly like Cumberland's English tutor's office at Oxford. Oak furniture and many bookcases lined the room. A leather wingback chair was in one corner and The Gek indicated Cumberland should sit in it. Discombobulated, Cumberland sat and The Gek sat behind the desk.

"You will kill the child."

"I'm here to kill Hitler."

"Yes, the child Hitler. You will kill the child"

"I will kill the child, how?"

"I will send you to Braunau Am Inn 21st April 1889, to the house of Alois Hitler and Klara Pölzl. Kill the child."

"Will it work?"

"The travellers were the same age once."

"Will I come back?"

"Eventually. All the travellers have returned to this moment from wherever they were. Some took a day, others many years but they returned."

The Gek took a pipe and placed some yellow crystals into it. He walked around the desk and passed the pipe to Cumberland who lit the crystals and took a big lungful of bitter, acrid smoke. The consciousness that had been Colonel Cumberland Smith left his body and materialised in another time and in another place whilst simultaneously not moving at all.

The Man from Another Time opened his eyes and looked at the house in front of him. To his left, a cobbled road with horses and horse drawn carts. To his right, more houses. The sun shone and a light spring breeze blew in the face of The Man from Another Time.

"Kill the child."

The Man from Another Time stepped forward and then took another step and another and eventually The Man from Another Time found himself at the front door. He opened it and walked inside.

The house seemed empty. The Man from Another Time looked down and realised there was a knife in his hand. The Father appeared from the kitchen and The Man from Another Time simply slit his throat. The shouting attracted the attention of The Siblings; The Man from Another Time simply slit their throats too. The floor of the house was covered in blood, The Man from Another Time realised he was naked and covered in blood. The Man from Another Time passed the knife from his right hand to his left and wiped the blood from his right hand onto the jacket of The Father who was dead on the floor. The Man from Another Time then passed the knife back to his left hand and, unconcerned, proceeded up the stairs. As he walked up the stairs, he became more aware of the wood of the floor, the paint on the walls and the sound of The Mother protecting her new-born baby. The Mother screamed and shouted at him, but The Man from Another Time couldn't speak German and nor did he care very much what was being said.

"Kill the child"

The Mother didn't understand him, but she launched herself at the naked, bloody murderer from Another Time and clawed and scratched at his face. She tried to take his eyes out, but The Man from Another Time was strong and military trained although he couldn't quite remember where, when or by whom he had been trained. He threw The Mother down and her throat was simply slit just like the rest of her family's had been. The entire Hitler family lay dead in their home and The Man from Another Time advanced into the child's room. The new-born Adolphus Hitler lay in his cot sleeping. He yawned when The Man from Another Time stood over the cot and gurgled when he raised the knife. The light glinting off the blade momentarily distracted The Man from Another Time, but he couldn't remember anything except for "Kill the child." Tiny Adolf Hitler didn't so much as a whimper as The Man that had been Colonel Cumberland Smith simply slit the baby's throat in the belief it would end a war that hadn't yet started.

The Man from Another Time turned and left the house. He walked the earth for many years, never finding his place and never quite knowing who or what he was. The three scars that ran across his face remained unstitched, uncleaned and unconcealed, left as a monument to the act that defined who

The Man from Another Time was. The baby killer. The Man from Another Time became The Old Man and he journeyed to Münster and there in the side of a hill he found a passage through thick foliage hanging over an opening. He walked far, due west in pitch darkness and eventually found himself in a vast cavern. Inside which were lots of people with white faces. So, as The Führer Gregor Strasser marched his tanks towards Stalingrad, The Old Man was standing on a raft in the middle of the vast cavern when Colonel Cumberland Smith came to end the war.

HOME-TIME
BY THE SPENCE BROTHERS !!

SCHOOL FINISHES AT FIVE PAST THREE. THAT'S MY FAVOURITE PART OF THE DAY. HOME TIME.

THE BELL RINGS AND AS WE FILE OUT, THE TEACHERS GIVE US OUR GUNS BACK.

I GO TO GUNNINGTON SECONDARY. IT'S NOT THE BEST SCHOOL IN TOWN BUT IT'S THE ONLY ONE WITH AN ACTIVE SHIELD-DEFENCE.

EVER SINCE THAT QUANTUM RESEARCH LAB UP THE ROAD BLEW UP, EVERYTHING'S BEEN A BIT MENTAL.

DAD SAYS THE EXPLOSION CREATED A SPACE/TIME DISTORTION FIELD AROUND OUR TOWN WHICH DEFIES ALL KNOWN LAWS OF PHYSICS.

MUM SAYS DAD SMOKES TOO MUCH WEED.

SPREAD-NOSE DARREN RECKONS THEM ALIENS PHASED HERE FROM CYGNUS V, BUT HE'S A DICK-HEAD AND NO-ONE REALLY LIKES HIM.

MOST DAYS WE HAVE TO DRAG LISA OUT OF DINOSAUR ALLEY COS SHE GETS ALL TRIGGER-HAPPY.

THERE'S ALWAYS KILLER ROBOTS ON A SIMOV STREET. THE ARMY SAID THEY DISMANTLED THEM ALL BUT THEY'RE USELESS.

AND THEY DON'T COME AROUND HERE NO MORE.

WE CHIP DOWN WOLFSPITTLE ROAD, WHERE I LIVE. MUM SEES ME COMING AND DROPS THE WARP SHIELD. MY MATES KEEP GOING, I'LL SEE EM TOMORROW.

MUM GETS VEX, BUT I CAN'T TAKE THE HOV-BUS HOME, I'D MISS ALL THE FUN !!!

187

Disconnected

KB Willson

Thank you for coming to see me. It's rare that I get any visitors these days, so it's nice to hear a new voice, especially one as well articulated as yours. You can ask me anything you like; don't be shy, I've heard just about every possible question over the years, so nothing you say could possibly shock me, but to get the ball rolling why don't I start at the beginning? Because that's what everyone is interested in: how it all started.

Back then I had no idea that my little proclivities would have such an impact on the future of mankind's race toward the stars, but I guess I'm happy to have been of use. Let's face it, in another time I would have been locked away in an asylum, so I'm thankful for small mercies. Oh, and as you've probably noticed, I do tend to ramble on... so feel free to chip in whenever you want to. I don't know whether you're on a tight schedule, but I've got all the time in the world.

So... I suppose it started with the germ of an idea, as these things often do. A strange fancy that became an obsession, a bizarre fixation which just got a little out of hand. It was like a buzzing in my head... an itch that needed to be scratched. I can't describe it any better than that, although by God, I've tried. Doctors, psychiatrists, psychoanalysts, they've all trooped by, and I've tried to explain it to all of them. Again and again. So believe me when I say that I *really* can't tell you what it felt like, what it was that made me embark on this most eccentric of journeys; but what I *can* do is to try to give you some idea of how I got here.

I was bullied as a child. That's the first thing. I mean, a yank in an English village school? It was always going to happen. I know it's nothing special… thousands of kids get bullied, and they all have their own way of coping. Probably. But all I can say is that when it happened to me, the effect it had was to drive me deep inside myself. And I can't say my mum and dad helped very much. "Big boys don't cry" … "Mummy's brave little soldier"… "Sticks and stones"… I heard them all a hundred times. So I hid myself away, metaphorically speaking. I became like the creature inside one of Doctor Who's Daleks: impervious to pain, with all the violence and hurt of the outside world bouncing off my impregnable outer shell. Such a strategy takes its toll, of course, and it was about that time when people began to regard me as, well, a bit *weird*.

From my point of view, though, this was one of the best periods of my youth. The kids at school had begun to leave me alone, and I spent most of my time on my own… thinking, dreaming, and developing the most incredible inner life; and it was during these wonderfully rich teenage years that I began to formulate the philosophy that was to stay with me for the rest of my life. You see, it began to dawn on me that I wasn't just the sum of my parts, but something *other*; and that I, that is to say, the *real* me, was somehow disconnected from the mechanics of my body. I inhabited an indefinable space somewhere deep inside, hidden beneath this outward facade, this protective shell of blood and bone and tissue.

The concept that I had of myself, that I still have if I'm honest, is of a coruscating ball of light, sparking rainbow colours like one of those stained-glass whatsits that you hang in the kitchen window. Internally I was dancing, dazzling… yet I remained locked away, protected from view by this extraordinary being that stared out at me from the bathroom mirror…That face and body were what people recognised as Glen Alexander, but I had become so far removed from my outward appearance that I hardly felt any emotional connection to it at all.

I hope I'm not getting too philosophical for you; most people begin to drift away after a time, and I wouldn't blame you. Apart from the professionals, of course: it's their job to listen.

Anyway, it's hardly rocket science (if you'll excuse the pun) to work out what sort of person this attitude would turn me into. If I had indeed buried my shining, dancing soul so deep that no one and nothing could *ever* touch it, then what would happen if I was ever to peel back that armour, to open up my shell; to reveal that inner beauty? I don't expect you to answer... I can only tell you what I thought, what I *feared*. I feared it would be crushed; stamped on and destroyed. Shattered into a million tiny fragments: impossible to mend. Because that is what we do to each other, we *humans*... we ridicule, and we destroy. So it had to be protected, you can see that, can't you? My secret self, hidden away: kept safe...

You can understand, then, why I opted for the life of a loner, keeping those around me at a safe distance; never letting them in. That's not to say that I didn't have friends, though they were invariably other loners: those who society branded misfits; those who didn't *belong*. They say that every animal seeks out its own kind and I suppose that we all crave acceptance, in some form or another. It's just that some of us attach more conditions to it than others.

There has even been the odd occasion when I've met someone really special, someone with whom I might have wanted to share... what exactly? My soul? Possibly. But if I'm being honest, every such relationship was doomed from the start. To misappropriate the words of Richard Dawkins: "There is something infantile in the presumption that somebody else has a responsibility to give your life meaning and point..."

I don't want you to feel sorry for me, though. God, no. My life has been brilliant, by any standards. I mean, how many people do *you* know who have walked in space? Seen the magnificence of the Earth from 200 miles above the atmosphere? Believe me, I'm not complaining. I grew up as a child of the Sixties, when to be an astronaut was every kid's dream. I remember on the night of the moon landing (and remember we were still living in England at the time), my family decided they were all going to bed. All of them. Not one of them could be bothered to sit up into the wee small hours to watch the greatest moment in Man's history: a man on the moon. I refused point blank; sleeping through such a climactic event was unthinkable. History was being made, and I was determined to be a witness...

As it happened, by the time Armstrong took his "small step for a man", the whole family was there, huddled round the television. I *knew* they wouldn't be able to resist. Such was, and is to this day, the lure of the space programme.

Then, some years later and quite by chance, I found myself living next door to a man who had worked on that mission, who had been instrumental in setting the Eagle safely down in the Sea of Tranquillity. He had a little bit of the Lander's wafer-thin material on a plaque on his mantelpiece, to celebrate the fact. He was the first man I knew who had worked for NASA.

But I'm getting ahead of myself. I was talking about my soul, wasn't I? Existential angst, that's what one psychiatrist called it, but what do they know? How can they possibly understand? Have they been up there? Sick with the weightlessness? Fumbling with padded fingers to control the knobs and switches that keep you alive?

I remember once, I think I was about eighteen, and able to drink legally in a British pub for the first time... not that I hadn't already had several years' experience, you understand: but always out of town, away from the prying eyes of family and neighbours. Anyway, I was standing at the bar in this seafront hotel when an older man came up to me; must have been in his late twenties, I suppose, and out of nowhere decided to pick a fight. Don't ask me why; in my experience people like that never need a reason. He looked me square in the eye and announced, to everyone within earshot, that he was about to give me the pasting of my life.

Now, given what I've already told you, you'll realise that this wasn't an unfamiliar situation, but rather than preparing for the inevitable beating, and to this day I don't know why I did it, I matched his gaze and said, quietly and simply, "You can beat my body; you can break my bones; you could even kill me, if you wanted to. I know you have the power. But whatever you do to this body of mine, you will never, *ever* be able to touch the real me. Because what is me... what is *really* me... is far beyond harm. You will never, *ever* touch ME."

There was a pause, the slightest flutter on the wind. "You're fucking mental."

He left me there, turned and left me; my armour intact.

And that was that.

Ironic, isn't it? Talking about my "armour". It seems my whole life has been one long procession of machine after machine, each one with me at the heart of it, each one designed to keep me safe. The shuttle; the space station; even the space suit itself... all intricately crafted to keep the hostile environment at bay: to enable me to survive. Enclosed and encased in a series of high-tech solutions to the most impossible of problems; and if a component failed, well, there was a backup system. There was *always* a backup system. Belt and braces, as my old grandpa used to say.

Do you know what you do in the blackness of space? Aside from shitting yourself with fear, of course, and trying to concentrate despite the deafening pounding from your heart, and the sting of the sweat. Well I'll tell you: you wonder. In both senses of the word. You wonder at the incredible majesty of the blankness around you, punctuated as it is by a billion billion points of light. Then if you look the other way, there is the Earth: the blues and whites and greens of our home, shining in the most beautiful way you can imagine. No, scrub that. You can't imagine it, not unless you've been there. You may have seen the pictures, but believe me, they're nothing like.

Then there's the other sort of wonder, too. You start to wonder about yourself; about your place in all of this. I'm not talking about religion, though I can, if you want me to. My thoughts on that score have changed dramatically since... well, since my *experience*. But that's when I started to develop my little peculiarity. I don't need to go into detail, I'm sure. You wouldn't be here if you hadn't done your homework. You see, as I've already told you, it was all to do with being encased... encased in machines; machines that provided the safe and supportive environment in which I could flourish. Machines that I could control, to a point, but which also continued functioning merrily along without my giving them a conscious thought. That's the trouble with the space station; for all the constant hubbub, for all that your day is scheduled to the nanosecond, there is far too much time to *wonder*.

Blood in a weightless environment is fascinating, do you know that? It was up there, in the space station, that I first began what they like to refer to as "self-harming". I wondered what it would be like, that's all. You see, given the way my personal philosophy had developed over the years, it was obvious that the human body is just another of those machines. A suit of protective armour with its own inherent life support system; my arms and legs no more or less than the robotic arms on an exploration pod, devices through which I could interact with and explore my environment. The real me, that creature who is Glen Alexander, somehow sits at the heart of this machine: driving it, if you will.

Stop me if I'm going too fast for you, won't you? I know you're probably recording it all, but it's important that you understand. God knows, I can hardly understand it myself.

You're right, of course. Cutting yourself hurts. You can experiment with ways of dousing the pain, and we had plenty available to us on the station, you can be sure of that, but ultimately, it hurts; and you can't keep it secret, not when you're so closely confined with everybody else.

"Houston, we have a problem!" It's a cliché now, of course. Everyone on the planet uses it as a joke, whenever something goes wrong. Dear Jim Lovell, bless his heart... he had no idea what he started. But up in the station, back then, when they realised what I was doing, the phrase seemed entirely appropriate.

And that was the end of my career. I mean, they couldn't have someone like me associated with the programme anymore, could they?

Poor old Glen, went a bit unhinged up there, didn't he? The Agency will look after him though. I mean, he's one of ours, isn't he?

They had no idea; no one did. It was only the beginning. They transferred me to this facility and gave me a lovely room, not like this one we're in today. I mean, what would I do with all those creature comforts now? But back then, oh my lord, I couldn't fault them. I had a fantastic view over the grounds, and although they kept an eye on me, I was pretty much free to wander wherever I fancied.

I used to sit for hours watching the groundsmen mowing and pruning; cutting back the trees and the shrubs. I could relate to that. Whole lengths of bough cut away without ever harming the tree, which would come back even stronger. It fitted with what I had always believed: you may harm the outward manifestation, but that doesn't necessarily affect the life within.

So once again I began to wonder: how far can you go? How far can you 'prune' the human body? I've got to admit that I did become a bit obsessive. But in those early days, when I was injecting local anaesthetic so that I could snip away at the tips of my fingers, I couldn't have dreamed of going as far as I did, had it not been for one brilliant stroke of good luck.

Charcot.

Have you heard of it? No, neither had I. But you see, I had been putting on quite a bit of weight… lack of activity coupled with a healthy appetite will do it every time… and with that came the diabetes and with *that*… Charcot. Named after the guy who discovered it, apparently. I'm not that bothered who found out about it, but the effect is that you can't feel pain in your extremities. I first found out I had it when I broke my ankle and had no idea: it's a bit like leprosy in that respect. But what a bonus! It meant that I could hack away at myself with much less discomfort and begin to get up close and personal with my feet and ankles in a way that required minimal pain control.

Sorry, I should rephrase that. I didn't mean to say, "hack away". That suggests a degree of butchery, whereas this was a clinical dissection: like in Leonardo's anatomical drawings. God, I've always loved those…

Anyway, my next check-up revealed the extent of my "tinkering", and I was moved to a secure medical unit, which to be honest was the next stroke of luck, as it was there that I met my great friend Schreiber. As mad as a hatter, of course, but with a fantastic surgical knowledge. He got it immediately: understood exactly where I was coming from… and the deal was struck.

You see? I couldn't do it on my own. No one could. There's a limit to what you can cut away by yourself: you need to keep your hands functional, for one thing. But Schreiber did it all. God knows how he got access to the stuff, or how he managed to secure the operating theatre for long enough to complete the task, though I have my suspicions. No one will tell me the truth, not even now, but it's not hard to put the pieces together. You see, at the time, they were desperate to find a way for humans to survive the journey into deep space. I mean, travel beyond the moon and on to Mars was just the beginning. My guess is that I handed them an opportunity, a chance for experimentation on a willing human subject. They could strip me down to the basics, get rid of everything that wasn't essential for life. The astronaut of the future, little more than a brain surrounded by a bit of essential tissue, plugged into the spacecraft's systems and ready to go. Am I saying that NASA was complicit in the work? That Schreiber was their man all along? To be honest with you, I don't give a damn either way. What I *do* know is that thanks to the work we did all those years ago, even the furthest galaxies have now been populated by creatures just like me. Humans who have been pared down to the barest minimum, then fitted with state-of-the-art casings to enable them to function in their new environment. My descendants, rulers of the universe.

There was a ceremony, I recall, many years ago now, when I was given a citation in honour of my part in the programme, and after that I began to be visited by people like yourself, writers and journalists who were keen to see where it had all begun, to interview the first of the line. But the fact remains that I really had very little to do with it. I owe it all to the exquisite surgical artistry of Schreiber, without whose extraordinary ability I could never have achieved my dream. He was the true pioneer, and the pruning could not have been done more expertly or to better effect.

And this is the result. What you see before you. In the words of the old song "I am what I am."

I know it can be shocking when you first see me, but at least they've tidied me up a bit. You should have seen me in those early days... I'm told you needed a strong stomach to be anywhere near me! But now that I'm inside this beautiful custom-built case they tell me I should survive for a fair old while yet. It fulfils my every need, you see: though, ironically, nothing like as well as my old body used to. The creature inside the Dalek: the metaphor becomes the fact. Obsession can lead you down some strange pathways, that's all I'm saying. Be careful what you wish for: you don't know what you've got 'til it's gone. Was that Joni Mitchell? I can't remember. Someone like that, anyway.

Oh no, I don't want you to feel sorry for me. After all, I got what I wanted, didn't I? How many people can honestly say that? The trouble is, where do I go now? In my mind I am free, still floating above the Earth, still playing among the stars; but in reality... well, I guess you would say that I'm a tad restricted. Schreiber? I never heard of him again. Do I feel anger toward him? God, no. He carried out my instructions to the letter. I knew what I was doing; understood the consequences. Except for one.

It's the loss of stimulation, you see. That's what really gets you. Okay, I may be able to hear, and I can speak, after a fashion; but not to be able to feel, not to be able to see, not to be able to interact with the world in any other way...

196

It's the memories that haunt you. Taunt you, even. I remember the breeze lifting the hairs on my skin. I remember the sun on my face. I remember the touch of a woman's hand. I remember... cliché after cliché, I know, but...

But...

You can make what you want of this, because it's not something that I've ever told anyone before, but there are times when what is left of my hearing picks up the sound of the machine. A gentle hum: electricity through wiring. Quite comforting, in its way; like the heartbeat in the womb. I imagine the cables that run between this box and the wall. Or the generator. Or whatever the hell it is that supplies the juice that keeps me living. And just occasionally I find myself wishing, hoping... yearning, I suppose... that someone would come in and listen to my story and be able to see beyond the bravado of the freak show... and hear the pain... and the loneliness... and the desperation... and that they would walk over to the wall, or the generator, or the power pack...and with hardly any movement at all, just a simple flick of a switch, or a pull on a plug, they would set me free.

Or to put it another way... I would finally, *truly* become...

... disconnected.

The Suns of Tardimanus

Michel Louis

Translation

"…and I saw a new heaven and a new Moon, for the first Moon passed away…"

- The Tardimanus

In the beginning…

The 21st century was common in many respects, not least because the majority of the people on earth were either engaged in surviving or else trying to divide and conquer. In fact, the humans were so busy arguing that they failed to see what was coming.

In amongst the noise and chaos of everyday life, a little fact crept in and out of the news barely noticed, like a mouse in the night… or a fart with its slippers on… silent but deadly.

Hardly noticed by anyone, this catastrophic event was the crash landing of a spacecraft called Beresheet on the Earth's Moon.

Beresheet was a name taken from Genesis, meaning *in the beginning*. It was a human-less lunar probe sent on a mission by space scientists to the Moon to carry out remote experiments, take measurements and send messages to outer space. While the mission succeeded in one part (getting the messages in to space including the entire dictionary in multiple languages, an encyclopaedia of the history of earth and ancient scriptures including all the religious texts), the space scientists completely underestimated the impact of the lesser-known aspects of the mission.

Unbeknownst to many, the spacecraft was carrying another experiment on board. This included thousands of tardigrades in a suspended state of animation. Encased in amber, the tardigrades could live for hundreds of years and be bought back to life given the right circumstances, the right conditions for life to survive.

At the very last minute, the space scientists sending the spacecraft in to space, also decided to include samples of human DNA.

The spacecraft was launched with much fanfare. A new dawn in space exploration had begun, starting with getting back to the Moon, which had been largely abandoned since the original Moon landings.

Upon attempting to land on the Moon's surface, the space scientists lost control and the craft hurtled towards the Moon's surface. As the spacecraft crashed, it exploded over the lunar surface. The contents burned and shattered into millions of tiny particles The fuel tanks burning and all of its experiments fused together in inexplicable chaos that was to change the course of life itself… and the fall out was only just beginning.

The tardigrades amber casing melted as the temperatures reached the thousands. Melting metal, DNA sent spiralling into molten amber containing the suspended tardigrades. The pressure of the blast had sent pieces everywhere, the contents of the spacecraft scattered far and wide, a crackling sea of sparks, smoke and soon, dying embers.

The chemicals from the spacecraft bleed deep into the molecules of the Moon, the half-burnt pages of the books were sown like seeds of half-remembered knowledge across her surface. The history of earth was laid bare in fragmented form, smouldering and rough around the edges.

As the flames burnt out and the ashes settled, the tiny tardigrades, thrown out by the blast, bounced around the lunar orb. Like specks of blazing hot fairy dust, they bounced as on a never-ending trampoline… like tiny tag nuts freed at last, until suddenly, they came to a halt as they crashed into something solid.

A mound of small brownish yellow boulders, no bigger than rugby balls formed a small barrier and the tardigrades and human DNA landed amongst them and seemingly disappeared into them as the boulders crumbled ever so slightly.

As a dark brown powdery substance seeped through the broken boulders, the truth slowly emerged… like a shart in white trousers.

The boulders it turned out, were not boulders at all. They were the remains of the nappies the astronauts had left behind on the Moon landings, almost fifty years before.

The still burning hot tardigrades and specks of human DNA merged into the powdered excrement, the melting amber soaking it altogether… like a bubbling primeval soufflé.

The fusion created a new form of life; the experiments of the humans had given birth to something entirely unknowable, unimaginable. The primeval soufflé kept growing and expanding, rising as it reached its peak. All of a sudden, the soufflé exploded in and out of itself all at once, a primordial fart that gave birth to an expulsion of gas that was quite indisputably… the mother of all farts. Forever named …. The Big Fart. The sound waves reverberated far and wide, and what came next, were the most gruesome creatures you could ever imagine.

These creatures were to become the destiny of a new race. One part Tardigrade, one part human, one part human astronaut excrement. The Tardimanus had been born.

The Tardimanus

The Tardimanus came to life after The Big Fart in the dying embers of the crashed spacecraft. The new spark of life created a gas cloud around each Tardimanus that allowed them to breath. As they grew and excreted more gas, their own personal clouds grew larger and even more dense.

The fusion of the elements surrounding the birth of this new species meant that the Tardimanus were able to grow larger than they would have done if they were still your average tardigrade. In fact all the Tardimanus grew to around the size of a house cat, albeit in a more vertical form. They all had tardigrade faces, but with human like mannerisms and expressions, as they had all come from the same fusion of DNA. Their little faces suckered and puckered in a never-ending quest for more.

Due to their hybrid DNA, the Tardimanus glowed like small amber orbs, lighting up their clouds of gas. They grew to develop human ways; the human DNA was fused with every particle and hot amber coursed through their veins.

The fusion also had one other unexplained factor, in that everything happened faster. Each twenty-four hours on Earth was a thousand years in their evolution, they grew bigger, they reproduced faster, and the gasses grew stronger by the second.

All Tardimanus were exactly the same, and all of them were duel-gendered, a hybrid of the male and female DNA on board the crashed spacecraft. They could self-reproduce and all gave birth and partook in this new cycle of life. They reproduced around every three minutes in our terms, and it took another thirty-three minutes for each baby Tardimanus to reach full maturity.

The Tardimanus didn't need new food supplies as they ate their own excrement in a never-ending cycle. Some even just spent their whole time with their head in their asses eating their own excretions or reproducing. It gave them a lot of pleasure and they never thought to question their existence. They were strangely self-sufficient in their own unique, disgusting and humanesque ways.

The Tardimanus had also collectively absorbed all of the information that was placed on board the spacecraft. They had the ability to work as a hive mind, all with the same weird knowledge, which was based on fragments of all the leftover parts of the data disks, bits of dictionaries, encyclopaedias and half burned scriptures that had survived the crash landing.

Still primitive, the new species spent lifetimes wandering the surface of the Moon, reproducing rapidly with nothing else to do except eat, sleep, excrete, eat, play and copulate, with no danger around them at all. They seemed immortal, at least none of them ever seemed to die. With no need to hunt and gather, and no weather to hide from, and being perfectly protected by their own gasses, the Tardimanus' reproduced into the googols.

Soon they covered the surface of the Moon and their clouds of gas all merged.

A new atmosphere grew around the Moon, a dark glowing amber and brownish cloud engulfed it and grew thicker by the moment. The new ecosphere evolved quickly. The gases built up, a cloud system was formed, methane rain came and went, and the winds of a trillion farts a second blew in all directions. The smells came like the changing of seasons, each fouler than the last. This was the very embodiment of the greenhouse effect; our Moon fell victim to the human curse.

Pockets of heavier methane clouds formed, warming up the atmosphere and creating storms and endless thunder that rattled the Moon like a thousand gods farting. The noise and wind were never-ending, and yet the Tardimanus thrived.

Every now and then, a fart flare would burst out from the Moon, sending gases spewing into space in every direction. Sometimes they flared towards the Earth, and for a few days parts of the Earth would hang heavy with a stench, which everyone described as 'not human', although we all knew different.

The Tardimanus thrived on the denseness of the gases, oblivious in their free and pleasure-filled existence. Their bodies evolved as fast as the methane-hurricanes that now swept the Moon's surface, adapting to the ever-increasing temperatures.

The Tardimanus didn't experience time and evolution like the humans or the others, they had no need for measurements of existence or for self-reflection, they simply accepted their reality for what it was. They had no concept of past and future. Time was not a construct they needed to adhere to. Death did not exist.

The Language of Farts...

They didn't need to learn to communicate in language other than farting at each other, as they all did the same thing and they all had the same experiences. The methane clouds meant that the atmosphere on the Moon developed a unique acoustic anomaly, where sound became magnified. It was a very loud place to exist.

The language of farts was actually quite complex, almost like a system of Morse code blended with a varied spectrum of sound, depth, vibration and longevity.

The complexities of the language of farts, meant that occasionally, on days nobody could never figure out a pattern to, the Tardimanus would gather in groups and spontaneously erupt in to performances of long orchestral pieces, with the high-pitched longer farts creating a mosaic operatic effect that reverberated to infinity.

The rumbling deeper farts provided a baseline to the music, whereas what humans call the "silent but deadly types" on earth, actually created a screeching sound on the Moon, a sound never before heard by human ears, as they were not attuned to its frequency. Many a human has escaped sure persecution and 'gaslighted' their loved ones due to this anomaly in the human hearing spectrum. We, however, could not help but hear it.

As the musical numbers built to a rising crescendo, many took for cover, although you could never run fast enough to get away, and you certainly could never hide. The best you could do was try and block some of it out. The smells that emanated from these performances were indescribable. They could even create temporary weather systems in space, with torrents of gases spewing in every direction like lunar flares, sending tornados of methane rolling in to space, all carrying the tune of the Tardimanus.

Space Exploration...

As they settled in to their new home, the Tardimanus curiosity evolved into developing new ways of exploring themselves and their surroundings. They started to create experiments of their own, as being born of experiments gave them an uncontrollable urge to develop new ones. Something in their make-up involving the faecal matter of the first men on the Moon and the experiments on the spacecraft gave them the idea for space travel.

One such experiment was to send some of the Tardimanus on space exploration missions. With their own personal atmospheres, they could survive in outer space and recycle their food supply, so there was no need for any specialist equipment. Tardimanus technology was rudimentary, but it was undeniably effective.

The launchpad was a hundred Tardimanus grouped in a circle, where they created a collective fart of such magnitude, they could launch a group of three Tardimanus to a distance of thousands of miles in mere seconds. These light speed farts, code named; "Death Fart One, Two Three etc…" were to reach every corner of the galaxy, and we all watched on in horror as their experiments began.

Their first mission was to Uranus, which the Tardimanus later went on to declare in a moving musical epic, as their true spiritual home. The combination of the Tardimanus methane clouds fused beautifully with the windy planet, which happened to have its very own handy source of methane. Colonisation and heat induction took precisely seventeen hours (or one Uranian day) to complete. The ice turned to pools of bubbling methane. Uranus was now theirs.

The Great Stink 'Returns'…

The Tardimanus then sent several expeditions to planet Earth. This had a strange effect on their gas clouds as it merged with the atmosphere of earth in that they became completely invisible. They were able to explore all sorts of places unseen, the only clue being a foul smell that could never be disguised.

On one Earth expedition, a group of three Tardimanus managed to sneak unseen in to The Houses of Parliament in England. They went exploring in every chamber, taking in all there was to see and leaving a stench behind that nobody could even describe. The humans were beside themselves. At first, they were all either blaming each other, politicians exchanged vicious words with each other, accusing each other of being the culprit, accusations of 'you smelt it you dealt it' flew around the chambers and tensions simmered like the new smell permeating parliament. Yet even after the Tardimanus were long gone, the smell lingered on. "The Great Stink Returns" the news outlets claimed, in reference to a similar incident in 1858.

No matter what the humans tried, however many times they cleaned it out or however much air freshener they used, nothing could get rid of that faint lingering smell. It eventually became something they came to accept; they really had no choice. The dank and heavy stench of methane clung to the ancient buildings like skid marks on a public toilet, stubborn and refusing to budge.

On other expeditions, the Tardimanus sent larger groups of one hundred Tardimanus at a time to various planets in the solar systems. They visited Mars, Venus and beyond the milky way. They visited planets the humans had not even discovered yet, as the Tardimanus gas based organic technology was far superior to the humans' homemade rockets. They had the benefit of the knowledge of all of the humans' mistakes, and they needed nothing other than themselves to achieve their missions. Once they landed on other planets, they would set up small colonies and begin the process of breeding.

They didn't have a grand plan to take over the universe, it was just something they did naturally. They didn't think about it, or have any meetings or have a set timetable, they simply just wanted to. It was almost as if it was engrained in their DNA.

Left unchecked, the Tardimanus eventually existed in every possible realm of the physical world. In all of time itself, no species had ever evolved this fast and wide and there was nothing all creation could do but watch with interest.

Theirs was a utopia never dreamed about before, yet it was to all come at a cost.

Nobody on earth noticed at first that the usually bright Moon was slowly turning a rather nasty shade of brown. Nobody looked up at the Moon anymore, they were too busy reading the horrors of the news. They were drowning themselves in a made-up fantasy world and over dosing on comments sections and pontificating their views to others, a vile mixture of bile and other people's words.

If anyone did notice, it was blamed on pollution and who could blame them. Most of the world was either burning, flooding, infected or dying and the skies were turning red and dark. Only a few noticed the Moon as the changes swept over her surface. A fading of her light, a hazy gaseous brown cloud circling and swirling across the surface, a slight amber glow. No more Moon bows, no more night light, no more silvery Moons.

The world-weary earth belched and complained, it had plenty of its own issues to contend with, yet still the humans didn't see. The shouts of the many were ignored by the few, and they never noticed until it happened.

The beginning of the end...

Sometime in mid-2020, the space scientists had sent another rocket into space, this one carrying vital oxygen supplies to the International Space Station.

As it neared its final destination, the rocket got caught up in a lunar fart flare and span off course, and started heading toward the Moon.

The humans were finally about to be woken up.

As the rocket hurtled towards the Moon, a few of the Tardimanus saw it coming, they watched in fascination, which you could tell as their faces all stopped moving.

Through the thick brown clouds of methane gas, the rocket broke through and crashed in to the Moon in a great big bang that echoed through the moons gaseous acoustics. The crash sparked a thousand fires and soon the entire Moon was a blazing ball of gas.

The humans looked up in horror and awe! The Moon was literally on fire and they thought this was the end times.

The Tardimanus, with their amber blood and methane infused DNA, all liquified and joined together, a mass chemical reaction causing the Moon to become one with the Tardimanus.

The Moon's burning atmosphere grew and grew and became like a small new sun in the sky.

The now all one mass consciousness that was once the Tardimanus and the Moon rapidly evolved to withstand their new atmosphere, now quickly co-creating more farts of epic proportions, and supplying the new Moon-Sun with a never-ending supply of methane gas.

The humans stood in shock. No longer would they have their Moon, the Moon as they knew it was gone forever. In its place was now a new Sun, a burning mass of gas and methane-based consciousness, a forever glowing amber ball.

The evolution of the Tardimanus on the Moon was so fast, that the last rocket crash destroyed the old Moon forever. A burning symbol now stood in the sky night and day to show all of us in creation the destruction the humans created. Night times became light, and no longer could they hide.

The humans had polluted earth's one satellite, and they finally understood it was too late. They had quite literally shit all over the universe, and the end of life as we knew it was nearing.

The destruction of the old Moon sent shock waves through all creation, as by now the Tardimanus had set up colonies all over space, and the very basis of space and ironically… time… was now under their control. With the methane clouds spreading, just one spark could set the whole universe alight, and there was nothing anyone could do about it but watch… and try not to breath in.

As the old Moon died and became one with the Tardimanus, fart gases flared and its spreading methane atmosphere took on a deadly new characteristic. After the new Big Fart, if anyone or anything became engulfed in the Tardimanus moon gas, or if they even slightly breathed it in, then they too, would become one with the Tardimanus.

It's almost too late for life now, it's just a matter of time. The Tardimanus "are taking over and soon all of space will be a mass of endlessly burning Suns of the Tardimanus", and all we have to look forward to now is a methane based collective consciousness and the language of farts.

The only hope that we, the Ancient Ones of creation have left is a prophecy of a time to come when a new Moon shall descend from the heavens towards Earth.

A lost Moon hidden away for millennia is said to return to the centre of the universe and balance will be restored to all creation. She will bring the antidote to the chaos bought on by the reign of the Tardimanus. We all await this day with bated breath and pinched noses, as until the new Moon rises, none of us is safe.

Until that day comes, we the Ancient Ones watch over creation… and wait… oh dear God, oh dear Me… what's that smell? What the fuuuuuuaaaaaart?

Translation

"I am the Tardigrade and the Human, the beginning and the ending…"

- The Tardimanus - 2023

The Adult Prodigy

K. S. Dearsley

Francine smiled as the last chords of the orchestwave died away and Alex's hopes shrivelled. There should have been a pause, an unwillingness to break the spell.

"It's wonderful, darling. Especially that bit in the slow movement, you know..."

Francine's surgically perfect features arranged themselves in an expression of delighted enthusiasm. Alex could have looked as good as she did, as she had often scolded him, if only he had not been so obsessed with his music.

"This bit?" Alex gestured, interrupting the instrument's coloured beams to repeat the pattern of sound. He accepted his fiancée's praise, but he had seen enough of true rapture as a child prodigy to tell the difference.

"See? I told you your block wouldn't last." Francine threw her arms around Alex's neck and hugged him. For a disturbing moment it could have been his mother when he was eight years old. Child prodigies had been freaks then, things to be fussed and wondered over. Growing up was always going to be hard, even before Dr Arnold Carmichael's 'miracle'.

Francine released him as if he had suddenly acquired a jacket of barbed wire. "Hadn't you better be going?"

Alex accessed the chronometer on his implant. "I'll make it. Will you be there tonight?"

Francine shook her head. "I promised I'd take mother to the Davey Richter concert–he's so cute–just like you were, I'll bet."

"Except my talent was natural." Alex put away his music.

"Imagine what you would have been like if edit removal surgery had been available then!" Francine rolled her eyes.

Alex left her preening herself for her night watching the prodigy perform, and ran for the nearest vacuum-train terminal. He passed billboards advertising communication implants and the omnipresent Davey Richter, the latest genius to emerge under Dr Carmichael's laser. Pigeons had been using it for a perch and the six-year-old's face had gained a guano birthmark. Alex smiled as he hurried on.

The Sweet Vibes Club was already busy when he arrived. The manager, Frank Sangster, glided over to him smoothly exchanging 'hellos' and smiles with the clients on his way. His slicked down hair matched the sheen on his pseudo-silk suit.

"Is it your chrono-implant that's slow or you?" He greeted Alex with a show of teeth. "Never mind." He gestured at the orchestwave console. "We've some important new guests. Impress them and maybe I won't replace you with a younger talent."

Alex winced. As he took up position, Sangster moved into the spotlight and activated his voice enhancer. "Ladies and gentlemen—I give you our very own resident prodigy—Alex Gyllian!"

There was a trickle of applause. The indifference was what had attracted Alex to the Sweet Vibes Club when the concert hall bookings had gone into a terminal drought. Davey Richter could have appeared among them, or a heavenly choir, and the audience would not have been impressed or distracted from the all-important consumption of food and drink. Alex could drift through his shift dreamily flicking melodies around the walls, and imagine the reverence of a full auditorium. Tonight, the gestures would not behave. They skipped and lurched making the melody tumble and jerk when it should have swung and crooned. Francine's words formed a counterpoint to the music.

"Imagine," she had said, "If edit removal surgery had been available then."

Did she think that he had not imagined it at least twice a day? Every time he had to make his way to the club he imagined. He tried to brush the words away. The sweet rill of piano waves transformed mid-phrase to wheezing bagpipes. Alex was so startled he let his arms drop. The sudden silence drew stares from the clientele.

Sangster scowled and signalled the spotlight. His smile lit as it touched him. "That's right, Alex, you're not seeing things, we really do have a celebrity in the club tonight. Ladies and gentlemen, let's hear it for our favourite raunchy, rhyming Magic Conundrum quiz show hostess–Margi Makepeace!"

As the spotlight zoomed to the former presenter of the most popular holoshow of the decade, she rose nervously. Her chemical blonde hair and pumped curves defied the traditional image of a poet, but so did her verse.

"Give us a rhyme," shouted someone.

"No, no–once I start, I can't stop. I'm thrilled to be here. I'm a big fan of Mr. Gyllian's. I used to go to all your concerts. Would you join me? Oh, that's indiscreet of me." She looked around as if expecting to be told to stand in the corner, her blue eyes doll-like.

"Do as the lady says, Gyllian." Sangster gave Alex his graveyard smile. "You know what her being here can do for this place? The publicity? Remember, if you mess up, I can replace you with a ten-year-old who'd settle for payment in lollipops."

Alex shrugged. He joined the quiz presenter. "I'm honoured."

"Oh no, the honour's all mine..." The words tumbling from Margi Makepeace's mouth were at odds with her expression, as if her lips were moving too fast for her to keep up with them. It was not only her cleavage that made Alex feel breathless.

"I've always been an admirer of yours too," he lied. "The way you produced those poems on whatever subject the audience shouted out, without even having to think about it. It takes me all day to come up with two words that rhyme."

"It got harder and harder. There's this fear, you see, that one day you won't be able to do it. That's why I went to Dr Carmichael. Oops, I'm not supposed to tell anyone. I'm always saying things I shouldn't."

"Dr Carmichael?" Alex leant forward. "I thought he only operated on kids."

"Oh dear, me and my big mouth. I just get worse and worse. Let me buy you a drink..."

"No, wait..." Alex put his hand over hers to keep her in her seat, but she kept on talking.

"Really, I shouldn't have said anything. He only did it as a special favour because I begged and begged and look what happened. Waiter! Bring us more drinks, there's a sweetheart. Please, you mustn't take any notice, forget I spoke, I wish I could. I..."

"Adults can have edit removal surgery?" Alex gulped his drink. With no more unconscious judge standing between him and his creativity, the whole universe of music would be open to him. Margi's flattery and excuses faded out to a static buzz as one word reverberated through Alex's head: imagine.

It took a long time to get an appointment with Dr Carmichael; six months at least, the receptionist said.

"Tell him Margi Makepeace sent me."

The next day he was sitting in Dr Carmichael's office calculating how the notes of the orchestwave would resonate off the walls and buzz against the glass on the genius-maker's framed certificates, while the man himself fiddled with an old-fashioned stylus on his desk. His frameless spectacles added to his gravitas, but did nothing to hide the unease in his eyes.

"What you ask isn't that simple," he said.

"Why not? An adult's brain is bigger than a child's, better formed. It should be easier to operate on."

"Which one of us is the expert here?" The doctor threw down his stylus, as if explaining for the umpteenth time. "Children are malleable. Bring them to me before they're two and I can make them linguists, artists, mathematicians—whatever their parents want. It's merely a matter of severing the block that prevents the unmodified from hearing and seeing, sensing and responding to all the influences around them, but there's always a price to be paid."

"You owe me." Alex slapped the desk. "Before you and your edit removal surgery I was special."

The doctor's manner relented. "Without the edit function things can become jumbled. Children are less formed, as you put it, and can adapt."

"You operated on Margi Makepeace. What did she pay you?"

Dr Carmichael glanced up. For a long moment, his gaze locked with

Alex's, then he looked away. "Margi was scared she'd dry up. I released the edit on her linguistic functions. You've heard the results. Why do you think she left the Magic Conundrum show? She can't stop herself. She'll say the wrong thing in every language from English to Inuit. The show's producers asked her to leave."

He paused. Alex remembered Francine's return from Davey Richter's concert.

"It was wonderful! You should have heard him." She had gestured extravagantly, sitting on the edge of a chair, then standing again. "... and he was such a little sweetie!"

Alex looked steadily at the doctor. "I'll take my chances," he said.

It was the music that woke Alex. He pushed his way up through layer upon layer of feather quilts to reach the sounds. Piercingly beautiful, they sang in his veins and flooded his eyes with tears. He lurched upright looking for the source of such beauty. Music swung and swooped around his head. He put a hand to his temple. As the effects of the sudden movement settled, the music returned to its soaring splendour.

"It's me," Alex whispered. For a moment he found himself trapped between his yearning to hear more and the need to record the music before its echoes stilled. He began searching for a noter.

Alex's concentration was so intense that the way Francine's lips were parted, and her eyes were shining meant nothing. The last notes became an emptiness on the air, and she sat back as if released from a trance.

"It's beautiful." She choked on the words.

Alex shook his head. He knew it could be better. His performance fell so far short of what he heard. "It needs a proper orchestra—real musicians."

"But darling, compared to..."

"What I wrote before?"

"I was going to say to Davey Richter—or any of those other so-called prodigies—I've never heard anything so... so..." She gestured at the air.

Alex observed the shapes her hands made, the set of her shoulders, and heard in his head the sounds they would produce on the orchestwave, discords and conflicting rhythms, not beautiful, not perfect. Not like the music that flooded his mind. He had to find the right musicians to perform it.

The volume of the applause was painful, filling the auditorium with the exhilaration of waves crashing against rocks. Pleasure shone from the performers' faces. The only member of the audience not clapping himself purple was Alex. Beside him Francine was applauding so hard Alex almost expected sparks to fly from her hands.

"Come on." He pushed through the rows of ecstatic fans, dragging Francine with him to the waiting limousine. The petrol-drinking monster was a luxury only those feted at the top of society were allowed to use, but settling back into its leather interior failed to smooth out his frown.

"What's wrong?" Francine demanded.

"Couldn't you hear it? The violins sounded like rusty chains."

"They sounded fine to me."

"If you'd heard the music in my head..."

"Well, I haven't, and neither has anyone else. The performance was a triumph and all you can do is complain about it." Francine pouted, and turned on the car's old-fashioned radio.

Alex tried not to listen. It was playing one of the grand masters of classical music and it was all wrong. There were arpeggios where the melody should have resonated simplicity, and allegros where there should have been adagios. Alex ground his teeth and glared out of the window: this was a composer revered as a genius for centuries and he couldn't orchestrate a nursery rhyme! And the musicians! How could the conductor tolerate such imbalance? Couldn't he hear it? Couldn't any of them hear?

Francine had gone. It was a relief to be free of her inharmonious movements and bad taste, her insistence that he should eat when he had to note down the music that filled his head before it flew away.

"There's more to life than music," she had said. "You don't care about anything else any more–certainly not me. What's the point of being successful if you don't enjoy it?"

To her that meant eating in swanky restaurants and going to clubs where the holo-jackals would jostle each other to get their image as they emerged–with Francine dazzling in diamond necklaces. It was not the kind of music that he wanted to hear.

Her parting shot before slamming the door was: "I could put up with you being a bore, darling, but frankly I can't stand the smell any more."

Alex had sniffed at his armpits. There was a discordant blast from the brass section, but that was preferable to the whine of the epi-scourer as it stripped away his dead skin cells.

He now knelt at a box sorting through the memories of before, ready to store in the attic–holophotos of Francine, scraps of his old music–all worthless–a holophoto of Alex and Frank Sangster on stage at the Sweet Vibes Club. Suddenly resolved, he picked up the box and carried it out to the garden. He emptied the contents in a heap. Smoke pollution was strictly illegal, but by the time the extinguishers arrived he would have finished. Alex flicked his igniter, hearing the spurt of flame as a crash of trumpets, and dropped fire into the pile.

Dr Carmichael had tried to warn him, but he had not listened, or was incapable of hearing, as his audiences were unwilling or unable to hear the flaws in his music. Someone had once said that the blemishes on a rose enhanced its beauty. Alex shook his head, sending notes tumbling over one another. He could hear perfection in his mind, and the blemishes of the world jumbled over it. If he could wipe out the flaws with one wave of his arm, like the notes on an orchestwave, perhaps he would have peace.

The bonfire danced and crackled as the flames purified his life of unwanted memories. He watched the clean red and gold liquid heat ripple along the edge of the holoframes and reach out greedy fingers towards the fence, urged on by a tremolo breeze. Alex heard violins and a stirring bass as the fire whipped itself to a frenzy, snaking towards him.

Francine sniffed back a tear. "Why did you put him in here?" She and Dr Carmichael were watching Alex as he sat wedged in the corner rapidly covering a sheet of paper in musical notation. "I blame myself–our trial separation..."

"Hah!" Alex shouted without looking up. There had been nothing 'trial' about it. Her head was no doubt as full of credit signs as his was of music. So what? Each to their own obsession. If only they would leave.

Dr Carmichael held a finger to his lips. "You saw the state he was in after the extinguishers found him."

"But a cell..." Francine's protest threatened to turn into a wail. Alex looked up sharply at Dr Carmichael. The doctor began to usher her out. "Will he recover?"

"No," Dr Carmichael said, and slowly let his breath out as Alex nodded. They would keep their bargain.

The doctor clicked the door behind them as quietly as he could. Alex's scribbling checked for an instant. Despite Francine's tears his accommodation suited them all. Francine could keep Alex's money; Dr Carmichael could keep his reputation and the padded walls gave Alex the only thing he craved–the silence which would allow his music to be as he created it–perfect.

Emergent Orange

T. M. Jordan

We do not know much about art and cannot easily work up ourselves into ecstasies over it.

Mark Twain, *The Innocents Abroad*

1.

I don't keep up much with the art world. But even I had seen the billboards promising the art of the future. Blue Hat, a self-described chaotic-neutral hacker and e-artist, was putting together a show that she called Viral. She promised it would rock the art world to its core.

Blue Hat was her artist and hacker name. Her real name, which also sounded like a hacker name in fairness, was Ziggy Billeaudeau. In her day job, she was, an associate lecturer at Oxford, who tolerated her work because of the money she brought in. Billeaudeau was fascinated in the crossover between technology and art, seeing it as an avenue that hadn't really been explored by artists who still liked mucking about with paint rather than code. Her speciality was attempting to bridge the two.

 She had settled on the name of *Viral* for the art project a year before, having no real intention to necessarily base a piece around the name. But it sounded sexy and dangerous, and had the requisite 'funny at first, but less every time you hear it' pun quality she enjoyed in titling things.

Blue Hat set about creating her own work. She took inspiration from Langton's Ant, but developed it further. Langton's Ant is an ant programmed to turn left or right depending on the colour of the square, whilst also changing it in the process. It creates seemingly random patterns, but complex lines begin to emerge after a few thousand moves.

She tweaked it, less interested in the mathematics and more in the patterns. Instead of squares, she used irregular decagons, multiple colours, and multiple ants. The effect was to create an ever shifting, flexing, and rippling canvas of chaotic colour. She placed this in a room with a top-down projection onto the floor, so that when people interrupted the light patterns, the ants would react and add an extra element of chaos. She was very proud of it.

Blue Hat had also curated interactive exhibits so that people could create their own computer art. There was digital drawing and painting on large interactive screens, where each piece would be catalogued and projected so that everyone had a chance to be an artist. There was a MIDI music creator that encouraged people to draw pictures in the MIDI sound files to create weird, discordant computer music. There was an opportunity to use an advanced form of Deep Dream, where a person could upload a photograph, any photograph, and tweak the image so that wild colours, patterns, and whorls (usually cats), can appear in the image. These were hugely popular with children.

But before she had embarked on this experiments, Blue Hat had also contacted artists all over the world for their contribution—some she knew already to be working with technology, others to challenge themselves in extending into a new medium. The first, by an underground-gone-mainstream graffiti artist called CK, short for Captain Kickass. CK had made their name scrawling trite political messages on the sides of government buildings, criticising fascism, and such. The art was so-so, but most admired by young people for the fact that CK was able to scale and tag rather extraordinary places, such as MI6 headquarters or the Home Secretary's home address, without being caught. The art was the icing on the cake of sheer bravado, albeit a watery, thin icing that didn't add a whole bunch, the equivalent of saying really mean things on a blog only your mum reads.

For their installation, the art gallery had installed a brick wall at "great expense." CK had built (or more likely had an assistant build) two machines that were in constant war with each other. The first sprayed along the wall with black paint in the pattern of a design that CK had created. The second machine filled with white wall paint would chase the other machine, trying to paint over the design. This piece was called 0800 34537, which as the little plaque pointed out was the phone number of a local graffiti removal company. The piece was in constant motion, but the design was never to be completed fully.

If you squinted at the white paint, the faint outline of the previously painted designs could be seen. It was a dragon. It looked like it was pulled straight from a book the Standard Tattoos for the Unimaginative.

One of the other pieces was by a well-known Internet artist, Frank Dasset. Basset had become obsessed with the MS Paint as a child. Where most people could only hope to create pretty colours in geometric shapes, Basset was able to churn out complex pictures showing surreal scenes of pop culture twisted to the macabre, the punny, the insane, the every which way that was imaginable. He posted a new piece online almost every single day, many going viral. What made him particularly popular was the little suggestion box that his website carried (250 characters max.) that allowed members of the general public to make suggestions for his next, daily piece. Each piece posted would carry with it the suggested description, though occasionally he would post his own original pieces inspired by dreams.

In the gallery program, his installation was simply labelled *Pieces by Frank Basset and company*. This did not do justice to its scale. One wall was covered from corner to corner; floor to ceiling, with his digital paintings, and each picture was printed on a four by three-inch canvas and framed, with barely a hair's distance between each one. It was suspected that, due to the number of nails driven into the wall to hang each picture, serious structural damage had been done to it that no amount of poly filler would fix. Each piece was credited to Frank Basset and whoever had made the suggestion. For example:

No. 356—by Frank Basset and Angela Sidebottom
Giant octopus with head of Jamie Oliver throttling to death various fast-food mascots. US Army attacking him in downtown Paris, and he roars in anger. Jet planes fly by and he's climbing the Eiffel Tower. French army armed with good food.

This had been reproduced perfectly, with other numerous details included as well.

Most critics had been quite sniffy about Basset's pieces, saying it "played to the crowd," and that it had too much "mainstream appeal." The gallery, which sold postcards of various prints of Basset's art, couldn't agree more.

Ilsa Hoštáková, taking her cue from Marina Ambrović's *Rhythm 0*, had created a performance piece that pushed the boundaries of the human body. Hoštáková had regularly pushed the human body to the absolute limits, and her body in places was a patchwork of scars from her previous performances. Most had explored the relationship between pain, pleasure, and the responsibility that both engender. She rarely commented on her work, though as she was the subject of her art, she was not elusive.

This latest piece, called *Suggestion Box* was a deliberate attempt to go viral. Hoštáková placed herself inside a large, glass-walled room. In the room were a number of objects ranging from paintbrushes and paint to hammers and nails. There was also a screen, which displayed a chatroom open to the general public. For six hours each day, she would take suggestions from the general public of what she was to do with each object, and she would perform these to the best of her ability. These would be broadcast around the world. Naturally, she would not be able to complete every suggestion, as they would come through by the thousands every minute. But she did not edit the choices, and performed each one without prejudice.

The little plaque beside the room gave the piece context, calling it "*A companion piece to* Rhythm 0 *for the modern age. Where previously Hoštáková's pieces examined the consequences of direct action within the room,* Suggestion Box *develops the idea further by looking at the effects when there is a degree of separation between the subject and the user.*"

Despite Hoštáková's protests, very strong filters were put on the chatroom so that she did not commit suicide on a webcam to the world.

By far the most interesting piece was a piece by a newcomer artist. Blue Hat claimed not to know who the artist was, just having received an e-mail from a burner e-mail address that promised the most wild and breath-taking piece for her show. The promising email was signed 'from Lovelace.' Blue Hat had naturally been sceptical, but kept up with correspondence with Lovelace out of curiosity until she was sure that what they were promising could be delivered. Once satisfied, they made the space available for Lovelace to deliver.

Lovelace did not arrive in person. Rather, they sent a truck with a wooden crate, the last in an extensive list of deliveries to confuse and obfuscate the original departure point. The guy delivering didn't even know what was inside the large wooden crate, and didn't seem to care. The crate was put into a large white space in the exact middle of the room, as requested by Lovelace, and opened. Only then did Blue Hat realise what she had been sent.

The show was opened to critics at first, to get the reviews and build buzz. The reviews were mostly positive about the art in general, but were positively enthused about Lovelace's piece. *"The most revolutionary and dangerous piece of art since Chris Burden nailed himself to a car,"* said one critic. *"At times confusing, but beguiling in all its complexity,"* said another. It was the talk of the art world, with pictures in outrage tabloids published and shared for everyone to be outraged. This was what I was here to see.

The piece was called *The Turner Test*.

Placed in the middle of the room was a desk. It was a plain desk, made from cheap wood and painted black. In one tray was a pile of plain, decent quality paper (replenished regularly), with a line of neatly sharpened pencils of different softness and colour, depending on what would be needed at the time. Sat at the desk was the rough approximation of a human from the waist up. Translucent Perspex covered mechanics of cogs and wires and motherboards that whirred and fluttered information throughout the entire body. The head was mostly taken up with complex cameras and microphones that fed to a central processing unit in the chest of the automaton. The face was not designed to be a realistic—it was like putting a mask on a toaster, a small effort to make the crude human machine more palatable to the public. It was a design that emphasised it was not real; a Brechtian human-machine.

Critics had already drawn comparisons with The Turk, the historical magic trick that fooled people in playing with a grand chess-master hidden under a desk. However, the desk here was open and plain, the mechanics of the automaton clear for all to see, if not understood. Unlike The Turk, which was nothing more than a parlour trick, this was actual magic. This machine could make, for you, "art."

2.

"Bluetooth," said my friend. "Definitely Bluetooth."

I had gone with a friend to visit the gallery, after the initial hype had died down. Though *Viral* was proving to be a popular exhibition, the undisputed highlight had been *The Turner Test*. People love robots. The popularity of the show had meant that paying visitors were given a number according to their visit, as well as a lottery for a small selection of random visitors based on when they entered, if they were lucky. There were only a small amount available each day, and I was lucky enough to be given number forty-four. My friend was one before me.

"You think?" I said. I had read all the articles, the speculation and conspiracy theories about *The Turner Test*. I know I had read lots of arguments that it must be a Bluetooth contraption; almost as many that said the test proved that it wasn't. Not many people actually seemed interested in what it produced though.

"Yep. There's some guy sat a desk listening to everything people say, does a pretty drawing and the machine just prints it. Easily done." Simon paused. "I mean, it's still a really cool trick, totally fits in with everything else in here, but yeah, it's a trick."

I nodded. "Still cool though."

"Yeah—still cool."

At that moment, Turner let out a small beep. It spoke to the person, telling it the title of picture (usually a simple description of what it contained). Then, one of the eyes extended a camera lens from its face and leaned over the picture. The other eye flashed, and Turner returned back to its seat. It then slid the picture across the desk to the person sitting opposite, who out of habit thanked Turner and left with picture in their hands.

"Number forty-three please." Turner's voice was an unnatural, flat buzz, like an evil machine from a budget TV series.

"That's me," said Simon and he took his place opposite Turner.

Turner lifted its head to look in Simon's direction.

"Describe your picture," said Turner. The harsh electronic buzz blurred the words into each other like a table saw.

Simon smiled and began to describe an outrageous picture of Abraham

Lincoln sitting astride a T-Rex fighting a purple robot gorilla, and also the T-Rex had machine gun arms.

Turner softly hummed as it processed the request and began its actual work. Within its machine brain, it ran through millions of pre-existing reference images from the Internet and created a picture in its machine brain. Appropriate pictures were selected within seconds and collaged to form a single cohesive image, like an autonomous photo editing program. With the image created internally, it then determined the most efficient way to transfer the image to the page, maintaining its integral quality as a picture whilst also developing a method where pencil textures created an effect that simple digital tools weren't able to, without looking obviously digital.

All this so that, after nearly five minutes, Turner had handed Simon an original image of Abraham Lincoln sitting astride a T-Rex fighting a purple robot gorilla, and also the T-Rex had machine gun arms. He held it up excitedly for me to see. He stood up, and as he came back to stand next to me as my number was called.

I walked towards Turner, took my seat, and watched its blank mask. It buzzed the same request it had buzzed for the hundreds before me, and surely the thousands after.

I began my pitch.

I had thought for a long time what I would ask Turner to draw for me. I had studied all the ones that people had posted online—a mixture of Thomas Kinkade twee crap from the unimaginative, bizarre mash-ups designed to assess Turner's abilities like Simon's, or a cheap alternative for family portraits. Nothing, however, that I or anyone else really thought of as 'art.'

Now, in fairness, the intention of *The Turner Test* is not the final piece created, but the robot and the process of Turner instead; similar to how Andy Warhol's mass production of a *Campbell's Soup Cans* was the art as opposed to the final product. But instead of it costing $11.8 million for a picture of soup, you got your own picture to put in a frame at home. Though the robot itself would cost thousands of dollars, each piece created was given away for free, and though each piece was unique the value was only intrinsic to the owner rather than anyone else. The end product art itself was, essentially, worthless. Critics agreed on this point—computers can't make art.

Which is why I found it to be the most interesting part. Worthless, pointless art created by a computer—arguably, the ultimate soulless commercialism that critics had accused Frank Basset's pieces of, taken to the absolute extreme. Computer-made art with barely any human input, certainly without any human artistry or skill, and it was thought of by the art world as worthless. Turner was the attraction here. But I wanted to see what it was really capable of. I wanted to try something I don't think anyone had tried yet.

I asked for it to create me something original.

At first, Turner just stared at me. There was a moment, however brief, that I felt that I had stumped it, yet knew as well that I was just waiting for it to process my request, as it had done with every single other request it had ever processed. But whether it was because it was my turn that coloured my perceptions or there was actual change in its processing, it did feel like it took slightly longer to take the request under consideration.

But eventually, Turner began to move its hands towards its artistic implements. It did not reach for a drawing pencil; rather, it picked up first a yellow pencil and shaded the entire sheet of paper lightly in yellow. It followed this with an orange pencil, covering the yellow so that orange appeared pale and sickly. Finally, it picked up the red pencil and here and there upon the page made slight line drawings, like hair caught on a film. The simplicity of its colouring made the process much quicker than had it drawn a picture.

I looked at it. It was a piece of paper, coloured in sickly orange with some red lines, random, scattered and barely discernible from the orange.

I looked to Turner, then back at the orange.

'What is this?' I said.

Turner looked at me with its blank face, and with its harsh buzz said, "*Emergent Orange.*"

"Yes, okay I can see it's orange—but what is it?"

Turner ignored me. Instead, one of the eyes once again extended, leaned over the orange paper, and took its picture. The other eye flashed, and Turner returned back to its seat.

"Number forty-five," buzzed Turner, signalling that my time with the machine was utterly over.

I stared at the robot for a moment longer, stood up from the desk, and went to where Simon stood. The next person, a woman in her forties, took a seat opposite Turner and began the process again.

Simon looked at my orange piece of paper.

"What's that then?" he asked.

"*Emergent Orange*," I said. "Apparently."

Simon sniffed. "Just looks like normal orange to me," he said. "Then again, you know what they say—true art is incomprehensible. What are you gonna do with it?"

I looked at it again, trying to discern any pattern in the stray red lines amongst the orange, but there was no shape, or pattern. It was just a bit of paper, coloured from edge to edge in orange.

3.

I got a very nice frame for my picture.

I spent the next week, when not completely engrossed in work or real life, thinking about the *Emergent Orange*. When I was at home, I would watch it as if the few, faint red lines would move to form a new picture that would explain it all. I thought if it was folded in a certain way, it might word like one of those *MAD Magazine* fold-ins, but that didn't work. I tried to go cross-eyed staring at them, like those old Magic Eye pictures from when I was a kid, but that didn't work either. I denied that it was nothing; got angry that it was nothing; depressed that I got nothing; but I could not accept that it truly was nothing. There had to be something in the orange that I could not see, something that was not visible to the human eye.

Emergent Orange. Turner had very definitely called it that.

So I did a bit of research about it. There's not much, but it's not an original idea. This guy, Jim Bumgardner (no, really), had superimposed pictures upon pictures, and found that the more pictures he superimposed over each other, the more the results turned to a sort of dirty bronze colour. He called this phenomenon *Emergent Orange*, and he had no explanation for how it worked, except that it did.

I looked at what Turner had given me, and this seemed like it perhaps made sense. I wondered how many pictures Turner must have run through to get to this bit or orange and what those red lines meant too.

4.

"Number twenty-three," buzzed Turner, and I took my seat opposite Turner. The blank face of the automaton stared at me, and I tried to read something in that vacancy there. There was, of course, nothing, not even a spark. "Describe your picture," it intoned.

I placed *Emergent Orange* onto the table and slid it towards Turner.

"I'd like this," I said. "But better."

Turner moved its head to study the image, scanning in detail as if it was entirely new. Once completed, it lifted its head to look at me.

"Additional information required."

A soft murmur went around the room. This had never been heard before from Turner. I was aware now that I had an entire room's worth of eyes watching what I would do next.

"Um, okay. This is from a drawing you did previously, about two weeks ago. You called it *Emergent Orange.*"

Turner looked back to the drawing. It gave no indication that it had heard me, or processed what I said, but this was to be expected—it was a robot. There was no spark of life, just diodes.

Turner picked up a piece of paper and retrieved the same three pencils it had used when it had first coloured *Emergent Orange* (which I noticed were considerably shorter than last time) and began. The process was very much the same as before, but with only the smallest of differences. There were a few new red lines, though very faint, and made more prominent the original positions of the red lines, with fragile veins emanating from them. In much the same timeframe as before, the picture was completed. I took my completed picture home and framed this one too.

This one was called *Emergent Orange 2.*

5.

After Emergent Orange 2, I decided I needed to contact someone about this. I didn't know nearly enough about art to figure anything out, nor anything about computers. I managed to track down Blue Hat's e-mail address, since Lovelace only existed in so far as a thought exists, and explained the situation to her along with scans of both pictures. She was intrigued, and agreed to meet me for coffee.

After I finished explaining the story again in person, fielding the occasional question and showing her the two pictures, she sat deep in thought for a long time.

"So, what does this mean?" I asked. Because I sure as hell didn't know what was going on.

She unlinked her fingers and ran them through her blue hair. Finally, arriving at the right words, she spoke. "Have you heard of the Turing Test? Never mind, I'll explain it, I love explaining things. Basically, if you were talking to a machine, would you be able to tell that it was a robot or would you be fooled into thinking you're talking to a person? which sounds clever and brilliant except it's not a perfect test, right, because people are idiots and can sometimes sound like a computer, and sometimes the computer can fool you and sometimes—most of the time if we're being honest—it can't fool you. You with me."

So far, I was. She did not wait for me to respond, because she did not ask me the question. She was used to giving lectures, at speed it seemed.

"So, robots can sometimes pass for human, sometimes can't. But you can trick a person easily, with voice stuff and brain stuff and algorithms—because it's easy. There's billions of information available for reference for how a human should speak, and if you get a robot to learn from that it can imitate it. But that's no better than a parrot—and parrots haven't managed to write *Hamlet*. And even then, robots still get it wrong, like that one that thought a picture of a cat was a pot of guacamole!"

I nodded as if this was a common reference point that I understood.

"If we're talking in terms of AI, then speech probably isn't the way to go. Because any fool can speak. So, how can we show if a robot has consciousness. Well, how about art? Humans have been making art since they could draw on cave walls and represent something. A chimp can paint, but only Pollock could create his drip paintings. What if a machine could create? That would be intelligence, don't you think?"

There was a pause, and I realised this time it actually was a question.

"Er. Maybe?' Blue Hat waited, and I continued talking until I said something intelligent. 'But it's still a machine, we can see that."

"That's not the point—it's not if it looks human, because that doesn't matter. But if you think it made art, then maybe behind that mask there is a spark of something."

"Okay," I said. "So if it doesn't matter that it doesn't look human, then what matters is the art. And the process too though."

Blue Hat was already ahead of me. "If we showed these pieces to an art critic, they'd just assume a person made it, regardless of whether they liked it or not, because they wouldn't be expecting a robot to have made anything. That's not a fair Turing Test."

I felt like I might be getting where Blue Hat was heading with her suppositions now. "But if the art came directly from the machine itself, and you can see its process, then maybe that makes it art, instead of just being a glorified printer. Because if you think its original, then the machine thought about what it wanted to make—"

"—and therefore, it has creative intelligence," finished Blue Hat. "Shall we go find out?"

"What, now?"

"Definitely. I curated the thing; I can do whatever I like." She stood up and headed for the door. I followed because she certainly wasn't going to wait for me. We got a ride to the gallery, which was closing soon and waited until we could use *The Turner Test*. There was forty-five minutes until the gallery closed, and in that time, we watched Turner go through eight iterations of creation with the general public. A few family pictures, a few tasteful images of countryside settings—people getting what they wanted from Turner rather than anything new. But whilst watching, I had a thought about these processes that Turner was running through. An artist learns from each piece, grows, and evolves to become better. Maybe these pictures provided it a fertile ground to practice its craft.

Time passed, and we were left alone with Turner. Blue Hat took *Emergent Orange 2* from my hand and sat opposite Turner. "Describe your picture," said Turner in its inhuman buzz.

"Refine this picture," said Blue Hat, sliding it across the table. "Twentieth iteration."

Turner studied the picture as both Blue Hat and I studied it. Eventually, it reached for the same three pencils it had reached for the previous times and began its process. The sickliness of the yellow was lesser this time, the orange placed on top now more vibrant and healthier, like a desert at sunset. But the orange did not cover the entire page this time—instead, lines of yellow emerged, like highlights beginning to form a shape. The red hairs were thicker, bolder, and the veins had spread across the page in a complex interlocking lattice, dancing around the brighter highlights. It had a mathematical, fractal beauty, too complex for a human to create. But it didn't matter if it was capable of a human, but whether we believed that the machine had created it for itself.

"*Emergent Orange 22*," buzzed Turner, and returned to its default position.

I joined Blue Hat and we looked at the picture, studying it, tracing the lines with our fingers. There was only one question on our minds.

Was it art?

6.

One year later, and Blue Hat and I open a new installation, with permission from Lovelace who had politely declined the invitation to be present at the show. With Turner at its centre, the walls had large versions of *The Emergent Orange Sequence* around the wall for people to admire.

Turner sat in the room as a display piece. The original purpose was gone now, and Turner was allowed to produce new variations on its pictures. The later variations of *Emergent Orange* had shown hints of portraiture, landscapes and surrealism emerging in the red and yellow lines. Blue Hat had told me the next step was to see how it could innovate further, maybe having something akin to Picasso's Blue Period. I wasn't sure how she was going to achieve this.

Blue Hat mingled through the guests, making polite conversation in her punk art dress and now pink hair. I floated through doing the same with less success when it became clear I didn't really know much about it all, besides being the person who tried to break the system in the first place. This was fine with me, as I found it far more interesting to listen in on conversations.

I stood behind one couple that were looking at *Emergent Orange Variation 16*, one of the earlier variations. Blue Hat and I had made sure that we tried to get as many iterations as possible, jumping back and forth between versions to see what Turner was capable of. I stayed a while to hear their conversation.

The first, an older man who had in his hand a champagne flute half-drained of prosecco sniffed loudly. "I don't know much about art," he said dismissively, "but I know what I like. I preferred Turner's landscapes."

The second, a youngish looking woman in her thirties murmured in agreement. "My four-year old could have drawn that."

What the Wind Can't Carry

Sophie Sparham

J ae's chest folded in like an origami bird retracting its wings before the illusion of flight. She bit down on her lip and resisted the urge to claw at her heart, to pull out the needle threading itself through her upper body, untighten the clamp around the four chambers. *Why now?* The Vipers had them surrounded. There were twenty of them to the Jackals' ten, their silhouettes illuminated by the floodlights of the Waste.

In front of her, beyond the barbed wire fence, the cooling towers rose above the desert, like two fingers cursing God. Machines which churned around the landfill, emitting black smoke, and leaking poisonous gases into the sky. No one could live this close to the Waste and survive more than a few weeks. Jae had met the Vipers down one of the narrow shanty town streets for a reason. The houses here were dilapidated and abandoned: broken glass, scrap metal and rags had been dumped across the cracked and dusty floor; parts of sofas left lying against doorways. Perfect for gang trade. An old wooden shop sign lay in broken pieces next to a burnt-out building on her left. No doubt torched in a raid long ago. She felt for the envelope beneath her leather jacket. She'd gotten what she came for. The problem was getting out.

The needle threaded back through Jae's chest. Beneath her gasmask, her breaths came in rasps. *Count*, she told herself. A simple technique. One that worked when the pain heightened, and she needed to regain focus.

One, two, three, four...

Jae took a step backwards and her knee buckled. A knife flew past her head. *Fuck.* She tried to right herself, sweat dripping down her face. The Vipers advanced.

Jae ducked a right hook as a rival gang member launched himself at her. He reached her neck, but Jae was too quick. She kicked at his shin, knocking him off balance. Sickness rose in her stomach as she staggered towards the wall of nearest building and reached out to the corrugated iron for support. A rat ran from the empty oil drums piled to her right. In the centre of the conflict, Kaylam, the Jackals' young prospect, was in a tug of war with a Viper, struggling to pull the suitcase full of kai out of his grasps. Jae tried to yell for backup, but couldn't catch her breath. The bodies of Finn and Marco lay dead in the sand. Blood seeped into the desert from beneath their jackets.

"I'm sorry," she whispered.

In the darkness, Jae saw flashes of the conflict as the Wall's sweeping searchlight beams staggered the length of the street.

The guards will be here soon, she thought. *This won't go unnoticed.*

Eyo Sanco, the Vipers' second in command, rose from the floor. "Oi, Jackal!"

Jae landed a jab and felt the Viper's jaw crack. Eyo staggered back, gripping her face.

Five, six, seven, eight…

The envelope slipped from her jacket and fell to the ground.

"Sharpe!" a young well-built Viper yelled. Jae reached for her blow gun but was unable to move her arm. Her vision blurred. She ducked, grabbing the envelope as he swung his fist. His punch missed but she saw his boot too late. Jae fell back. The world went silent. Above her the constellations shone, framed between the sandstone buildings. Floored and winded, she tensed, anticipating the next blow. The guard siren sounded.

Jae groaned as she sat up, her attacker lay unconscious amongst the oil drums. Zuki, the Jackals' head medic, stood in front of her.

"Fall back," Zuki ordered. She bent down to Jae.

"I'm fine." Jae croaked. "Find Kaylam, the kai, get the others back to the den. Do it!"

"Everyone out!" Zuki yelled. The Jackals scrambled out of the fight and ran past them, northwest, back into their territory towards the Jackal's Den.

Zuki stared at Jae.

"Go!" Jae said.

"Where are they?" a guard yelled from a side street.

Get up.

Jae forced herself to her feet and limped away from the Waste, towards the totem poles that marked the beginning of Jackal territory. Shapes in the darkness shifted and pounced as she passed beneath the Sky Road, its neon lights blurring together above Nihil. Bile rose in her mouth, sour and acidic. She dragged herself down a side street, ripped off her gasmask, and vomited behind the bins.

Nine, ten, eleven, twelve...

She clutched the envelope tight against her stomach and passed out.

Jae awoke to Zuki staring down at her. She was back in her quarters. The stone in Jae's bracelet was dark blue, almost black.

"How long?" She rasped; a cough rattled her chest.

"Jae, I don't–"

"How long?" Jae raised her voice.

Zuki screwed up her eyes. "Months... but another heart attack like that..." her voice trailed off.

Jae couldn't meet Zuki's eye. "Who did we lose?"

"Marco, Finn... Keat..." Zuki paused. "You broke Eyo's jaw."

Jae glimpsed at the scar beneath Zuki's cheekbone, not meeting her eyes. "I swear, I'm gonna..." she gasped for breath.

"Did yer get it?" Zuki asked.

Jae pulled out the brown envelope from her jacket pocket. Zuki nodded as she inserted the earbuds of her stethoscope.

"How'd yer get me back?" Jae asked.

"Kaylam and I carried yer."

Jae felt as though an anvil sat on her chest. "Blood and sand," she exclaimed. She tried to turn to the edge of the bed, but her body was like lead.

Zuki put a finger to her lips as she listened. "Yer need a transfer," she said. "I 'eard a trucker talkin' about it–"

"I need ter get this envelope to Mother."

"She'll be asleep, there's still two 'ours of light."

"How long have I been out?"

"Rest" Zuki said. "The envelope can wait."

Jae closed her eyes and sank into unconsciousness.

The silence of the corridor outside meant that it was daytime. Jae woke in a cold sweat. Her head pounded. She wheezed as she reached for her clothes, pulling her vest top over her head. Jae grabbed her cigarettes and pushed herself to her feet. Dizziness caught her off guard. The needle threaded back through her chest. Wincing, she reached the top of the last flight of stairs and opened the hatch overhead to the Jackals' club bar. Daylight shone through the windows. Empty bottles, cards and half-finished cigarettes littered the tables. She lowered the hatch and walked outside. A young Jackal on day watch nodded as Jae put on her sunglasses.

Jae dragged herself to the black bench beneath the Den's awning. This was the quietest time in Nihil. Most residents slept and the machines of the Waste were switched off before dusk. Jae pulled a cigarette from her pocket. Her hands trembled as she lit the match. At the bottom of the road hundreds of ether addicts lined the Wall, still as statues, faces red raw. The drug allowed users to live out dreamlives through hallucinations. The temptation to take it grew stronger by the day; at least then she would know peace, just for a while. In her fantasy she was a ruler with a large, loyal gang beyond the prison walls. Her afro would be braided and her clothes clean. She would be healthy, free of fear, able to walk her territory as she chose. Able to love whom she chose.

Jae spotted Pan in the crowd. He stood arm outstretched and mouth open, as though speaking to an audience. They'd been brought up together in the kid gang, Fennec. Pan had showed her how to set snares for desert rats. But the day the Jackals came, Jae had been chosen and Pan left behind. Now his skin was as cracked as the desert floor, chunks of his hair were missing and few of his teeth remained. Down the line, Lanna balanced on one foot, stretching her hands towards the sun. Jae remembered her dancing around the campfire, telling stories to the younger children. Next to her were Vurlace, Meradith, Adran… The list went on. Most of them wouldn't make it to the end of the year. Ether addicts got hooked young and died young, mostly due to skin cancer. Jae massaged her heart, wondering about the secret lives they now dreamt. Soon the sun would set, and their craving would begin again.

The ether addicts' numbers grew each night, and their attacks were becoming more violent. Jae had put a knife in the back of a woman who'd raided one of the Jackals' junkshops in search of kai. She remembered the pleading look the woman had given her; her bloated stomach. How far gone had she been? How long until the birth? It was the kindest thing to do for them both. At least that what she told herself. Jae flicked the fag-end to the floor. In New Town there were three ways of living; the gangs, the Waste, or the ether real. Those lucky enough were given the choice. She shuddered as she got to her feet. Jae took one last look at her old friends as she entered the Den.

Dusk fell over Nihil. Jae tied a golden scarf over her mouth, hitched up her leather jacket and stepped into the streets. She moved slowly, conscious of the limp in her step. New Town had been built at the same time as the Waste and had now overtaken Old Town's population by two thirds. The houses and shops were no higher than ground level, giving the guards a view of the entire city from the Wall. Newly arrived prisoners had assembled the buildings whilst they still had the strength. Jae passed Armeen's shop, smelling the spices purchased from Old Town market.

"Yer reet Jae?" he asked. The searchlights of the Wall brushed his face.

Jae nodded. Zuki was right, she should have stayed in bed. Armeen pulled a sack inside and closed the door. A black and gold rag was nailed into the wood. A few doors down, Satara arranged recycled furniture. A welded metal chair was placed next to a table with an odd leg. Knives made from old truck parts hung from string in the window.

As Jae grew closer to the market, she saw candles being lit in shop windows. This time was the in-between. The hour no one had a shadow. A few miles away, the Waste's siren sounded, conveyor belts rumbled, and furnaces churned back to life. An engine above roared, as a truck flew over the prison towards the floating harbour. The truckers were the only people allowed in Nihil who weren't guards. They delivered supplies, dropped rubbish at the Waste or used Nihil as a pitstop on their way through the Althea desert. Jae had heard them talk of the fierce sandstorms that buried cities. Truckers weren't granted access to the desert floor. They spent their stay on the Sky Road, the long bridge arching over Nihil. The neon lights of the strip flickered on, and the first truckers made their way to bars, gambling wheels and private shows. Every night the same circus. The few prisoners stupid enough to jump from the Sky Road had been killed by the fall. Most didn't see the point. They had a saying in New Town: find a way to live in the prison or die in the desert.

Three people stood in the centre of the road, their eyes closed, limbs limp, as if they were hung from the air, slumped like coats on hangers. A skinny hunchback scuttling between the men nodded at Jae. She followed him down a back alley.

"Be quick," she said, her eye moving to a shadow behind the Wall's barred windows. It slowly circled the perimeter.

"A gram," the man stuttered.

"Twenty kai."

Jae reached her hand out and the man shook it. She pocketed the money. Dealing ether real was punishable by death but every gang did it. Her eyes moved back to the Wall; the shadow stood still.

"Count ten kai for the lead, four kai for the wood..." she muttered. "The Price of the Twelve" was the first song taught to gang kids, to remember guard rotations.

The market was quiet. People walked between stalls with baskets under their arms and children by their side; whilst gang members marched up and down, overseeing trade. A Scorpion with a long brown plait scowled at a Viper as he played with his knife. The market was neutral territory, but that didn't always mean people stuck to the treaty. Jae's nose wrinkled. Someone was cooking desert rat.

"Want some?" A woman asked, stirring a large pot of stew.

"Bit early for me."

Jae walked through the centre of the market, passing venders.

"Five for two, vine fruit! Fresh from the stem!"

"Carpet tiles, guard rations!"

"Get-em before they go!"

At the market's south-east edge, a stairway descended into the desert floor. Jae raised her hood. Two Vipers were standing outside the Black Dog Inn on the boarder of Scorpion territory. They glared at her as she disappeared below ground. A hand stopped her at the bottom of the stairs.

"Name?" a cloaked figure spat.

"Jae Sharpe to see Verai Culow."

A bolt rattled and the door swung open. She entered the Black Market.

The Black Market was illegal, but enough guards were paid off to turn a blind eye. The smell of incense masked the damp of the tunnels. Candle sconces were fixed to the stone walls and dripped wax as she passed. The people in the market wore hoods and cloaks, gang colours tied around their wrists or boots. Viper purple, black and gold for Jackals, the red and mustard yellow of Scorpions. Traders skulked past her, leading customers to private rooms. Others leaned against the walls or gathered at corners. Down the tunnel, symbols were carved into the lintels above doorways: a dagger, a vulture, a skull. Jae stopped at a bottle.

"Verai?"

"Enter," he called back.

Small glass bottles lined the walls of the room. Each bottle had a paper label with an illustration. The green liquids had images of plants and leaves, the black and clear bottles had images of scorpions, wolves, and skulls. Verai was sat on a stool, measuring a white powder on iron scales.

"What will it be?" he asked, placing his loupe on the table.

"Two vials of stalker, one vial of horned viper and some form of tranquilliser."

Verai raised his eyebrows and smiled to reveal pearlescent teeth. He opened the drawer by his knee and pulled out a pair of white rubber gloves.

"Let me see…" His eyes scanned the shelves and reached for four bottles right at the top.

Verai sold poisons and cures, like his mother and grandmother.

"Suppose someone wanted a remedy for their heart, to prevent attacks," she asked, "do yer have owt for that?"

The glass vials clinked as Verai placed them on the table.

"Do you want to lower blood pressure, fight infection, treat thickened blood?" His brown eyes met hers.

"I– they don't know," she replied.

"I've labelled them," Verai passed the vials to Jae.

Jae placed them in her pocket.

"Jae, forgive me, but are you alright?"

Jae forced a smile. "Never better."

Book Synopsis:

What the Wind Can't Carry is dystopian lesbian romance about the quest for freedom.

Feared gang member and second in command of the Jackals, Jae Sharpe, has three months to live. Her only lifeline is Athermite's Plot, a fable handed down by her ancestors of a site where an ambulance is rumoured to have crashed generations ago and may contain the medication she needs. Jae is determined to find it, save her life, and become rich from selling the remaining medicine.

But Jae lives in Nihil, a desolate prison town in the middle of the desert, whose main trade is toxic waste disposal and showing passing truckers a good time on the Sky Road bridge, a neon circus of casinos and strip clubs. She has already navigated herself through gang warfare to retrieve the pages of Arthermite's diary, which are deemed useless to Nihil's illiterate population.

However, Jae refuses to beg the guards for help, knowing they'd rather watch her die than translate the text. Instead, she's found the one prisoner who is rumoured to read and has taken her hostage.

That prisoner is Tobias Flinn, a female shadow puppeteer, who has taken on a male identity. Toby lives in Old Town, a place in Nihil where conscientious objectors are attempting to live communally. She begrudgingly agrees to help Jae, but at a price. She wants the Jackals to liberate the children of Nihil.

Together, they must put aside their differences and join forces to find freedom.

Biographies

Tom Clarke

Tom Clarke is a teacher from Northampton.

K. S. Dearsley

K. S. Dearsley's writing is the result of reading too much as a child. It has appeared in publications as diverse as *The Binnacle Ultra-shorts* and *Diabolical Plots*. For more years than she cares to admit, her day job was as a feature writer for the local press. She is the author of the *Exiles of Ondd* series, available on Amazon and Smashwords. Find out more at www.ksdearsley.com.

Alistair Fruish

The love of science fiction helped the young Fruish overcome aspects of his dyslexia and learn to read fluently. He spent the last part of the 70s with his head stuck in a *Doctor Who* comic or a Terrance Dicks novelisation. These were the keys that eventually opened up the whole of literature for him.

T. M. Jordan

T.M. Jordan has long been a NoHo Arts Lab botherer since its founding, having been a contributor in some manner (writer, actor, editor, etc.) to all their issues and performances so far, including creating and overseeing the writing of *Memories of a Bottlecap Queen* and responsibility for the song "I Want to be Free (Like an Octopus is Free)". He is currently reading and writing essays on all of Stephen King in publication order (horrorinclined.wordpress.com), and hopes to find the time to write a novel soon (though makes no promises).

Twitter: @PickmanP_Brush.

Michel Louis

I came to this planet apparently of my own free will, yet I do not remember making this choice.

I spend my time here examining this reality and finding some words to express my absolute horror at humanity. This takes various forms, and I always make it a point to never reveal my identify in case 'they' find me.

Sci-fi is not my genre, but if it was this is what you would get… because this has happened in another part of the multi-verse, and it could happen here too if the humans don't stop trashing the shit out this Godforsaken planet… and its Moon!

And it is forsaken, because I did that…

You're welcome…

M

Cavan McLaughlin

Cavan McLaughlin is filmmaker, artist, author, creative media practitioner and Senior Lecturer in Media Production. Editor of the recent volume *Trans-States: The Art of Crossing Over* (2019), he has also published on Crowley, solar symbolism and narrative, open-source occultism and contemporary occulture. As a media professional of over twenty years, he has been involved in almost all aspects of audiovisual production, specialising in video art, music videos and visual poetry. He is the founder and Chair of Trans-States C.I.C. (trans-states.org) as well as co-founder and editor-in-chief of *Monad: Journal of Transformative Practice* (monadjournal.com). Cavan has a profound affection for cows, fungi and rainbows.

James Milton

I grew up and continue to live in Oxfordshire, I always dreamed of being a writer and telling stories. I went to school at Bartholomew school and graduated from Staffordshire University with a degree in Film Studies, focussing on scriptwriting and Hollywood history. Since then I have spent my working life in a variety of library and librarian roles but have continued to write for myself. I had a series of articles published on a football supporters' website and appeared in a published omnibus of work from that site called *These Turbulent Times*. I have continued to tell stories, completing first drafts of two novels and I continue to work towards finishing and publishing those books.

Alan Moore

Alan Moore is an English writer, magician and performer. He is widely regarded as the best and most influential writer in the history of comics and won a Hugo for *Watchmen*. His seminal works include *From Hell*, *Lost Girls*, and *The League of Extraordinary Gentlemen*. He is also the author of the best-selling novel *Jerusalem*. Between 2011 and 2018, Moore has also created five short films and one feature-length film, *The Show*, with film director Mitch Jenkins. Alan Moore was born in Northampton and has lived there ever since.

Laura Roklicer

Laura Roklicer (born 5 July 1996) is a fiction writer, screenwriter, lyricist, and poet. By age 17, Roklicer had written a stage play and began writing lyrics in a music studio. Shortly thereafter, she began collaborating with international artists independently and through her start-up words4thoughts. Her time at the European Space Agency and her travels inspired the poetry collection *The Broken God* (2019), many screenplays including the award-winning The Therapy (2019), the short film *The Odd One Out* (2020), the short story "Tally Marks" (2022, *The VAINE Magazine*), scripts for a science YT channel with 10M subs, and an article on the distinguished philosophy blog Imperfect Cognitions. With a BA in Creative Film, BSc in Psychology, and an MA in Philosophy of Mind and Cognitive Science, she continues to connect art and science through her doctoral studies, in which she is devising lucid dreaming techniques to aid authentic fiction writing.

Kevin Rooney

Kev Rooney is a Northamptonshire based artist and writer who has been exploring dark fiction for over two decades. Never happy to settle in one medium or style for too long, his latest experiments revolve around the creation of meaningful narrative through tabletop miniature gaming. Follow his progress, and enjoy links to free comic anthologies, art and short fiction, over at www.phantasosengine.com.

Donna Scott

Donna Scott is a writer, editor, comedian, podcast presenter, storyteller, performance poet, and actor, originally from the Black Country, now living in Northampton. She was the first ever Bard of Northampton, a finalist of both Old Comedian of the Year and BBC New Voices, and is also part of the multiple award-winning The Extraordinary Time-Travelling Adventures of Baron Munchausen comedy group. Her podcast, The Lemonade Budget for Champagne Social Butterflies has been top ten in the Apple Stand-up podcast charts, and top-twenty in the all-time charts. Her stories have been published in many anthologies and magazines, and she is the editor of the Newcon Press *Best of British Science Fiction* series. She is a Director (and former Chair) of the British Science Fiction Association. www.donna-scott.co.uk.

Sophie Sparham

Sophie Sparham is a poet and writer from Derby. She has written commissions for BBC Radio 4, The V&A and The People's History Museum. She co-hosts the night Word Wise which won best spoken word night at the 2019 Saboteur Awards. Her latest collection *The Man Who Ate 50,000 Weetabix* came out in April via Verve Poetry Press.

Sophie's work has been published in *Orbis*, *Under the Radar* and *The Morning Star*. Her poem *Sunrise Over Aldi* won third place in the 2020 Charles Causley International Poetry Competition.

The Spence Brothers

Born and raised in Northampton, England, the Spence brothers had their minds twisted horrifically and beyond recognition by the medium of comics at an early age. Their shared insanity led them to the works of Jack Kirby, Frank Frazetta, Jim Starlin, Alan Moore, Frank Miller, Mike Mignola, Richard Corben, George Perez and Jamie Delano.

Their hideous and broken minds were further unhinged by authors Harlan Ellison, Kurt Vonnegut, Harry Harrison, Isaac Asimov and Richard Matheson.

At various times the Brothers have been known to lurk at the fringes of the Northampton arts and music scenes but nothing was proven and no charges were brought against them.

After years of battling a ravaging addiction to laziness, the Brothers have reinvented themselves and plunged head-long into the rapidly-expanding field of mind damaging.

The Brothers remain crumpled and belligerent, happy in the knowledge that nothing is trying to eat them anymore.

Joshua Spiller

Joshua Spiller writes prose fiction, comic books, and abject failures. *The 8th Emotion*, a kind of visionary sci-fi thriller, was his debut novel. It was also a Grand Prize Finalist for the 2020 Eric Hoffer Award. You can check out more of his work at joshuaspiller.gumroad.com.

KB Willson

KB Willson is the pen name of Northants born actor/entertainer Kevin Burke. As his 'day job' requires him to be professionally jolly – everything from theatre to circus via magic and fire-eating (including spending 10 years as Northampton's Official Jester) – writing enables him to indulge his darker side! His SF story "Wheat" won the NewCon/IAgrE short story competition (2013) and was subsequently published in the NewCon Press anthology *Looking Landwards*; his horror short "Father's Day" can be found in the Little Red Writers collection *Dorset Shorts* (2019); and in September 2020 he had a piece of horror flash – "Oubliette" – published online by Timber Ghost Press. He currently lives by the sea in Dorset with his little dachshund dog, who likes to sit on his lap while he is writing

For more information visit www.kbwillson.com or follow him on twitter @kbwillsonauthor

Yoshe

One of the founding members of the Arts Lab, Yoshe is a big believer in the power of the arts to improve our lives and the world around us. Since starting out as a travelling busker, she has worn many hats along the way, as a radio presenter, university lecturer, gig promoter, researcher of subcultures, long-distance unicyclist and sofa for cats.

These days, Yoshe spends most of her time making music, painting, writing and dancing around her living room. She is a great disappointment to both her parents and her school careers advisor.

She has always been intrigued by the internet – interviewing people in online subcultures on the deep dark web for her Master's research, and working this fascination into her writing, art, and general daydreams.

"The Thunderous Applause" is the first short story that she has let out into the world.

Milton Keynes UK
Ingram Content Group UK Ltd.
UKHW020310151123
432568UK00007B/10